Judith Stacy fell in love with the West while watching TV Westerns as a child in her rural Virginia home—one of the first in the community to have a television. This Wild West setting, with its strong men and resourceful women, remains one of her favorites. Judith is married to her high-school sweetheart. They have two daughters and live in Southern California. Look in on Judith's website, www.judithstacy.com.

With a degree in early childhood education, **Lauri Robinson** has spent decades working in the nonprofit field, and claims once-upon-a-time and happily-ever-after romance novels have always been a form of stress relief. When her husband suggested she write one, she took the challenge, and has loved every minute of the journey. Lauri lives in rural Minnesota, where she and her husband spend every spare moment with their three grown sons and four grandchildren. You can visit Lauri at laurirobinson.blogspot.com.

Like many writers, **Debra Cowan** made up stories in her head as a child. Her BA in English was obtained with the intention of following family tradition and becoming a schoolteacher, but after she wrote her first novel there was no looking back. An avid history buff, Debra writes both historical and contemporary romances. Visit her website, www.debracowan.net.

All a
COWBOY
Wants for
Christmas

JUDITH STACY
❧
LAURI ROBINSON
❧
DEBRA COWAN

HARLEQUIN®
entertain, enrich, inspire™

ISBN-13: 978-0-373-29707-8

ALL A COWBOY WANTS FOR CHRISTMAS
Copyright © 2012 by Harlequin Books S.A.

The publisher acknowledges the copyright holders
of the individual works as follows:

Recycling programs
for this product may
not exist in your area.

WAITING FOR CHRISTMAS
Copyright © 2012 by Dorothy Howell

HIS CHRISTMAS WISH
Copyright © 2012 by Lauri Robinson

ONCE UPON A FRONTIER CHRISTMAS
Copyright © 2012 by Debra S. Cowan

CONTENTS

WAITING FOR CHRISTMAS

Judith Stacy

Dear Reader,

For me, the best part of Christmas is the gifts. Not the kind that come wrapped in colorful paper with big bows—though those are always nice. The gifts most meaningful to me are the ones that don't come in packages. They are the joy I feel from donating to the homeless shelter, hearing the sweet voices of the children's choir performing traditional carols and seeing my loved ones gathered around the red-and-green lights twinkling on our Christmas tree.

In *Waiting for Christmas,* this same joy is experienced by Marlee Carrington, who reluctantly travels to Texas to spend the holidays with distant cousins and meets handsome businessman Carson Tate. They're drawn together by the town's Christmas festival, yet Marlee's past makes her reluctant to commit to a future with Carson. All of that changes when Marlee receives a special, long-awaited gift that only the man who loves her can bestow.

Waiting for Christmas also brings the return of Ian Caldwell and Lucy Hubbard. Readers met this troubled couple in *Maggie and the Law,* and again in *A Hero's Kiss,* and have anxiously wanted to know how things turned out for them. Their story is concluded here.

Best wishes to you and your loved ones for a warm, happy holiday season.

Judith

DEDICATION

To David, Stacy, Judith, Seth and Brian.
Thanks for always making this fun.

Chapter One

Harmony, Texas, 1889

Five weeks. Just five weeks, then she could leave.

Marlee Carrington gripped the handle of her carpetbag and reminded herself that five weeks wasn't so very long. She'd certainly managed to live longer than that in places far worse than this wild, uncivilized land called Texas.

Around her on the platform the passengers she'd spent the long journey with hurried to meet friends and loved ones, their expressions bright with joy despite the gray winter sky. Porters carried luggage from the baggage car. The locomotive hissed, shooting steam into the cold, crisp air.

Marlee stepped away from the crowd, keeping to herself.

The town of Harmony, what little she could see of it from the railroad station, spread westward. The wide dirt street was bordered by watering troughs and covered boardwalks, and lined on both sides with wooden buildings, a few of them two stories tall. She'd expected as much, but seeing it sent a tremor of uneasiness through her.

The arrival of the train had attracted a great deal of attention. Townsfolk flocked to the station. Young boys and girls raced through the crowd. Several dogs followed them, barking.

All manner of people moved about. Rugged-looking men dressed in coarse clothing, some with long, unkempt beards. They hustled about, intent on their work, driving horse- or mule-drawn wagons to the train station, yelling, cursing. And all of them had pistols strapped to their sides. Some carried rifles—right out in the open, in broad daylight.

Marlee gasped. Good gracious, what sort of place was this?

Four weeks. Maybe she would only stay four weeks.

Shouts drew her attention to a group of men near the baggage car involved in a heated discussion over something. Marlee glanced at them, then looked away, not wanting to draw their attention by staring, afraid—

Well, she didn't know what, exactly, she was afraid of. She was just afraid.

In the crowd of people still streaming toward the train station, Marlee spotted a number of men who, judging by the nicer clothing they wore, were probably merchants and businessmen. They joined the fray around the platform, shouting directions to their drivers and the porters unloading the box cars.

Clutching her carpetbag tighter, Marlee ventured to the edge of the wooden platform and craned her neck, searching for a familiar face in the crowd. She expected her aunt and uncle to meet the train. She'd hoped her cousins, Audrey and Becky, would come, too.

A jolt of unease shot through Marlee. Would she recognize them? Years had passed since she'd seen them—she'd been only a child when they'd made the trip to Pennsylvania to visit.

The sea of strange faces seemed to double, the shouting intensified, the children raced faster, dogs barked louder. A wave of anxiety crashed over Marlee.

What if her aunt and uncle had forgotten she was coming? What if they'd left town? What if they hadn't really wanted her to visit them, after all? What if they were just being nice when they'd invited her here? What if they'd changed their minds and fled, leaving her stranded here in this frightening place amid a town full of strangers?

Marlee drew in a quick breath, forcing herself to calm down.

No, of course her aunt and uncle hadn't left town. They simply were late arriving at the train station to meet her. That's all it was.

Surely.

They'd asked her to come here and spend the Christmas holiday with them. That meant they truly wanted her here.

Didn't it?

Didn't it?

"Oh, dear…" Marlee mumbled and turned away.

Her heart beat faster in her chest, racing along with her runaway thoughts. She'd only been here a few minutes but already she didn't like it. She didn't belong here. She didn't fit in. No one—not even her cousins, probably—would accept her.

An idea struck her.

She could leave sooner than planned. Much sooner. In a week. She could make up a story about receiving a telegram from Mrs. Montgomery stating that Marlee was desperately needed during the Christmas holiday after all, and she could tell her aunt and uncle and cousins that she was leaving.

For a moment, Marlee let the vision play out in her head. She could return to Philadelphia, to her home—though it wasn't her own home, of course. Yet the Montgomery mansion in which she had a small room was the closest she'd come to feeling as if she had a home in many years.

She'd worked as the personal secretary to the wealthy and socially prominent Mrs. Montgomery for several months now. It was a job she was lucky to have gotten immediately upon graduating from the Claremont School for Young Ladies, with an education she was lucky to have received.

Girls with her background—no father, a working-class mother, a childhood spent shuffling from one distant relative to another—seldom received so golden an opportunity. Mrs. Montgomery had taken a chance in hiring her. Marlee had not—and would never—give her one tiny reason to regret her decision.

Another wave of anxiety washed through Marlee, this one stronger than the last, remembering how circumstances had forced her into the journey that had landed her in this place.

Mrs. Montgomery had decided to spend the Christmas season with friends in Canada. Marlee had assumed she would accompany her, as she always did to handle correspondence, schedule social events and organize her charity work. For a few hopeful days, Marlee had thought the dear old woman would take her along, that this Christmas might somehow be different from all the rest.

But Mrs. Montgomery had decided that this holiday visit would be for enjoyment only and had informed Marlee that she would not be needed.

Marlee paced the platform as the vision filled her mind of what awaited her in Philadelphia, if she cut short her visit here in Texas.

Mrs. Montgomery's grand home would seem awfully sad and lonely at Christmas. A few of the servants had been left behind, but they had families nearby to spend the holidays with. One of them would surely invite Marlee to their home. But she wouldn't feel wanted or accepted there. Wouldn't that be the same as spending the holiday here in Harmony? How would that be different from all her other Christmases?

Well, for one thing, Marlee told herself, there wouldn't be any gun-toting men in buckskins. Or dogs roaming the streets. Or children unaccompanied by nannies. She wouldn't be forced to live with family members she didn't really know, in a town that surely had strange customs, with no friends, nothing that would make her feel welcome, wanted or accepted.

Marlee's heart soared as another thought struck her.

She could leave. Now. Right now.

She could go inside the station and buy a ticket back to Philadelphia. She could make up a story about receiving a telegram from Mrs. Montgomery stating that Marlee was desperately needed over the Christmas holiday after all, and she could ask the station master to notify her aunt and uncle that she was returning home. And she could leave.

Marlee turned and headed toward the ticket window when the roar of the crowd seemed to dip and the chaos around the station diminished. She spotted a man striding toward the railroad station. Heads turned. People moved aside and let him pass.

He was tall—good gracious, he was tall—dressed in dark trousers, a crisp white shirt and a dark blue vest. Though the air held a chill, he wore no coat, just a black Stetson pulled low on his forehead.

He carried no gun. Was he unafraid here among all these men who brandished weapons? Maybe he was simply arrogant. Or was it confidence?

The man moved with great purpose through the crowd, then vaulted onto the platform with practiced ease. The men gathered there hurried to him. He turned, and for an instant, faced in Marlee's direction.

Was he looking at her?

Her breath caught and her heart raced—but for an entirely different reason this time.

Handsome. A strong chin, thick brows and blue—they were blue, weren't they?—eyes that seemed to slice right through her. Marlee's heart raced faster, somehow. Her knees trembled, sending a strong quake through her. She stood mesmerized, unable to take her eyes off him.

Her thoughts scattered.

Was he simply looking in her direction? At something behind her? Or was he gazing at her?

Another thought jolted her back to reality.

Good gracious, she probably looked a fright. She'd spent days aboard the train. Her dark green traveling dress was limp and wrinkled. She'd done what she could to freshen up as the train neared the station, but she no doubt looked pale and drawn. Was her hair disheveled? Her hat straight?

The man shifted his weight drawing attention to his wide shoulders, his long legs.

A few days wouldn't be too long to stay here in Harmony, would it?

Marlee watched as the man turned back to the men who crowded around him. He spoke, and they quieted. He spoke again and one of them answered, then they all nodded in unison. He pointed and they turned, and with one final word, the men headed off to do his bidding.

A longing, deep and strong, bloomed in Marlee. Such command. Such presence. Such power and strength.

The man, whoever he was, was important. Very important. And everyone in the town of Harmony knew it.

She watched as he moved down the platform, talking to the train conductor.

Two weeks. Two weeks here wouldn't be bad—not bad at all. In fact—

Squeals of delight jarred Marlee from her thoughts, forcing her back to reality as two young women raced through the crowd and dashed up the steps onto the platform.

"Marlee!" one of them cried.

"We're so glad you're here!" the other said.

Her cousins. Audrey, only one year younger than Marlee's own twenty years, and Becky barely a year younger still, wearing gingham dresses and matching bonnets. Both girls threw their arms around Marlee and hugged her tight. Becky pulled the carpetbag from her grasp.

"We thought this train would never get here," she declared.

"How was your trip?" Audrey asked. She leaned back a little, looked closer at Marlee then let out a little squeal. "You look so much like Mama. Doesn't she, Becky?"

Her sister gasped. "She does! And that means you look like *us!*"

Marlee saw the resemblance immediately. All three of them were tall and slender, with light brown hair and deep blue eyes.

"It's like we're really sisters," Becky declared, and gave her another hug.

"You must be starving," Audrey said, and linked her arm through Marlee's as they crossed the platform. "Mama's been cooking all morning."

"We've fixed up a room for you," Becky said.

"It's small," Audrey pointed out.

"But it's so pretty," Becky said. "Audrey made new window curtains."

"Becky hooked a new rug," her sister said.

"I love your dress," Becky declared. "You have to tell us about what the girls in Philadelphia are wearing."

"Wait until you hear what the town is doing for Christmas this year," Audrey said.

"This is going to be the best Christmas we've ever had," Becky declared.

With a cousin on each side of her, Marlee descended the steps and headed toward town. She glanced back over her shoulder and spotted the man still talking to the conductor.

Five weeks. Five weeks, as originally planned. Five weeks in Harmony, Texas. It really might be the best Christmas she'd ever had.

Chapter Two

"This Christmas is going to be marvelous," Becky declared, as Marlee walked with her cousins down the boardwalk away from the train station.

Marlee spotted a few women wearing simple dresses covered by long cloaks. Some carried market baskets; most tended the small children who swarmed around them. The street was filled with carriages, horses and wagons.

"Here we are," Becky announced and gestured to a large display window filled with blue speckled pots and pans, an array of colorful blankets and knitted hats and scarves. Harmony General Store was painted on the glass.

Marlee followed her cousins inside. She'd read about the store her aunt and uncle, Viola and Willard Meade, owned in the letters she'd received from them over the years. It was exactly as she'd imagined, with aisles and shelves filled with merchandise, everything organized and spotless. But she hadn't expected the place to look so warm and inviting.

"She's here!" Becky shouted.

Customers turned to stare. At the rear of the store, the woman behind a counter looked up and smiled. Marlee knew immediately that this was her aunt Viola. Tall with slightly graying hair, she resembled Marlee's own mother.

"Oh, Marlee, welcome," she said, as she hurried down the

aisle. She threw her arms around her. "We're so blessed to have you here this Christmas."

"Thank you. I'm pleased to be here," Marlee said, and decided there was no sense mentioning that only a few minutes ago she'd seriously considered jumping aboard the next eastbound train to escape this place.

"Your uncle Willard is seeing to the arrival of the new merchandise," Viola said. "You girls show Marlee her room and get her settled."

They passed through the curtained doorway into the family living quarters, a large room with a wooden table and chairs, cupboards, a sideboard and a cookstove. Ruffled curtains covered the windows. A narrow staircase led up to the second floor. The room was warm; the aroma of baking ham hung in the air.

"We used this for storage," Becky said, as she headed toward the rear of the room. "But we emptied it so you could have a place of your own."

Marlee lingered in the doorway as Becky and Audrey went in ahead of her. The room was small, but larger than the quarters she'd been assigned at Mrs. Montgomery's Philadelphia mansion—and much more inviting.

Dark green curtains hung on the windows, bringing out the warm colors in the patchwork quilt and rug. A bureau stood against one wall, and on another a small writing desk and stool; a rocker with a soft cushion sat in the corner.

Emotion rose in Marlee. They'd put this room together for her? *Her?* It seemed too good to be true.

"It's lovely," she said, in little more than a whisper. "Absolutely lovely."

"We picked green because it's Christmas. We even decorated a little," Becky said, pointing to the bureau where a golden star was nestled among evergreen boughs. "You're going to love our Christmas this year. We're having a big festival. The whole town is going to be decorated."

"We're going to have music almost every night," Audrey said.

"Real musical performances at the social hall," Becky said, then gave her sister a teasing smile. "Performances that will include a certain man."

Audrey blushed. "Nothing is going on between Chord Barrett and me."

"Nothing?" Becky said. "Well, he certainly finds every excuse possible to stop by the store a dozen times every day."

"He's just seeing to his duties," Audrey insisted, then said to Marlee, "Chord is one of the town's deputies."

"A deputy and a musician?" Marlee asked.

"Chord's whole family is singers and musicians," Becky said. "The Barrett Family Singers, they call themselves. Malcolm and Selma—that's Chord's ma and pa—gave all their children musical names. Chord's younger brother is named Allegro, but everybody just calls him Al."

"Then there's Melody, Lyric and Aria," Audrey said.

"Piccolo and Calliope are twins," Becky added. "The family has performed everywhere. Malcolm is in Colorado lining up more performances for them."

"Chord doesn't travel with the family as much as he used to now that he's a deputy sheriff," Audrey said.

"And because he likes to be in Harmony near you," Becky pointed out.

A little grin crept over Audrey's face, but she ignored her sister's words.

"You get settled, Marlee, and rest up a bit from your trip," she said. "We'll all have supper after the store closes."

She and Becky eased out of the room and closed the door.

Marlee unpinned her hat and took off her shoes. She needed to unpack, but the bed looked awfully inviting. She lay down and fell asleep.

Marlee came awake with a start in a pitch-black room. A minute passed before she remembered where she was. She didn't know how long she'd slept but her growling stomach told her it must have been a while.

She rose and eased open her bedroom door. Wall sconces were lit in the kitchen, but she saw no one and hoped she hadn't slept through supper. The sound of voices drew her across the kitchen, and she realized the store was still open for business. She parted the curtain at the doorway—then gasped.

He was here. That handsome man she'd spotted at the train station. He was in the store standing at the counter, talking to her aunt and an older, slightly balding man who was probably her uncle Willard.

Good gracious, he was even more handsome up close.

Marlee's head felt light as she stared. She couldn't take her eyes off him. A strange heat rushed through her.

Then he shifted and his gaze cut to her. Marlee froze in the doorway, a handful of curtain fabric twisted in each fist. For a few seconds—or was it hours?—their gazes locked. His expression darkened and his eyes dipped to her feet, then rose to her face again, as if he was seeing straight through her.

Goodness, she looked terrible. Here she stood in her stocking feet, in a rumpled dress she'd actually slept in, with loose strands of hair curling around her face. She'd hardly been at her best today on the railroad platform when she'd thought he'd looked at her—and now, somehow, she'd managed to look even worse.

Marlee jerked the curtains closed and dashed back to her room.

* * *

"Did you see who came in the store today?" Uncle Willard asked.

Marlee sat at the supper table with her aunt, uncle and cousins, and the meal of ham, sweet potatoes, green beans, fried apples and corn bread smothered in butter spread out before them.

"Carson Tate," Uncle Willard said, not waiting for anyone to answer his question.

"He was at the train station today," Audrey said. "You might have seen him, Marlee. Tall, dark-haired, wearing a black hat."

"And looking too handsome for his own good," Becky added with a giggle.

Marlee froze. So, Carson Tate was the man she'd managed to embarrass herself in front of not once but twice—and on the same day.

"He's the biggest businessman in town," Audrey said. "He owns—well, he owns just about everything."

"He said he's got some investors coming to town," Uncle Willard said, "and he wants to show them how prosperous the merchants in Harmony are."

"If they're here during the Christmas festival, they'll easily see what a wonderful town Harmony is," Audrey said.

"I doubt they want to look at tinsel and evergreen boughs," Uncle Willard said. "He didn't say exactly what kind of investments they were looking to make."

"More like he wouldn't stand still long enough to explain it," Aunt Viola said. "That man is always in a hurry, always rushing from place to place."

When their meal was concluded, Marlee helped clean up. She'd pitched in to get supper on the table as well. Back in Philadelphia in Mrs. Montgomery's mansion, there'd been cooks and assistants, serving girls and servants who'd handled everything. She'd not been needed—or wanted—in the kitchen.

"I think Carson Tate is the most handsome man in town,"

Becky declared in a little singsong voice as she washed the dishes.

The cup Marlee was drying slipped, but she caught it before it hit the floor.

"Everybody's mama is hoping he'll take a shine to her daughter, that's for certain," Audrey said.

"He's not courting anyone?" Marlee asked.

"No," Audrey said.

Marlee let out the breath she realized she'd been holding.

"I'm telling you the man is too busy for courting," Aunt Viola said, as she carried plates to the cupboard. "He's always running toward the next money-making deal as if the devil himself were nipping at his heels."

"Having money is good," Becky pointed out.

"But it's not everything," Audrey said.

"Audrey Meade, you're sweet on Chord Barrett," Becky said. "Admit it."

Audrey blushed, then smiled broadly. "Yes, of course I am," she said.

"I knew it!" Becky declared.

Becky and Audrey broke into laughter. Aunt Viola slipped her arm around Audrey's waist and gave her a hug. Marlee watched this intimate moment between sisters, between mother and daughter, and her heart ached a little for her own mother, whom she hadn't seen in months, and for the siblings she'd never had. How wonderful it must feel to be a part of a vibrant, loving family.

They finished washing the dishes and put everything away while Uncle Willard helped himself to the last of the fried apples. He and Viola went upstairs.

"Do you need anything?" Audrey asked, as she stood on the stairs.

Marlee shook her head. "Nothing."

"Good night, then," Audrey said, and followed her sister up the stairs.

In her room, Marlee lit the lantern on her bureau. The soft glow of the flame spread its warmth. The gold Christmas star nestled in the evergreen boughs Audrey and Becky had placed on her bureau sparkled in the light. Memories of past Christmases floated in Marlee's head.

They were of Christmas mornings spent with near strangers, mostly. Marlee's father—whoever he was—had left before Marlee was old enough to register a memory of him. Her mother had been forced to take a job as a servant and leave her daughter with relatives. All of them had been kind to Marlee, but none had been loving and accepting. She'd always been the outsider on those Christmas mornings, when gifts were handed out to squeals of delight from the rightful daughters and sons of those relatives who'd taken her in.

Rarely had Marlee seen her own mother on Christmas. As part of a large household staff, her mother had been expected to fulfill her duties as seamstress to the mistress of the house, not cater to the wishes of her daughter. Marlee had understood, just as she'd accepted that this year her mother was in Europe attending to the wardrobe of her employer, but it had made for lonely, quiet, often tear-filled Christmases, just the same.

The memories crowded Marlee's mind and seemed to sap her strength. Fresh air would do her good, she decided. She fastened her cloak around her shoulders, put on her bonnet and grabbed her handbag as she left her room. All was quiet in the kitchen. No sound floated down from upstairs.

Certainly her aunt and uncle wouldn't approve of her walking the streets alone at this late hour, but she wouldn't be long. Just a quick stroll and she'd come back. They wouldn't even know she was gone and, besides, what could possibly happen to her in this little town with the quaint name of Harmony?

Chapter Three

Cold air enveloped Marlee as she slipped out the kitchen into the alley behind the general store. Stars spread across the black sky. Lantern light glowed in some of the windows that faced the alley, allowing Marlee to get her bearings. Across the narrow dirt lane stood animal pens and outbuildings.

She stood by the door listening, but heard nothing. In the dim light she spotted no one in the alley. Relieved to have the place to herself, she set off.

At the corner of the general store she turned left, intending to make her way to Main Street. Ahead of her, something moved in the shadows. Alarm rose in her as all the things that could happen to her blossomed in her head.

A drunk cowboy. A criminal escaped from jail. The whole town, surely, in bed asleep. No one who'd hear her scream. Why hadn't she thought of those things before she left the safety of her aunt and uncle's store?

Marlee stood very still, hoping the shadows from the building behind her would make her invisible. Her eyes and ears strained for any sight or sound. Nothing. A thread of relief ruffled through her. Perhaps whoever it was had gone. Or maybe no one at all had been there. Had it all been her imagination—

"What are you doing here?" a deep voice demanded.

Marlee jumped and her heart thumped in her chest. Good

gracious, it was a man. Close by. And not sounding all that pleasant.

Should she run, try to reach Aunt Viola's kitchen before he caught her? With her long skirt and petticoats, she knew she'd never make it in time. Marlee drew herself up. There was nothing she could do but talk herself out of this.

"I might ask you the same," she replied, trying for the same haughty tone she'd heard Mrs. Montgomery use on servants and underlings.

She knew she'd failed when she heard footsteps drawing nearer.

"Don't come any closer," she said. "I've—I've got a—a gun."

The man continued walking, as if her threat had only enticed him.

Marlee pulled her handbag from her wrist and struggled with the drawstring. "I'll use it," she called. "I mean it. Don't come closer."

He covered the distance between them in two long strides. The heat of his body washed over her.

"You shouldn't make threats you can't back up," he said, leaning down.

Marlee stepped back and bumped into the wall as light from the neighbor's window shone onto the face of her would-be attacker towering in front of her.

Her knees weakened. She thought she might swoon—but not because her life was in danger.

Carson Tate.

He glared hard at her, then recognition registered in his features—but not pleasure at seeing her.

"You're Willard's niece," he said. "I saw you this morning at the train station, then in the store."

Oh, fabulous, Marlee thought. The two times she'd looked her worst—and he remembered them both.

He introduced himself, then frowned again.

"I know you're new here," he said, "but you shouldn't be out on the street alone at this time of night. And don't pretend you have a gun, when you don't."

"But I do," she insisted.

A little snicker slipped from his lips and he yanked her handbag from her grasp. His grin froze as he held it, feeling its heft.

"What the hell?" he muttered. Carson reached inside and pulled out a Derringer pistol. "You've got a gun in here," he declared.

"I told you I did," she said.

"You've got a gun," he repeated, more outraged this time. "What are you doing with a gun in your handbag? It's dangerous. You might shoot somebody."

"That was the plan," she informed him.

"Is this thing loaded?" he demanded, and opened the chamber. "Empty. Did you really think you could scare somebody away with this thing?"

"Well, it hasn't worked so far," she admitted.

"Do you even know how to use this?" he asked.

Quincy, Mrs. Montgomery's butler, had asked her the same question when he'd learned of her trip to Texas and offered the little gun.

"You just point it and pull the trigger." It was the same answer she'd given Quincy. Carson didn't seem as satisfied as the old butler had been.

"There's a lot more to it than that," he told her, and his tone lightened a little. "And it helps if you put the bullets in."

Carson dropped the pistol into the pocket of his coat.

"It's really not a good idea for you to be out here by yourself at night," he said, then cupped her elbow and urged her through the alley.

Heat rushed up Marlee's arm. Even through the fabric of

her cloak she could feel the strength in his hand, his fingers. They walked to the rear entrance of the general store. Carson lingered near the door but didn't open it. Instead he eased closer to Marlee.

A strange heat, deeper than would be expected on a cold winter's night, wafted from him and, somehow, penetrated her cloak. It drew her nearer.

Carson leaned down and touched his lips to hers. She gasped but he didn't stop and she couldn't find the strength to pull away. His arms encircled her. She stood in his embrace, lost in his kiss.

He stepped back. Cold air rushed between them, bringing her back to reality. She hurried into the kitchen and closed the door behind her.

He'd kissed her—and he'd stolen her gun.

Marlee worked alongside Audrey and Becky the next morning, washing the breakfast dishes. She struggled to keep up with their well-practiced routine, but her cousins didn't seem to notice. They chatted about most everything, but Marlee couldn't keep her mind on the conversation as the events of last night played over and over in her mind.

When she'd awakened this morning, she'd wondered if she'd dreamed the whole thing—meeting Carson in the alley, the warmth he gave off, the kiss he'd given her. She'd never been kissed before, *really* kissed. It had all seemed like a fairy tale—until she looked in her handbag and saw that her pistol was gone.

Marlee picked up the cups Audrey had dried and took them to the cupboard.

She had to get her gun back. It belonged to Quincy, and he'd only loaned it to her for the trip. He'd expect it back when she returned in January.

For a moment she considered reporting it to the sheriff,

but then she'd have to explain why she was in the alley alone late at night, and eventually her account of the incident might lead to the kiss.

Oh, that kiss.

A wave of warmth rushed through Marlee at the memory. She grabbed a dry plate and rushed to the cupboard, sure her cheeks had flushed pink.

The nerve of that Carson Tate, she thought. He'd put her in a difficult position. Now she had to find him and demand her gun back. Only—

What if he kissed her again?

Memories of last night whipped through Marlee again, warming her cheeks anew. What if he tried to kiss her? Should she let him? She hadn't exactly put up a struggle last night. Maybe that meant—

"Marlee? Marlee!" Becky shouted.

She spun and found her cousins by the back door putting on their cloaks and bonnets. They looked as if they'd both called her name several times.

"We can't be late for the meeting," Becky said.

Marlee didn't dare ask questions, given that she suspected Becky had explained everything earlier when her thoughts had been occupied with Carson.

"We'll stop by Flora's place first," Audrey said.

Marlee hung her apron on the peg, and grabbed her bonnet and cloak as she hurried out the door after them.

Flora's Bake Shop smelled of cinnamon and vanilla and made Marlee's mouth water as she walked through the door with her cousins. The display cases held cookies, cakes and pies.

"Everything's ready," called the young woman behind the counter. She was several years older than Marlee, with dark hair and wearing a blue dress and a crisp white apron. She placed a package wrapped in brown paper and tied with a string on the counter, then paused. "Oh, you must be Marlee. Welcome."

"This is Lucy Hubbard," Audrey said, taking the package and leaving coins on the counter. "She's the best baker Flora has ever had in her shop."

Lucy managed a tired smile. "I'm certainly the busiest."

"Flora's been in Papa's store twice this week, stocking up on sugar," Becky said. "She doesn't want to run out, with the festival coming."

"All the merchants in Harmony have their hopes pinned on Christmas this year," Lucy agreed. "Hope it goes well this morning. Give my best of Mrs. Tuttle."

Marlee and her cousins headed west through town. They'd gone no more than three steps when Becky reached for the package her sister held.

Audrey yanked it away. "These cookies are for the ladies. We can't eat them. Mrs. Tuttle will smell it on your breath and you'll never hear the end of it."

"She's the mayor's wife," Becky explained. "The festival was her idea."

"Mayor Tuttle wasn't excited about the idea," Audrey said. "Nothing much excites the mayor."

"Can you blame him? Being married to Mrs. Tuttle?" Becky blurted out.

Audrey and Marlee both gasped, then all of them broke into laughter.

Main Street was moderately busy this morning with shop-keepers sweeping the boardwalk and arranging crates and barrels of merchandise just outside their doors. Marlee was surprised to see that Harmony had so much commerce. She spotted a dress shop, a millinery store, two more mercantiles and several restaurants. The Bank of Harmony occupied a large space across the street, and beside it stood a building with Tate Enterprises written in gold letters on the front window.

Marlee's breath caught. That must be Carson's office. Was he inside now? Working? Or, perhaps, thinking of their kiss?

She felt her cheeks flush at the memory, then forced it aside. She should be thinking of how she'd get Quincy's pistol back. At least now she knew where to go to demand its return.

Becky took up a running commentary on the people who occupied the businesses on Main Street, filling Marlee in on the history of the townsfolk, and throwing in a little gossip as well.

"Dorrie Markham owns the dress shop. It was one of the first businesses to open in Harmony," Becky said. "And Lucy Hubbard. She's got a secret past."

"You don't know that for sure," Audrey told her.

"She moved here from Colorado, telling nobody anything about herself," Becky said. "Then, not a few weeks later here comes Ian Caldwell asking for a job as deputy sheriff. And he's from Colorado, too. Now, is that really just a coincidence? I don't think so."

Marlee remembered that Audrey's beau was also a deputy in Harmony. "What does Chord say about this?" she asked.

"Ian hasn't given a single word of explanation," she replied. "But it's obvious that Ian and Lucy are in love."

"Only they try to hide it," Becky said. "At least, Lucy does."

They passed the last of the businesses on Main Street and stepped off the boardwalk onto the road that led out of town. On the left, a white clapboard church, set under towering trees. On the other side were a number of large homes with front porches and fences, surrounded by trees and shrubbery.

"That's Carson Tate's house," Becky said, pointing to a two-story home painted dark blue and white. "It's the biggest one in town."

"Which doesn't suit Mrs. Tuttle in the least," Audrey added, as they paused in front a nearby house. It was nice, but not as grand as Carson's. Around them, other women smiled and nodded as they went through the open gate and up the walkway to the front porch.

"Usually, everyone here is just as nice as can be. Usually," Audrey said in a low voice. "But today, well, there might be a bit of tension in the room, but—"

"What my sister is trying to say," Becky said, "is that this is a meeting of the ladies who are organizing Harmony's first ever Christmas festival, and things might get heated. The mayor and town council were against it, but the ladies pushed until they got the town's approval, and now we're stuck with it."

"Stuck with it?" Marlee frowned. "But you said the festival was going to be wonderful."

"It will be, if everything goes as planned," Audrey said. "The entire town is going to be decorated, merchants have stocked up on Christmas gifts and decorations. Restaurants and the bake shop have bought more food. The Barrett family will perform concerts. Everybody in town has put a lot of money into making this festival a success. If something goes wrong, every merchant, businessman and shop owner could go broke. And that would be the end of Harmony—for good."

Chapter Four

"**M**rs. Tuttle, I'd like you to meet my cousin from Philadelphia, Marlee Carrington," Audrey said.

Mrs. Tuttle looked and dressed the part of wife of the town mayor. Her graying hair was fashioned atop her head and secured by several jeweled combs. The garnet-colored dress she wore fit her generous figure well.

"We're happy you could join us," the older woman said.

Marlee left her cloak with the young maid waiting nearby and walked with her cousins through the wide doorway into the parlor. The large room was decorated with floral prints of dark blue and gold. Heavy drapes hung at the windows. Beyond, through another doorway was the dining room with a large table, chairs, sideboard and a hutch filled with china.

Dozens of ladies were in the parlor and the dining room, chatting as they helped themselves to coffee and refreshments. Audrey presented the package of cookies they'd picked up from Lucy at Flora's Bake Shop to the serving girl tending the table, then took Marlee to make introductions.

The faces and names became a blur. Marlee concentrated on memorizing as many as she could. She smiled and exchanged pleasantries, somewhat surprised that everyone was so welcoming.

Presently Mrs. Tuttle headed toward the front of the room. Marlee squeezed between her cousins on the settee.

"Welcome, and thank you for coming this morning," Mrs. Tuttle said. "I would also like to welcome our guest, Miss Marlee Carrington, niece of Viola and Willard Meade, here visiting with us from Philadelphia."

All the ladies turned Marlee's way and favored her with smiles. It was a little odd to be recognized in a meeting, since she'd been but a secretary to Mrs. Montgomery. Marlee smiled at the ladies in return.

"As you all know, the town will be decorated for Christmas a full week before the holiday, and the biggest celebrations will take place during the all-important three days prior to Christmas Eve," Mrs. Tuttle said. She gestured to the woman seated nearest her. "Melva, would you give us your report?"

Marlee remembered that this slight, dark-haired woman was Melva Walker, wife of Harmony's barber.

She rose and consulted the tablet in her hand. "Everything our town merchants ordered for the festival arrived as expected, in good condition. Stores will be fully stocked and our restaurants' larders will be filled to overflowing."

A murmur went through the gathering and heads nodded in agreement.

"Volunteers will put up the town decorations. Chord Barrett assures me his father will return from Colorado in time for our musical performances," Melva said. She looked out at the ladies and announced, "I believe we're all prepared."

A polite round of applause rippled through the room.

"Good," Mrs. Tuttle said, as Melva sat down. "How are we progressing with the donations for the orphans' asylum? Heddy, would you kindly—"

"Excuse me, Mrs. Tuttle?" a woman called from the back of the room.

"That's Harriet," Audrey whispered. "Her husband owns Goodwin's Dry Goods."

Harriet, a slip of a woman with iron-gray hair, stood. "I agree that the town is prepared for the festival. I think we're *overly* prepared."

A few gasps rumbled through the gathering.

"My husband has spent a fortune on Christmas decorations, Christmas toys, Christmas everything," Harriet said. "We've gone out on a limb for this festival and we're worried the town won't get the turnout we're expecting. What if we're stuck with all these Christmas things that we can't sell? We'll be ruined."

The gasps in the room grew into grumbles.

"Mama and Papa are worried about this same thing," Audrey said quietly.

"They are?" Becky asked, her eyes wide with alarm. "We could lose the store? Our home? Where would we go?"

"I've been worried about the same thing," another woman called.

"My husband says this festival is too risky," someone else added. "He was up last night pacing. This whole thing might be too hard on his heart."

"I'm sorry to say this," Melva said, "but lots of folks are worried and asking if the town can get enough visitors to make this profitable."

The room erupted.

Becky gasped. "Is Papa worried like that? Could he get sick? Could he even—die?"

"Nothing bad has happened yet," Audrey said. She reached across Marlee and patted her sister's hand. "Calm down."

"We discussed this," Mrs. Tuttle called, and the ladies quieted. "We decided there are plenty of townsfolk, along with ranchers and farmers from outlying areas, to ensure we'll have a wonderful festival."

"I can't calm down," Becky whispered. Big tears pooled in

her eyes. "If anything happened to Papa, I don't know what I'd do."

Marlee's heart went out to her younger cousin.

"I just don't believe there're going to be enough visitors to town," Harriet declared. "True, a family might come during one of the festival days, but what about all the other days?"

"We discussed this, too," Mrs. Tuttle pointed out. "Folks will come to hear the Barrett Family Singers. We've secured them for a number of performances."

"I think we ought to cancel," Melva shouted. "Now, while we can still return all this Christmas merchandise."

"What about the restaurants?" someone asked. "They can't return all the extra food they bought."

Another round of chatter rose in the room.

Tears flowed down Becky's cheeks as she leaned across Marlee and grasped Audrey's hand.

"We have to cancel this festival," she said. "We have to."

"Becky, please," Audrey said. "You're getting yourself all worked up and nothing has happened yet."

"But it might," she insisted. A big sob tore from her throat.

Marlee took Becky's hand. "Nothing bad is going to happen to your pa," she said. "The Christmas festival is going to be wonderful. I helped Mrs. Montgomery with a dozen charity events in Philadelphia."

"You did?" Becky asked, blinking back her tears.

"Yes. Hundreds of people turned out," Marlee said.

"They did?" Becky asked, sniffing.

"They did?" Audrey echoed.

"Yes, of course," Marlee said. She patted Becky's hand. "So don't worry about your papa. Everything will be fine."

Becky shot to her feet. "Marlee knows how to fix the festival!"

A stunned silence fell over the room. Every head, every eye turned toward Marlee.

A knot jerked in Marlee's stomach. Oh, good gracious, she hadn't meant to butt into the ladies' festival preparations. She'd only wanted to comfort Becky.

Mrs. Tuttle glared down at her. "Is that so, Miss Carrington?" she asked.

"Marlee works for a rich lady in Philadelphia," Becky called. "She's done hundreds of festivals just like this one."

"No, Becky," she murmured. "I said I'd done a dozen, not—"

"And thousands of people have come to them," Becky announced.

"It wasn't thousands," Marlee whispered, "it was—"

"You've done all that?" Audrey asked. "Really?"

"Well, yes, but—"

Chatter rose from the ladies once more, a cacophony of questions, comments and demands for information.

Mrs. Tuttle raised her hands, quieting the group.

"Please, Miss Carrington, do tell us what you think," she told her.

"Come on, Marlee," Becky said, grabbing her hand and yanking her to her feet. "Tell them."

She'd never been called upon to speak at a meeting before, to offer an opinion or a suggestion. In Mrs. Montgomery's employ she'd been relegated to keeping notes. She couldn't recall a time when she'd even spoken aloud. But what could she do?

Marlee faced the group and drew in a calming breath. Dozens of faces stared up at her, waiting for her to speak. Marlee's heart raced. She hardly felt adequate to speak to the ladies. She'd only been in Harmony a short while, and she could only imagine how much effort the ladies had already put into the Christmas festival. But she had, after all, organized a number of charity events before and she did, in fact, know what to do.

"It seems to me that securing the Barrett Family Singers is your best bet for bringing in a big crowd. I think that's the key to the success of the festival," Marlee said. "The only situation to deal with is how to find more visitors and get them to Harmony."

"And how do you propose we do that?" Mrs. Tuttle asked.

"I think we should bring them in by train," Marlee said. "There are three towns nearby, the farthest less than an hour away. We could get the railroad to put on extra runs during the festival."

"But how would we get the people to come?" someone called. "We can't round them up like cattle and herd them onto the passenger cars."

"We could get the Harmony newspaper to print flyers and posters and have some of your young men distribute them in those towns. We could purchase small advertisements in neighboring towns announcing the festival and the performances by the Barrett Family Singers," Marlee said.

"Everybody will want to come hear them sing," a woman in the back of the room called out.

Marlee gestured toward Heddy Conroy, the minister's wife she'd met earlier. "You could write to the churches in those towns and ask their ministers to announce our festival to the congregations."

Mrs. Tuttle's frown eased a little, but she still didn't say anything.

"Someone from Flora's Bake Shop or one of the restaurants could ride the trains and sell cookies or candy, or something more substantial to eat during their journey," Marlee said. "Maybe members of the church choir might be onboard as well, and lead everyone in Christmas songs."

"That would really put them in the Christmas spirit—before they ever set foot in Harmony," Harriet Goodwin said. "They'd tell their friends back home."

"I think the mayor, or you, Mrs. Tuttle, might be on hand at the train station to greet our visitors," Marlee said. "Perhaps some of the business owners might send a representative to direct them through town. Who knows, some of them could decide they like Harmony enough to move here?"

Mrs. Tuttle drew in a breath, then let it out slowly. She nodded at Marlee before turning to the ladies.

"I think our Christmas festival would benefit greatly from Marlee's suggestions," she said. "I say we put them into action at once."

A round of applause followed Mrs. Tuttle's words.

"Oh, Marlee, I'm so glad you're here," Becky declared.

Marlee glanced around the room at all the smiling, happy faces turned her way.

"I'm glad I'm here, too," she said.

Chapter Five

⁓⁓⁓⁓⁓

Carson muttered a curse as his elbow slid off the edge of his desk, jarring him back to reality. Annoyed, he pushed himself upright and grabbed a paper from the large pile stacked in front of him.

He'd set up his office this way, with an outer reception area and this inner office where he worked. He'd placed his desk in a certain spot, at an angle that allowed him to look out the window to Main Street for those few moments when he needed a break from his work and a glimpse at another human being.

For the last few days, all he could do was stare out the window.

What the hell was wrong with him? He'd been so intent on gazing out the window that he wasn't tending to business. He had a lot of things to take care of, all of them far more important that the goings-on outside on Main Street.

Carson's gaze swung from the letter in his hands, out the front window again. Work had been underway along Main Street for days now as Christmas decorations were being displayed. Large wooden red-and-white-striped candy canes had been nailed to all the posts along the boardwalk. Men had climbed ladders to string evergreen boughs across Main Street. Merchants were putting wreaths and candles in their windows.

Leaning slightly to his left, Carson caught a glimpse of several young women on the boardwalk across the street carrying market baskets. He followed them with his gaze searching their faces. They were clustered together so he couldn't see all of them clearly. They came closer and he recognized Audrey Meade and her younger sister.

Carson sprang from his chair. If the Meade girls were there, that must mean—

He dodged around his desk and planted himself in front of the big display window that bore the name of his business. His gaze swept the group of young women across the street. Audrey, Becky, the barber's daughter whose name he could never remember, that girl who worked at the—

Marlee.

His breath caught at the sight of her and a heat enveloped him. The same heat had plagued him for days, kept him awake at night and prevented him from tending to all the important matters that required his attention.

Still, he couldn't drag his gaze from her. He watched as Marlee and the others set about tying wide red ribbons to the posts outside Flora's Bake Shop. The task must have been more fun than he imagined because all of them were smiling, chatting. Becky said something. As he watched, Marlee's grin turned into a full smile, then she broke out laughing. All the girls laughed with her.

What was it? Carson wondered. What had Becky said that transformed Marlee's already lovely face into one of such merriment?

The day was cold but windless and the high sun overhead sent its rays down onto the girls. When Marlee turned her head, her hair seemed to shine with hints of red, at least all he could see of it under her bonnet.

He wondered what her hair looked like beneath that bonnet. He'd caught a glimpse of it in Willard Meade's store when he'd seen her peek through the curtained doorway from the back room. Silky and soft, surely. He'd had an overwhelming urge to go to her, touch her locks, coil them around his fingers.

An urgency grew in him with predictable results at the memory of later that evening when he'd found her alone in the alley. How lovely she'd looked in the moonlight. Then, how she'd tried to pull a gun on him to scare him away.

Carson's desire for her grew. She was a proper young lady raised among polite society back east. He hadn't expected her to attempt to bluff her way out of their encounter in the alley. She had spirit—something else he hadn't expected of her—which was probably the reason he'd kissed her.

Placing his palms against the cold glass of the window, Carson leaned in as he watched Marlee and her friends across the street. He'd kissed her, all right. It was hardly the way he conducted himself, certainly not the sort of thing he made a habit of doing. Surely every mama in town had pushed a young lady or two his way, hoping for a match. Carson didn't have time for matters of the heart. Business, making money, securing a solid financial footing was what mattered.

Carson drew in a long, heavy breath as he studied Marlee. Her slender hands, the sway of her skirt, the little glimpse of her ankle he'd caught, the bodice of her dress that swelled to—

"You okay, Mr. Tate?"

Carson snapped back to attention as Drew Giles, his office helper, walked through the door, staring as if he'd suddenly lost his mind. Not that he blamed him. Carson wasn't given to long moments of gazing idly out the window.

Barely twenty years old, Drew was a tall, slim young man with a shock of thick blond hair. He'd helped out at Carson's office for several months now and seemed to have a good head on his shoulders.

Drew walked closer, then glanced out the window. A knowing grin spread over his face. "I see you're admiring the town's Christmas decorations."

"That's exactly what I'm doing," Carson told him.

"Bigger things to come," Drew said. He nodded out the window. "The whole idea of running the trains was Marlee's idea."

Carson frowned—both because he didn't like that his feelings were so obvious, and that he had no clue what the "train idea" was.

"Seems some of the ladies were worried about enough folks coming to the festival," Drew said. "The way I hear it, Marlee had the idea to run trains to all the nearby towns and bring them in for the day. Hundreds of people will be coming to Harmony."

Carson glanced out the window again. Marlee had thought of that? It was a damn good idea—yet fraught with problems.

"We'll get all kinds. Pickpockets, scam artists, thieves. The sheriff will have his hands full, that's for sure," Carson said. "But at least my investors aren't coming until next month. I sure as hell don't want them here deciding on whether to invest in my weaving mill with a town full of criminals."

"They changed their plans," Drew said. "They'll be here during the festival."

Carson's head snapped around. "What the hell?"

Drew pulled a telegram from his back pocket and presented it to Carson.

"I just picked this up," he said.

Carson scanned the telegram, then crushed it into his fist. "Damn it. This is going to play hell with getting my mill going. I can't have those men here with scalawags and riff-raff running loose in our streets."

He grabbed his Stetson and headed out the door.

Carson spotted Chord Barrett outside the jailhouse nailing Wanted posters beside the door as he made his way down the boardwalk. He'd left his office in such a hurry he hadn't picked up his coat, but he was still so fired up about trainloads of strangers coming to town that the cold barely registered.

"Hell..." he muttered as he saw that Sheriff Thompson's horse wasn't tethered to the hitching post in front of the jail. He'd wanted to speak to the man personally. Not that he had anything against Chord. He'd proved himself a good deputy, despite the fact that he had the voice of a lark and toured the country doing musical performances with that family of his.

A man couldn't pick his family—as Carson well knew—and he doubted Chord would have selected those peculiar parents of his who'd given their children musical names. He doubted, too, that Chord would otherwise have been part of the family in which all the kids—sons and daughter alike—favored each other so strongly, all of them tall, with light brown hair and cool blue eyes.

"Afternoon, Carson," Chord called. "How you doing?"

"Not so good," he replied.

Chord turned away from the Wanted posters and laid the hammer aside. "Sheriff's out at the Dawson ranch. What's on your mind?"

"What the hell is the town thinking, bringing in trainloads of strangers?"

Chord threw up his hands in surrender. "I'll be damned if I know. Those ladies on the festival committee should have talked to the sheriff before doing all of this. It'll be nothing but trouble, that's for sure."

"More than you think," Carson told him. "Those investors who're interested in the weaving mill are coming smack in the middle of the festival."

The deal for the construction of a weaving mill on the outskirts of Harmony had been in the works for months. Carson had arranged for investors from back east to come take a look at the place and hear the details of his plan. He wouldn't be the only one to benefit from the mill, of course. It would bring new jobs and new wealth to Harmony.

Chord muttered a curse under his breath, then opened the door to the jailhouse. "Ian, get out here, will you?"

Harmony's other deputy, Ian Caldwell, strode outside. He was a tall man, solid, and knew how to take care of himself. Carson had seen him drag drunk cowboys out of the Gold Garter Saloon and toss them into jail with little effort.

Carson told him what he'd just explained to Chord, and Ian shook his head. A quiet moment passed, then he muttered, "Women."

As one, they all turned to gaze down the street.

Marlee, Audrey and Becky stood outside Flora's Bake Shop. Lucy Hubbard had joined them. Moments dragged by in silence, until finally Ian spoke.

"Why won't a woman just do what you tell her to do?" he mumbled.

There was no hostility in his words, no anger, not even any confusion or wonderment, only a longing and a hurt that seemed to roll from him in waves.

Everyone in town had speculated that something had gone on between Ian and Lucy back in Marlow, Colorado. Nobody knew for sure, one way or the other, because neither of them spoke of it.

"I'll talk to the sheriff when he gets back in town," Chord said. "He could order the musical performances canceled— which would suit me just fine—but that's what's bringing everybody to town."

Ian shook his head. "I don't see the sheriff doing that."

"He may not care so much about disappointing folks who want to hear Christmas music," Chord said. "But he sure as hell doesn't want to hurt the merchants who've spent so much money to get ready for this festival. I'll let you know what the sheriff says when he gets back."

"Appreciate it," Carson said, and headed back down the boardwalk.

Marlee and the others were still outside Flora's. Carson intended to give Marlee a piece of his mind, even though he understood that she was new in town and didn't know everything that was going on. A great deal was at stake for Harmony with the weaving mill he was trying to get built, and he didn't need any more surprises where the investors' visit was concerned.

This would be a business discussion, he told himself. Just business. Nothing more. And he sure as hell wasn't going to end up kissing Marlee again.

"Afternoon, ladies," Carson said. He touched the brim of his hat and managed a smile as he joined them on the boardwalk.

"We were just going inside Flora's for a bit to eat," Audrey said. "Would you care to join us?"

"No, thank you," he said, then turned to Marlee. "I wonder if I might have a word with you, Miss Carrington?"

Audrey and Becky threw her a concerned look, but Marlee said, "I'll be inside in just a minute."

Carson grasped Marlee's elbow and steered her to the corner of the building, then stepped off the boardwalk into the alley, bringing her with him.

She smelled delightful.

The thought slammed through Carson, chasing away the good intentions he'd had of educating Miss Marlee Carrington about the error of her ways, as well as life in Harmony, Texas.

He refocused his thoughts on the task at hand, and reminded himself again that, no matter what, he would not kiss her.

Marlee stared up at him, her eye wide, her lips pursed. Though she was covered up with that large cloak, he knew how shapely she was beneath it. He imagined what it would feel like if he slipped his hand—

"You wanted to talk about something?" Marlee asked.

Carson gave himself a little shake. "Yes, I do. You and the

other ladies should have discussed the notion of bringing train-loads of strangers to Harmony for the Christmas festival with the sheriff before you went and did it."

"And why is that?" she asked.

"Because all manner of thieves will probably come, too," Carson said.

She drew herself up a little and looked him straight in the eyes.

"If you're concerned about being a victim of a crime," she said, "I'd like to point out that you do, after all, have my Derringer to defend yourself with."

Carson's resolve crumbled.

He pulled Marlee into his arms and kissed her on the mouth.

Chapter Six

He'd kissed her—again.

And she'd let him—again.

Marlee moved the small stool farther along the row of tall shelves in the Harmony General Store and stepped up on it. Around her, shoppers were busy making their selections, talking with Aunt Viola behind the counter. Marlee had gladly pitched in and offered to dust the merchandise because she wanted to help out, of course, but mostly because it was a mindless task that allowed her the opportunity to think about what had happened two days ago.

Carson had kissed her. He'd said he wanted to talk with her when he'd approached her and her cousins outside Flora's Bake Shop, but after they stepped into the alley he'd hardly said anything at all. He'd just kissed her.

Then he'd walked away. He'd left her standing there alone, her heart racing, too stunned to figure out what had just happened.

And to make matters worse, she hadn't seen him since.

Was it right that a man would maneuver her into an alley, steal a kiss then disappear? What did it mean?

Marlee brushed the feather duster over the tin coffeepots on the shelf. Maybe it didn't mean anything—to him anyway. She'd never felt this way about a man before. Of course, her job with Mrs. Montgomery allowed few opportunities to meet anyone. Before she'd taken the job she'd been enrolled at the Claremont School for Young Ladies where all facets of her life were strictly controlled. There was talk among the girls and information was shared, but opportunities to mix with the opposite sex were limited.

If only there was someone she could talk to.

The vision of her mother floated into Marlee's mind. They had shared so little time, but that didn't mean they weren't close. She wished her mother was here so they could talk.

For a moment, Marlee considered broaching the subject with Aunt Viola. She was a wonderful aunt, and Marlee could see how Audrey and Becky adored their mother, yet Marlee couldn't bring herself to share her feelings.

Besides, she didn't know exactly what her feelings were for Carson. His presence in her life had caused her nothing but confusion and upset. Did that mean she should avoid him at all costs? Or should she confront him and demand to know— well, she hadn't any sort of idea what she would say to him.

Aunt Viola's voice broke into her runaway thoughts.

"You've been dusting those same pots for fifteen minutes now. I think they're clean enough," Aunt Viola said.

"Oh, I have?" Marlee felt color rise in her cheeks.

She gave her a warm smile. "Go out for a little walk. Stop by Flora's and talk to Lucy Hubbard. I think a chat with her will do you both good."

The scent of apple pie wafting from Flora's Bake Shop drew Marlee through the front door and out of the cold. She found Lucy sitting on a chair behind the counter, gazing out the window into the alley.

Her cousins had told her that everyone in town suspected Lucy had a secret past. Marlee thought she saw those memories in Lucy's face now as she stared outside at nothing.

Lucy blinked a few times, then spotted Marlee. She hopped out of the chair and walked to the counter. "What can I get for you?"

"I just came by for a visit," Marlee said.

Lucy looked a bit surprised, as if she didn't get too many folks in the shop just to visit. She smiled and said, "That'd be nice. How about some coffee?"

Marlee circled behind the counter while Lucy poured coffee from the pot on the cookstove. She pulled up another chair and they sat down.

"So," Lucy said, "are you enjoying your stay in Harmony?"

"Everyone has been so welcoming," Marlee said. "*Most* everyone."

Lucy frowned. "Has someone been unkind to you?"

"Well, not, not exactly," Marlee said, and felt color rise in her cheeks.

"Has someone been a little *too* welcoming?" Lucy asked softly. "Carson Tate, perhaps?"

Marlee gasped. She set her cup aside and plastered her palms against her cheeks. "How did you know?"

"I saw him kiss you in the alley," she said, and nodded out the window.

Marlee's face burned. She'd been seen? In the alley? Kissing Carson Tate? Had other townsfolk seem them? Was she the object of gossip?

"I only saw it because I was looking out the window," Lucy said.

Marlee gazed into the alley. She noticed that the view also took in part of Main Street and, in the distance, the jailhouse.

Her embarrassment fled and sadness enveloped her heart.

"You're in love with Ian Caldwell, aren't you," she said.

Lucy turned her head away. A moment or two passed before she faced Marlee again. "Yes," she whispered. "And you're in love with Carson Tate."

Lucy's words stunned her and she hardly knew what to say. She searched her feelings and knew something was in her heart for Carson. She'd felt it the moment she'd laid eyes on him at the train station. But was it love?

"Carson is always rushing around," Lucy said, "taking care of one problem after another, with some kind of business deal in the works. He's always in a hurry. But lately—since you got here—he's come into the shop almost every day, and he always manages to work the conversation around to you. I can see he has feelings for you, and I know you feel something for him. Maybe you two are meant to be together?"

Marlee shook her head. Now she was more confused than ever.

"Yet you're in love with Ian and you do nothing about it," Marlee said.

Lucy drew back a little. "Things are different with Ian and me."

"But he loves you," Marlee said. "Everyone in town says so."

A little grin pulled at Lucy's lips, yet it faded quickly. She set her coffee cup aside and drew a breath, as if she were drawing on some inner strength.

"Ian and I knew each other in Colorado, in a little town called Marlow," Lucy said. "I was married."

Marlee tried not to let her surprise show. "What happened?"

"Raymond turned out to be something less than a good husband," Lucy said. "I knew Ian cared for me, as I cared for him. He was a perfect gentleman, and I'd taken vows before God, so nothing came of our feelings for each other."

Lucy seemed lost in thought for a while, then spoke again.

"Ian was helpful after my marriage ended," she said. "I couldn't stay in Marlow, not after everything that had happened. So I moved here."

"And Ian followed you?" Marlee asked.

"He's a determined man," Lucy said. "You should stay in

Harmony and see what happens between you and Carson. If it's love, you can't let it get away."

"Yet you can't do that with Ian?"

Lucy shook her head. "I'm afraid. Afraid things might turn out the way they did with Raymond. I can't make that kind of mistake again."

"Ian's a good man," Marlee said. "He loves you."

"My first husband seemed like a good man, too. He said he loved me, and things turned out...well, they didn't turn out the way I expected."

The bell over the door jingled, taking Lucy's attention. As she went to wait on the customer, Marlee gave her a wave and left the shop.

She'd hoped that talking with Lucy might clarify her feelings for Carson, but now she was more confused than ever. And she was sad, too, for Ian who seemed to love Lucy so much that he'd stood by her through her marriage, then followed her to Harmony. Sadness filled her for Lucy as well, who'd been so damaged by that marriage she was too fearful to take another chance on love.

Darkness had fallen bringing a deeper chill to the air as Marlee slipped into the store. A dozen women were gathered near Aunt Viola at the counter. Marlee spotted Mrs. Tuttle, Heddy Conroy, Harriet Goodman and Melva Walker among them. Every woman frowned. Chatter flew back and forth between them.

Becky broke away from the group of women and hurried down the aisle.

"Marlee, something terrible happened." Her words came out in a rush.

All sorts of images filled Marlee's mind. Had someone been injured? Taken ill? Been killed?

"It's Malcolm Barrett, Chord's pa," Becky told her. She

swiped at the tears that sprang to her eyes. "He's hurt, hurt real bad."

"What happened?" Marlee asked, frantic for more information.

Becky wrung her hands. "He's still in Colorado. Remember he went there looking for places for the family to perform? Chord just got a telegram from the sheriff telling him his papa got run over by a runaway freight wagon. It said the whole family should come right away because their papa might not make it."

"Where's Audrey?" Marlee asked. "She must be so upset."

"She's at the train station," Becky reported. "The whole Barrett family—every single one of them—is leaving on the next train. It should be pulling out any minute now. Oh, Marlee, this is terrible. Just terrible!"

Marlee slipped her arm around Becky's shoulders and gave her a hug.

"We have to be strong, Becky, and send good thoughts and prayers."

Becky drew in a ragged breath. "I'll say an extra-big prayer."

Marlee joined the ladies clustered in the back of the store.

"Chord will keep us informed by telegram," Mrs. Tuttle reported.

"We'll have a prayer vigil at the church tonight," Heddy said.

"As soon as the family returns, we'll take food over," Melva said.

Several of the women chimed in with food items they would take to the Barrett home. Marlee wished she could cook well enough to volunteer to take something. With their plans made, the women left the store.

"I'll go to the train station and check on Audrey," Marlee said. "She must be so worried about Chord's papa, plus upset that he's leaving."

"We're all worried," Aunt Viola agreed.

Something in her aunt's voice caused Marlee to stop and turn back.

"What is it?" she asked.

"Of course, Malcolm's health is our first concern," Aunt Viola said. "But with him injured so severely, and with no way of knowing when—or if—he'll recover, I don't see how the Barrett family will return to Harmony anytime soon. And without the Barrett Family Singers, our Christmas festival will be a disaster."

Chapter Seven

"Ladies?" Mrs. Tuttle clapped her hands together. "Your attention?"

The women gathered in the parlor of the mayor's wife quieted. Marlee, squeezed between her cousins on the settee, felt the tension in the room.

"Is there anything new to report on his condition?" Mrs. Tuttle asked.

Audrey shook her head. "Still the same."

Several days had passed since the entire Barrett family boarded a train for Colorado. Chord had sent telegrams but they all gave the same report. Malcolm was alive but clinging to life.

"As you all know, canceling the Barretts' performances at our festival will have a devastating effect on its success," Mrs. Tuttle said.

A grumble went through the room. Marlee had heard many of the same comments at the store between Aunt Viola and Uncle Willard. Everyone in Harmony was worried about their financial investment in the festival.

"This is awful," Becky murmured. "Just awful."

"Don't get upset," Marlee whispered. "Not yet anyway."

"What if Mama and Papa lose their store?" Becky said. "What if—"

"Calm down," Marlee told her quietly.

"I have good news," Mrs. Tuttle said. "I've located another musical group. The Laughlin Singers are very well thought of, have toured extensively, and come highly recommended. And they are willing to come to Harmony on this short notice and perform in place of the Barrett family."

A round of applause went through the room. Excited chatter broke out.

"However," Mrs. Tuttle said, "unlike the Barretts the Laughlins will not perform free of charge. They expect to be paid—and paid well."

A groan swept through the crowd.

Becky covered her face with her palms and shook her head. "We're going to lose everything. Papa might be so upset he'll—die!"

"Oh, Becky," Audrey snapped. "Would you just hush up?"

Becky turned tear-filled eyes to her sister and gulped hard.

Marlee gave her an encouraging smile. "Something can be done."

"Do you think so?" she asked, wiping her eyes.

"Something can *always* be done," Marlee assured her.

"How much money does this Laughlin bunch want?" Harriet demanded.

"Do we have any money to pay them?" Melva called.

"I don't need to remind you that the town council wasn't in favor of this festival to begin with. So no money will be coming from them," Mrs. Tuttle said.

Becky groaned and shook her head fitfully. "Oh, I just know something terrible is going to happen to Papa. I just know it."

"We'll have to ask for donations," Mrs. Tuttle said.

"From *who?*" someone called. "Every merchant and businessman in town has already stretched themselves thin getting ready for the festival."

"Not *every* businessman," Mrs. Tuttle said. "Not Carson Tate."

Marlee gasped. Carson was reportedly the richest man in Harmony, and he hadn't donated to the Christmas festival?

"Marlee can do it!" Becky sprang from her seat. "Marlee can get him to donate lots of money! She did charity work back in Philadelphia, remember?"

Marlee felt every gaze in the room bore into her.

Mrs. Tuttle said to Marlee, "The town, the merchants, the families who are coming here expecting a joyous Christmas celebration—a great deal is at stake."

Warmth grew inside Marlee. How good it felt to be wanted, needed, especially for something so important. No one—certainly not Mrs. Montgomery—had ever thought so highly as to assign her such an important task or have faith that she could accomplish it.

She knew she could get Carson to donate the money. She'd seen Mrs. Montgomery wheedle funds from the most reluctant benefactors. Not that she'd need any such tactics on Carson. Surely he simply hadn't known about the festival during its planning stage.

"I should warn you that Mr. Tate might not be anxious to make a donation," Mrs. Tuttle said.

Marlee doubted that were true. Everyone said he was terribly busy, always rushing about, so he probably hadn't had the opportunity to make a donation. The festival was a very worthy cause, so all she had to do was ask and he would give generously.

"I feel confident I can handle it," Marlee said.

Mrs. Tuttle didn't seem convinced. "You're quite certain?"

Marlee rose and faced the women. "Absolutely," she declared.

"Very well, then," Mrs. Tuttle said. "The Christmas festival will proceed."

Applause broke out. Women swarmed around Marlee, thanking her, offering words of encouragement and praise.

Contentment and joy settled around Marlee's heart. What a marvelous feeling. How wonderful to be a part of something, to feel wanted and needed.

Maybe she'd stay.

The idea flew into Marlee's head as she basked in the glow of the gratitude that filled the room. Maybe she'd stay in Harmony—permanently. She could make it her home, never again to return to the tiny, impersonal room she lived in under Mrs. Montgomery's roof. She could stay here among family and friends—people who wanted her around, who made her feel as if she belonged.

Perhaps she could even convince her mother to come live in Harmony.

Love and longing filled Marlee anew. What a lovely—perfect—life she would have. All she had to do was convince Carson Tate to donate money for the Christmas festival.

How difficult could that be?

Mrs. Montgomery used to say that sweetening the pot was a good way to snare reluctant donors, Marlee recalled as she left the Harmony General Store with her aunt's market basket looped over her arm. The afternoon was cold, the sky overhead gray, but Marlee felt warm inside and anxious to complete this most important of tasks.

The bell over the door of Flora's Bake Shop jingled as she went inside and bought a half dozen sugar cookies from Lucy.

"Still warm," Lucy said, wrapping them in the red checkered cloth Marlee had given her. "Fresh out of the oven."

Outside again, she gazed across the street at the office of Tate Enterprises. Movement in the window caught her eye, then disappeared.

Was that Carson? Had he been standing there, gazing outside?

Everyone said he was extremely busy. But if he had time to waste staring out the window, perhaps this was, indeed, a good time to pay him a visit.

She smiled to herself. She'd carefully planned out exactly how she'd handle this meeting with Carson. It seemed she was off to a good start.

Marlee hurried across the dusty street and walked inside. Drew Giles sat behind a desk in the reception area. She'd met him a few days ago when he'd come into the Harmony General Store.

"Afternoon, Miss Carrington," he said, rising from his chair.

Marlee smiled. "I wonder if I might speak with Mr. Tate?"

"Well, I don't know," Drew said. "He's mighty busy."

Marlee held out her basket and pulled back the cloth. "Would you like a cookie, Drew? Fresh from the oven at Flora's."

"Miss Lucy makes the best I ever tasted," Drew said. He took a cookie, bit into it and sighed. "Well, I guess Mr. Tate can spare a few minutes."

Drew rapped on the adjoining door, then pushed it over. "Miss Carrington here to see you, boss," he said around a mouth full of cookie.

Marlee mentally reviewed the plan she'd made to get Carson to donate the money for the festival's musical group. She also recalled her vow to stick to business and not lose herself in thoughts of the kisses he'd given her.

Her resolve crumbled when she walked into his office and found him standing behind his desk. Such a handsome man. What would it be like to lean against that wide chest of his? To lay her head against those shoulders?

Marlee started, realizing where her thoughts were going. She had to stick to business—no matter how fast her heart raced in Carson's presence.

"Good afternoon," she said, and felt her cheeks color a bit at hearing how her words had come out in a breathy little sigh.

Carson didn't seem to notice. He just stood there staring at her. Then he hustled around the desk and pulled out a chair for her. Marlee lowered herself onto it, grateful to take a seat since her knees had started to tremble.

Carson threw a harsh look at the doorway. "Don't you have work to do?"

Drew's grin widened. "Sure do, boss," he called, as he backed away.

Carson sat down in the chair behind his desk. "To what do I owe the pleasure of your company, Miss Carrington?" he asked.

"I thought you might enjoy some cookies." She placed the basket on his desk and pulled back the cloth. The delicious scent of the cookies wafted out.

He glanced at the cookies, then at her.

"I appreciate that," he said. "Was there another reason for your visit?"

Marlee was slightly miffed he hadn't taken one of the cookies, then reminded herself that Carson was known to be a man in a hurry. She decided it was best to get right to the point.

"I'm sure you know about Mr. Barrett's accident, and how the family has rushed to his bedside," Marlee said. "And I'm sure you also know that the family had agreed to perform at the Christmas festival, but now can't possibly do so."

Carson just nodded.

"It's become necessary to hire another musical group to perform," Marlee said. "The good news is that Mrs. Tuttle has found a wonderful replacement who has graciously agreed to come to Harmony on very short notice."

Carson stared at her. She'd hoped he'd ask some questions, or at least express some pleasure that the Christmas festival would go forward. Surely he knew what it meant to the town of Harmony.

"However, this new musical group is charging for their appearances," Marlee said, "which makes it necessary to ask for a donation—"

"No."

"—from—"

"No."

Marlee huffed. "You don't even know what I was going to ask."

Carson looked properly contrite, and gestured for her to continue.

"What were you going to ask?" he said.

"I was going to ask if you could find it in your heart to donate the money—"

"No."

Anger spiked in Marlee. "You haven't heard the amount."

"Fine, then," Carson said. "How much?"

"Only one hundred dollars—"

"A *hundred* dollars? For people to come here and *sing?*"

"They'll perform a number of concerts," Marlee pointed out.

"Hell," Carson grumbled. "Maybe I'm in the wrong business."

"Those performances will bring lots of visitors to town," Marlee said.

"No wonder old man Barrett was always trotting those kids of his from place to place to perform," Carson said.

"It will mean a great deal of business for our merchants," Marlee said.

Carson shook his head. "Look, Miss Carrington, I—"

"It's for Christmas," she implored.

A moment passed, and finally Carson said, "I can't help you."

"But—"

"I *make* money. I don't give it away." Carson gestured to her market basket. "Did you think some cookies would convince me to donate that kind of money?"

Yes, she did think that it would at least help, but now she felt the gesture had made her look naive and silly. Still, she wasn't going to tell him that.

Marlee pushed her chin up. "It's accepted tradition to offer refreshments during a business discussion," she told him.

"A business discussion involves two people each getting something out of the deal," Carson told her. "What are you offering—besides cookies?"

Wild notions flew into Marlee's head, things she'd only heard whispered about among the girls at the Claremont School for Young Ladies. And now she was actually thinking about them—and doing them—with Carson.

The room seemed to grow warmer as Carson leaned his elbow on his desk and edged closer.

"Well, Miss Carrington?" he asked.

His voice sounded deeper, richer. His eyes looked darker. The heat he gave off pulled her closer, as if she were bound to him, unable to break away.

"What else are you offering?" he asked.

A spark of heat forced its way through her muddled thoughts. Had he just made an indecent proposal?

Marlee replayed his words in her mind. Good gracious, he *had*.

Of all the nerve. How dare he? Anger, outrage—something—raced through her. She should slap his face and stomp out of his office, and never speak to him again.

But what about the money for the musical group? The festival? The town of Harmony that was counting on her?

Well, she would have to give him a piece of her mind later—which she certainly would do.

Marlee tamped down her feelings and looked at Carson across the desk.

"If you weren't aware, Mr. Tate," she told him, "I'm currently in the employ of Mrs. Lillian Montgomery of Philadelphia, where I perform social and business duties with the utmost efficiency and competence, having been trained at the Claremont School for Young Ladies."

"The Claremont School for Young Ladies, huh?" Carson reared back in his chair.

"It's a very prestigious institution," Marlee assured him.

"I'm sure it is." He shook his head. "But I've got Drew to handle my business, and I don't have a need for social help, whatever that is."

"Oh, but you do," Marlee assured him. "Your home isn't decorated for Christmas. I could do that for you—and in good taste."

"I don't need my house decorated," Carson said.

"I could purchase gifts for everyone on your Christmas list," she said.

Carson shook his head. "I don't give Christmas gifts."

"You don't give gifts?" Marlee blurted the words out.

He sat forward. "How about cooking? Are you good at it?"

Cooking? Who said anything about cooking? Why would he mention it?

"How about scrubbing and washing?" he asked.

She kept her belongings neat and organized, but Mrs. Montgomery employed servants who did the heavy cleaning.

Marlee's spirits dipped considerably. If her cooking and cleaning skills were what it took to convince Carson to give her the money she needed, the Christmas festival was doomed.

"My request for a donation is made in the spirit of Christmas, and for the betterment of Harmony," Marlee said. "I think you're missing the point."

"No, I believe you're the one missing the point," Carson told her.

Not a hint of a smile showed on Carson's face. His expression hardened. He exuded a toughness, a strength that she hadn't seen before. Marlee knew she was gazing at a man who knew how to drive a hard bargain, to force a deal to go his way, to get the upper hand and keep it. She imagined other, less hardy men cowing down, giving him his way.

Yet something inside Marlee seemed to rise up, anxious to take him on.

"I run a business, not a charity," Carson told her. "The *gifts* I give folks in Harmony are jobs so they'll have money in their pockets, food on their tables. I bring new business to this town so it will grow, so more families can have better lives. I work hard at that. Very hard. And I'm not about to give away a hundred dollars so that a bunch of people can come here and sing songs."

Marlee's anger boiled over. She shot to her feet. "How can you claim to care about the citizens of Harmony when you have no real idea what's at stake?"

"I assure you, Miss Carrington, I know exactly what's at stake," he told her. "One hundred of my hard-earned bucks."

"This isn't about you, Mr. Tate, or what you want," Marlee said, glaring down at him.

Carson lurched from his chair and circled the desk in three quick strides to stand next to her. The force of his presence mere inches from Marlee nearly overwhelmed her, but she stood firm, refusing to give him the upper hand by backing away.

"I always get what I want," he told her.

He was close, so close. The scent of him as strong, luring her nearer with its familiarity—a familiarity she wouldn't give in to this time.

Marlee gazed up at him. "Don't even think about kissing me again."

Carson's expression shifted, as if the hunger that had come over him now threatened to consume him—and suddenly all

Marlee could think was that if he *didn't* kiss her again, she couldn't stand it.

Goodness, what was she thinking?

Forcing aside her feelings, Marlee narrowed her eyes at him in what she hoped was a threatening glare.

"I want my gun back," she told him.

"When you're all riled up like this?" he asked, and uttered a little laugh. "I don't feel like getting shot right now."

"You're despicable," she told him.

Marlee reached for her market basket. Carson snatched the cookies from inside.

"I never said I didn't want the cookies," he told her.

"Oh!"

Marlee stomped out of the office and slammed the door behind her.

Chapter Eight

She'd failed. Completely and miserably.

Marlee hurried along the boardwalk, Carson's words still ringing in her head. He'd refused to donate to the Christmas festival, and nothing she'd said had changed his mind—she hadn't even instilled a moment's hesitation in him.

Except when she'd mentioned kissing her again.

"Oh, dear..." Marlee fretted as she continued on her way to—well, she didn't know where she was going. Nowhere, really. She just needed to walk, to keep moving, to somehow deal with her encounter with Carson.

And put off the inevitable.

She'd have to go to Mrs. Tuttle's home and confess that she'd failed at getting Carson to donate the money to bring the Laughlin Singers to Harmony. Marlee cringed at the thought. The mayor's wife, her cousins, the women at the meeting, the town merchants had put their faith in her, and she'd let them down.

Marlee's steps slowed, recalling how the mayor's wife had cautioned her that Carson would be difficult to convince. Everyone in town knew he was focused heavily on his business. Surely they would understand why she hadn't been able to elicit the funds from him.

And there was perhaps still time, Marlee told herself, to

find another musical group who might come to Harmony on a few days' notice and perform for free. If not, then surely the church choir would sing. It wouldn't be as grand a performance, of course, and the visitors from neighboring towns who'd come in response to the newspaper advertisements and flyers would be disappointed, but Mrs. Tuttle could make an announcement before each concert explaining the situation and everyone would understand. Wouldn't they?

Marlee's anger rose again. This was all Carson's fault. He'd put her in this difficult position. He flew into her thoughts and she was so annoyed with him at that moment that she wanted to kiss him.

Kiss him?

Marlee stopped dead in her tracks. Why on earth had that notion sprung into her mind?

"Oh, dear…" she mumbled again, shaking her head. She forced her thoughts back to the task at hand.

No sense waiting, she decided. She'd go to Mrs. Tuttle's house now and break the news, and face the disappointing look she'd surely get in response.

Marlee spotted Audrey walking toward her. She could see the worry that had been etched in Audrey's face since Chord left Harmony with his family.

"I've just spoken with Mrs. Tuttle," Audrey said, stopping next to her outside Goodwin's Dry Goods store. "Everything is arranged."

An odd, uncomfortable feeling swept over Marlee. "Arranged?"

Audrey nodded. "She's heard back from the Laughlins. They're on their way to Harmony and ready to perform all the concerts we asked for."

Marlee's heart lurched and panic swept through her. "Mrs. Tuttle already hired them?"

"Of course." Audrey's expression relaxed a little. "You've done the town such a huge favor, taking on the task of arranging Carson's donation. I don't think anyone else would have attempted it, knowing him like we do."

"But—"

Audrey's brows drew together. "Is something wrong?"

"Well, actually," Marlee said, "I thought Mrs. Tuttle would wait until I brought the money to her before she hired the Laughlins."

"She didn't want them to go elsewhere," Audrey explained. "And everyone knew that, with your experience in fundraising, you could get the money, even from tight-fisted Carson Tate. So, everything is settled."

Marlee opened her mouth to speak but nothing came out.

"I've got to get back to the store," Audrey called as she hurried away.

Marlee staggered into the alley beside the dry goods store and fell against the wall, fearful that she might faint. The singing group was coming. Everyone thought she'd saved the festival. And, really, she'd failed completely.

What would happen when the singers arrived? Mrs. Tuttle, humiliated beyond belief, would have to inform them that, not only were they not going to perform at the festival, but there were no funds to pay for their train tickets or a night's lodging and meals.

The entire town would find out. Even folks in the neighboring towns would hear of it. The festival would be a failure. Merchants would lose their businesses. Families could be devastated. The whole of Harmony would turn against her.

She would have to return to that tiny little room in Mrs. Montgomery's mansion, with only the other servants to count as friends. Years—decades—would pass before she saw Audrey and Becky, her aunt and uncle again. This small glimpse of living among family here in Harmony would be but a memory.

Tears burned in Marlee's eyes. She'd thought she could make Harmony her home. She'd thought she'd finally found a place where she felt wanted and accepted. Now all those hopes were gone.

Pain stabbed her heart and twisted inside her. She'd actually pictured her mother coming to Harmony to live, so that at long last they could be together.

Marlee burst into tears. She hurried deeper into the alley and cried. The anguish of birthdays, Christmases, special moments spent without her mother or any close family tore from her in relentless sobs.

Carson pushed himself out of his chair and stalked across the room. How the hell was he supposed to get any work done when all he could think about was Marlee?

His office still smelled of her. The vision of her seated across the desk loomed in his head. Her dainty hands. Her pink lips. Those blue eyes of hers. Wisps of her hair curling against her cheeks, cheeks flushed bright with anger.

She'd actually had the nerve to raise her voice at him. Few people did that. Marlee had held back, as she'd surely been trained to do at that school she was so proud of and at that job she had back in Philadelphia, but finally she couldn't contain her feelings any longer. Where had all that emotion come from?

Where could it lead?

A familiar, pleasurable ache filled Carson as he gazed out the window.

What would it be like to have her in his bed? What would it feel like if—

"Damn it," Carson muttered, pushing the image from his mind. If he didn't get Marlee out of his head he'd never get any work done.

Carson pulled on his Stetson and left his office. He headed down the boardwalk anxious to put some distance between himself and his office—and the vision of Marlee across the desk from him. He needed to center his thoughts on the weaving mill he was trying to bring to town, and he wouldn't likely get things handled if he couldn't stop wondering what Marlee would look like naked.

"Mr. Tate? Mr. Tate?" someone called.

He paused and looked around the busy boardwalk, then spotted Audrey Meade heading toward him. She was a pretty woman with a good head on her shoulders. Carson knew Chord was courting her and, at that moment, it hit him that Chord was a fool for not asking her to marry him yet.

"I just wanted to thank you for what you've done." Audrey gave him a pleasant smile, and like most everyone else in Harmony, hurried away, not wanting to keep him from his business.

Carson had no idea what she was talking about and was in no mood to ask, so he started walking again. As he passed Goodwin's Dry Goods, a flash of blue caught his eye. Blue, deep blue, like the dress Marlee had on in his office. He stopped and, sure enough, spotted her at the far end of the empty alley.

Anger rose in him, a welcome relief from the other emotions raging within him. What was the matter with her? Why was she alone in the alley? Didn't she know it was dangerous?

Carson stalked toward her ready to chastise her for being so foolish, then stopped still in his tracks. Her back was to him and her shoulders shook. She was crying.

Fear and anger rocked him with a strength he'd never experienced. Had someone hurt her? Carson was overwhelmed with the need to protect her, and kill anyone who'd dare to lay a finger on her. He closed the distance between them in three long strikes, grasped her arm and whirled her to face him. Tears poured down her cheeks and her eyes were red and puffy.

"Get away from me!" she said, and tried to yank her arm from his grasp.

Carson held her firmly. "Are you hurt? Did somebody hurt you?"

She looked up at him as if he'd lost his senses. "No!"

"Then why are you crying?" he asked.

"Because!"

That didn't exactly answer his question, but he was relieved no one had attacked her. Still, she kept crying and Carson didn't know anything else to say so he wrapped both arms around her and pulled her against his chest. Marlee tried to jerk away, but he held on and she came full against him, sobbing into his shirt.

When her tears finally stopped she eased away. Carson took his handkerchief from his pocket and gave it to her.

"Now," he said softly. "Tell me what's wrong."

"Nothing," she told him, dapping at her eyes with the handkerchief. Then she sniffed again and said, "Everything."

Carson was overcome with the need to fix what was wrong—whatever it might be. He had to make things better, no matter what it took. Then it hit him that *he* might be the problem; it didn't make him feel very good about himself.

"Is this because I wouldn't donate the money you asked for?" he asked.

Marlee sniffed and drew herself up. "You are certainly entitled to spend your money as you see fit, Mr. Tate."

She'd responded to his question but hadn't really given him an answer. Carson knew something else was going on. He thought back to when she'd been in his office, how she'd stormed out in a huff. She'd seemed to accept his decision, though certainly it hadn't pleased her. Nothing else had happened—

"Audrey," he said, and managed not to utter a curse. "I saw her. She thanked me for something. Does she think I agreed to donate the money?"

"Apparently the ladies of Harmony had a great deal of confidence in my fundraising ability," she said, and looked away. "Mrs. Tuttle booked the Laughlin Singers on the assumption I could secure your donation."

Maybe he should have told her.

The thought sprang into Carson's mind and for a long moment he considered telling her the reason he'd refused to make the donation.

He'd never told anyone in Harmony why he lived his life the way he did, but at this moment telling Marlee seemed like the right thing to do.

Still, Carson couldn't bring himself to say the words, to tell her what had happened all those years ago. And besides, it wouldn't change the problem she faced.

He drew in a heavy breath and said, "I'll donate the money you need."

"No."

He looked down at her, not sure she'd heard him correctly. "I said I would donate the money—"

"No," she said again. Marlee straightened her shoulders and faced him squarely. "I don't want your pity—and that's exactly what your offer is about. I've spent my life handling my own problems and I will continue to do so."

"This isn't a good time to let your pride get in your way," Carson said gently.

That seemed to fire her up again, which was far better than seeing her cry.

"I will raise that money somehow—without your help," she told him.

Marlee glared up at him, defiance etched in the tight line of her mouth and the hard look in her eyes, and all Carson could think was that he wanted to kiss her.

Then she seemed to crumble again and took a step back.

"Immediately after Christmas, I'm leaving Harmony. I'm going back to Philadelphia," Marlee said, then hurried toward Main Street.

Carson watched her walk away and a heaviness crashed down on him.

She was leaving.

And he was falling in love with her.

Chapter Nine

Marlee sat on a stool in the Harmony General Store gliding
a feather duster along a display of matchboxes and candles. A
dozen or so customers roamed the aisles. Their words carried
to Marlee as she crouched in the back corner, cringing at everyone's topic of conversation.

The festival. The festival that everyone assumed would be
a success because she hadn't yet told Mrs. Tuttle that she had
failed to get the donation from Carson. After her confronta-
tion with him in the alley, she simply hadn't had the strength
to give the mayor's wife the bad news.

Of course, it didn't have to be bad news, Marlee reminded
herself as she shifted on the stool. Carson had said he'd donate the money—but she'd turned him down. Why had she
done that? All her problems—and Harmony's—would have
been solved.

Yet Marlee knew she couldn't allow herself to be in his
debt, emotionally. She couldn't let him rescue her, save her
from admitting she'd failed. She had to stay strong, handle her
own problems as she'd always done. It would do her no good
to rely on Carson, or anyone else, who wouldn't be around in
the future.

All those thoughts had struck her in a flash as she'd stood
in the alley gazing into Carson's handsome face, still feeling

his arms around her, basking in the warmth of the heat he gave off. For a moment, Marlee let the memory fill her mind, and the feelings encircle her heart.

How wonderful that he'd held her while she cried. He'd been concerned that something had happened to her. She'd seen that he'd wanted to fix the problem, whatever it was. No one had ever done those things for her before. She'd felt special in his arms, as if she belonged there, as if he wanted her there.

What would it be like to step into his warm, strong embrace again and again? How wonderful it would feel if Carson would always be there for her.

Marlee forced aside those thoughts as a more troubling one presented itself. In turning down Carson's donation for her own personal reasons, she was being selfish. She'd let her feelings overwhelm her good sense. Yet she couldn't imagine going back to Carson and asking for his money, even if it was for the good of Harmony. Not until she'd attempted to get the funds elsewhere first.

"You okay, boss?" Drew asked.

Carson let his gaze drift to the young man standing in his office doorway who was looking as if he'd found him dancing a jig atop his desk. Carson didn't blame him, though. It wasn't often he sat back with his feet on the corner of his desk, staring out the window.

"It's just that, well, you haven't been out of your office all day, and every time I look in here you're just sitting there doing nothing," Drew said. "You've got those investors coming and—"

"I'm heading out in a minute or two," Carson told him and turned his attention to the window again.

Folks passed by on the boardwalk but Carson didn't really see them. He was lost in thought—and it didn't concern the investors he was expecting.

Marlee. She filled his mind. When he'd kissed her all he could think about was bedding down with her. But after seeing her crying in the alley, holding her, comforting her, something in him had changed. At the time the notion that he was falling in love with her had sprung into his head. Now he knew it was true. He loved her. And she was leaving. She'd be gone right after Christmas, she'd told him. Carson didn't remember a time when he so assuredly did not want Christmas to arrive.

Of course, he could solve Marlee's problem by simply going to the mayor's wife, giving her the money for the singing group and telling her that Marlee had done her job. But what if Marlee had already told Mrs. Tuttle she'd failed? He couldn't make her look like a liar.

He could go to Marlee and insist she take his hundred dollars, but he doubted she'd take it. The woman had a lot of pride, which he couldn't fault her for, but she also had a stubborn streak a mile wide. Still, he'd have to find a way to make the donation. Then Marlee would stay. He'd see to it.

Voices outside his door caught his attention as Ian Caldwell strode into his office. Carson slid his feet off the corner of his desk and sat up as Ian took the chair across from him.

"I talked to the sheriff about keeping a lid on trouble during the festival," Ian said.

"Yeah?" Carson mumbled. "Trouble?"

Ian just looked at him for a moment, then frowned. "What's got your attention? I know it's not me or the festival."

Carson realized he'd been gazing out the window again, and shook his head to clear his thoughts. "Nothing. I'm listening."

Ian gave him a harder look. "It's Marlee Carrington, isn't it?"

Carson was taken aback by how readily the deputy had read his thoughts. He opened his mouth to protest, but Ian waved him off.

"Don't bother to deny it," Ian told him. "I see how you look at her. I know what that means."

Carson let a minute pass while he debated denying everything Ian had said, then decided against it. The two of them had been friends for a while and it was obvious that Ian was head over heels in love with Lucy, so he knew what Carson was going through. Maybe he'd have a little wisdom he could pass on.

"It just occurred to me that I'm in love with Marlee," Carson said. "Problem is, she just told me she's going back to Philadelphia right after Christmas."

Ian's expression darkened. "You can't let her leave. If you care about her, you can't let her get away."

Carson figured this was good advice. Everyone in Harmony knew that Ian had followed Lucy here from Colorado.

"And marry her quick," Ian said. "So she can't leave again."

Carson frowned. "You're worried Lucy might leave Harmony?"

Ian shook his head. "Things are different between Lucy and me."

"Seems to me you ought to take some of your own advice," Carson said. "Marry that woman. Don't let her get away."

"I don't know what I'd do if Lucy left again," Ian whispered.

Carson had never seen his friend look so troubled, so lost. For a moment he felt those same worries, wondering what would happen if Marlee really did leave after Christmas. Carson knew he couldn't—wouldn't—let that happen.

"Marry her," he said, and stood up. "Before it's too late."

Carson grabbed his hat and coat and strode out of his office, leaving Ian sitting in front of his desk staring at nothing.

No two ways about it, Carson silently swore as he made his way across Main Street, he wasn't about to let Marlee leave Harmony. He'd make her want to stay—and to do that, he needed more information.

He cut through the alley and knocked on the back door of the Harmony General Store. At this time of day he knew the Meade women would be in the kitchen preparing the family's evening meal, and after she'd looked so stunned when he'd asked if she could cook, he was sure Marlee wouldn't be among them.

The door opened and Audrey smiled at him. Warmth from the kitchen and the aroma of frying chicken wafted out around her.

"I need to speak with you," Carson said.

Her smile vanished. "Did something happen to Chord? Or his pa? Did—"

"No, it's nothing like that," Carson told her. "It's about Marlee."

Audrey disappeared for a moment, then stepped through the door with her cloak draped around her shoulders.

"I figured we'd have this conversation sooner or later," she said.

Carson shifted uncomfortably. Did everyone in Harmony know how he felt about Marlee?

"First off," Audrey said, "I'll ask you to state your intentions."

He'd always known the eldest Meade daughter brooked little foolishness from most everyone. Now he saw a strength in her that he admired, much the same as he saw Marlee. He thought, too, that Chord Barrett must be as crazy as a mouse in a milk can for not marrying her already.

"My intentions are honorable," Carson assured her.

"I'm pleased to hear you say that. Marlee hasn't had much family life. Her papa disappeared when she was just a baby so her mama had to work, which meant Marlee spent most of her life living with distant family and, well, just about anybody who would take her in, until she went to a school for young ladies. Her mama saved for years to pay it." Audrey smiled.

"Having her live here in Harmony would be wonderful—for Marlee and my whole family."

"She seems to be real caught up in this Christmas festival," Carson said.

"Christmas has always been a difficult time for Marlee. Growing up living in homes where you weren't wanted and never felt like you belonged was tough on her," Audrey said. "You should have seen the look on Marlee's face when she told the ladies she could secure your donation. She looked so happy, as if she'd done something useful to make everyone like her and want her around."

Carson nodded, taking it all in, feeling like a blind man for not seeing those things about Marlee himself.

"Maybe next Christmas, Marlee's mama could come to Harmony. She'd be absolutely thrilled to have her close by, finally," Audrey said. Her cheeks flushed and she glanced away. "Maybe I'm getting ahead of myself."

"Thank you," Carson said. He touched the brim of his hat and left.

Everything made sense, Carson realized as he left the alley and headed toward Main Street. He understood why Marlee had been so anxious to have him donate to the festival and why, when he'd turned her down, she'd become so upset. A hell of a lot more was at stake for Marlee than those singers.

But Carson didn't like that she seemed to feel she only mattered if she was doing something for somebody, that performing tasks was the way to gain friends and feel accepted. Marlee had a lot more to offer than that—despite what had happened in her childhood.

Carson paused. He didn't often think about his family back in Richmond—not that he didn't care about them, because he did. They exchanged letters so he kept up with the news. But that was it. He didn't have time for more than that. A man couldn't build a business by wasting his time on other things.

Still, it was the choice he'd made for himself, unlike Marlee. But he didn't like the choice she'd made and he knew he had to tell her so—along with a few other things. Carson headed back to the Harmony General Store.

Heat swept up Marlee's back and a scent caught her nose. She knew before she spun around that Carson Tate had walked up behind her.

She gazed up at him and felt her cheeks burn, her knees tremble. Quickly she glanced around the store, worried that someone had seen the look on her face. Only two customers remained and they were busy at the counter with Aunt Viola.

"I need to talk to you," Carson said in a low voice. "I know you told all the ladies that you could get me to donate money for the Christmas festival."

Marlee's cheeks burned anew. Bad enough that she'd bragged about her fundraising ability, had failed and now everyone in Harmony would suffer for it, but somehow Carson had found out and now she'd have to endure further humiliation?

He eased closer. "Look, Marlee, I know you wanted to do the right thing by helping out with the festival. But you don't have to try to please everyone for them to like you and want you around."

She gasped softly and fell back a step, as if he'd slapped her. She felt as if he'd somehow managed to peer straight into her heart, her soul, and see how desperately she wanted to belong somewhere. She'd never felt so vulnerable, so exposed in her life.

Marlee forced away those feelings, latching on to anger instead.

"At least I'm trying to be a part of something," she told him, her words tumbling out in a harsh rush. "Unlike *you*. All you care about is making money. You live in this delightful town, among wonderful people, and you don't appreciate any of it. You're so busy rushing from place to place you don't see what's in front of you."

He eased back a little, and Marlee saw a flash of anger, pain, disappointment—something—flash across his face. She expected him to deny what she'd said and tell her she was wrong, but he didn't.

"I've got a job for you," Carson said.

Stunned, Marlee just stared up at him. "A—a job?"

"I've got investors coming to town," he told her. "I need you to get my house ready for company and get a supper cooked."

Marlee shook her head. "You know I'm not trained in domestic chores. I can't possibly accept a job under those circumstances."

"You'll figure it out," he told her.

"But—"

"The job pays a hundred dollars."

Marlee's spine stiffened. "I told you I won't accept that money from you out of pity."

"This isn't pity," he said.

"Yes, it is," she insisted. "I already told you I can't cook or clean."

Carson angled closer and leaned down. Warmth washed over her.

"Is there some other task you'd like to perform for me?" he asked, his voice low and husky.

A tingle rushed through her, bringing with it a flood of highly pleasurable tasks the two of them might perform.

"Be at my house tomorrow morning," he said, and walked away.

Chapter Ten

The front door of Carson's house jerked open as Marlee came through the gate, leaving her to wonder if he'd been watching for her this morning, perhaps unsure if she'd show up—not that he'd given her much of a choice. She should have been nothing but thankful that he'd given her this opportunity to work for him, and by doing so had saved the Christmas festival and her from public embarrassment. Yet Marlee wasn't all that happy that Carson had wormed his way into her personal life enough to learn her innermost frailties.

Carson stepped out onto the porch as she came up the steps. She spared him a glance as she walked past. His face was freshly shaved, leaving her with the almost overwhelming desire to press her palm against his cheek. It didn't help that the delightful scent of soap clung to him.

He followed her inside and closed the door, then helped her off with her cloak. An ornately carved staircase rose in front of her. To her left was a dining room and on the right a large parlor. The furniture was lovely in both rooms, obviously expensive and selected by someone with good taste. Still, the whole place had an empty feel to it, as if it were occupied, yet not lived in.

"I'm not here much," Carson said, as if reading her thoughts.

"I take my meals at the restaurants in town. Reverend Conroy's sister cleans for me."

They walked through the wide doorway into the parlor.

"The furnishings are lovely," Marlee said. "I didn't realize you had a flair for decorating."

A tiny grin pulled at his lips. "My sisters and my ma back in Richmond picked out everything and shipped it here." He waved his hand around the room. "Change whatever you think needs changing. Same for the Christmas decorations. Get whatever you need."

"What sort of budget have you set?" she asked.

He shrugged. "Just get what will make the place look good. I want those investors to see Harmony as a nice place to live."

Marlee took in the room's settees, the chairs, side tables and lamps in one sweep, then walked past Carson into the dining room and stood for a moment or two looking over the walnut table and chairs, the sideboard and the hutch filled with delicate china.

"I stopped by Flora's this morning and asked Lucy if she'd come cook the meal. She's by far the best cook in town," Marlee said. "I thought we'd serve—"

"Serve whatever you think is best," Carson said, then added, "As long as there're meat and potatoes somewhere on the table."

"I'll go shopping now," she told him.

"Already? That's all the time you need to look the place over?"

"I have a trained eye," she pointed out.

"Fine, then," Carson said. "Let's go shopping."

"You're going with me?" she asked.

He grinned. "Who knows? I might want to go into the Christmas decoration business."

Carson helped her with her cloak again, then shrugged into his coat and hat, and they headed toward town. The morning air was cold and crisp, the sunlight weak in the cloudy sky.

Marlee stopped in her tracks as they stepped up onto the crowded boardwalk. All manner of men, women and children streamed in and out of almost every store along Main Street.

"Look at all the people. It's the first day of the festival," Marlee said. "The train must have already arrived."

"Did that singing group make it to town yet?" Carson asked.

"Yes. Their first performance is this afternoon," Marlee said. "Are you going?"

Carson rolled his eyes. "Damn right I'm going."

Marlee couldn't help but giggle. "Then we'd better get your house ready."

Since she'd worked in her aunt and uncle's general store for a while now, Marlee knew every item in stock so she'd already decided what she would purchase from them for Carson's house. But she also knew that since she was shopping on Carson's behalf, she had to spend some of his money at the other businesses in town. Carson wouldn't want to show favoritism.

The aisles of Goodwin's Dry Goods store were crowded with shoppers as they made their way inside. Marlee was pleased to see that the shelves overflowed with merchandise and that a touch of Christmas had been added to most everything in the store.

Green ribbons had been tired around lanterns and coffee-pots. Red bows adorned stacks of gray blankets. Children were crowded around a display of toys, dolls in fancy dresses, clowns and jumping jacks painted bright colors, an army of pewter soldiers and wooden horses, horns and drums, a dollhouse with tiny furniture, and a mechanical circus train complete with miniature wild animals.

Beside the toys sat boxes of colorful glass ornaments shaped like acorns, stars and balloons. There were wax angels with spun-glass wings, tiny candles in tin holders, silver tinsel garlands and large gold stars perfect to top any tree. With so many beautiful items, Marlee wasn't sure what to get.

"Which do you like the most?" Marlee asked.

"Definitely the circus train," Carson replied.

She looked up at him sure she was seeing the expression he'd worn on Christmases in his childhood.

"You've been very good this year," Marlee said. "I'm sure Santa will bring you whatever you wish for."

His expression changed. Gone was the magical look of a little boy at Christmas. He was all man now, and she was sure the thing topping his wish list would not be found under a tree.

"Let's keep looking," Marlee said, and felt herself blush.

She selected tinsel, ornaments and spools of red ribbon. Carson carried them to the counter, paid and told Mr. Goodwin to deliver them to his house.

Outside, the crowds were larger. Marlee and Carson made their way down the boardwalk among shoppers carrying large market baskets and brown wrapped packages. A line had already formed outside the Blue Bonnet Café and at Flora's Bake Shop.

Marlee joined the gathering of women gazing into the display window of Markham's Dress Shop. Red and green bell-shaped swatches of fabric had been sewn on the pockets of crisp white aprons; tiny jingle bells had been added at the bottom.

"Did this store open just for the festival?" Carson asked.

Marlee's cousins had told her Markham's was one of the first stores opened in Harmony. How could Carson not have seen?

"It's been here for a long time," she told him. "You didn't notice it?"

"Surely you'll agree that thinking up new businesses for Harmony is more important than knowing there's a dress shop in town," Carson said.

"I'll admit no such thing," she told him, then conceded, "Both are important."

She turned to the window again and gazed past the display

to the bolts of fabric stacked on the shelves. The image of her mother flew into her mind.

"Something wrong?" Carson asked.

She glanced up and saw genuine concern on his face. While it was her custom to speak little of her past, she figured that since he already knew one of her innermost secrets, telling him another wouldn't do any harm.

"My mother is a seamstress," Marlee said. "She works for a wealthy woman in New York and makes the most beautiful clothing for her. They're in Europe now. She always brings back exquisite fabric."

"You miss your mama, don't you?" he asked softly.

For an instant, Marlee thought she would cry, but she managed to hold in her tears.

"Everyone misses their mother. Don't you?" she asked.

He looked puzzled, confused, as if this was a question he'd never been asked nor had he ever considered. But Marlee didn't press the issue, fearing it was not a comfortable subject for him to discuss.

"We'd better finish up our shopping," she said. "I know you're in a hurry to get on with your business affairs today."

Carson shook his head. "No hurry. I'd like to look around, see what else is going on in town. Let's have a look at the Stafford Emporium. They've got toys in their window."

To Marlee's surprise they went from shop to shop taking in all the sights in town. Finally they made their way to the Harmony General Store. The aisles were jammed with customers.

Marlee spotted Audrey at the rear of the store. She waved and Audrey's face lit up. She waded through the throng of people to meet them.

"Isn't this fantastic?" she said. "The store has never been this busy. It's all we can do to keep up with sales. Papa and Mama are thrilled."

"Every store in town is packed," Marlee said.

"All because of your generous donation," Audrey said to Carson. She gave Marlee a big smile. "And your help, too, of course."

"Are you going to the afternoon performance?" Marlee asked.

"I don't think Papa will let any of us out of the store. He doesn't want to miss a sale. We'll go to tonight's show after closing," Audrey said. "You two must be hungry. Every seat in every restaurant in town is taken, from what I hear, so go on back to the kitchen. Becky is cooking."

"I've got something to do," Carson said. "I'll meet you here in a bit."

Before Marlee could answer, he left.

"They were wonderful, didn't you think?" Marlee asked.

Carson gazed down at her as they moved with the crowd leaving the social hall and couldn't help smiling. The Laughlin Singers had put on a good show, no doubt about it. Yet all the songs they'd performed didn't please him near as much as the look on Marlee's face.

She talked about the musical numbers as they made their way through town. True, he'd listened to the songs and he'd been pleased with the performances, but mostly he'd sat there thinking.

Carson looked around at the busy street. A lot of folks were still out, though night was falling. Men and women walked arm and arm, mamas shepherded their children, held their hands as they crossed the street. Candles burned in the shop windows and warm lantern light shown from the living quarters above. Bonfires had been set along Main Street and folks were gathered around enjoying the warmth, the fellowship; some were singing Christmas carols.

For all the time he'd spent staring out at Main Street, this was the first time Carson noticed—really noticed—the town's

Christmas decorations. The big wooden candy canes, the red ribbons, the green boughs made him think of his own boyhood, and Christmas mornings with his family. On the heels of those thoughts, others presented themselves, troubling him now as they'd done sitting in the social hall, listening to the Laughlins.

"I'd like to get your house decorated tonight," Marlee said. "You don't have to stay. I know you spent a lot of time away from your office today."

"I'll stay," he told her.

When they arrived at the house Carson saw that everything he'd purchased today—well, almost everything—was stacked neatly on the front porch. He carried the packages inside, lit the lanterns and they set to work. Of course, Marlee was doing most of the decorating. Carson had never felt so useless in his life. But he took a great deal of pleasure watching Marlee display everything they'd purchased, since it involved a lot of bending, reaching and swaying of hips.

"I think that's it," Marlee declared as she stood in the center of the parlor assessing the decorations. She turned to him. "What do you think?"

He thought she was beautiful. Her face glowed and her blue eyes sparkled in the lamplight. He thought he'd like nothing more than to sweep her into his arms and carry her upstairs to his bedroom.

"You were right," Carson said.

Marlee frowned and she touched her fingertip to her chin. "About the angels? Or the tinsel?"

"About what you said to me," Carson told her and walked over. "About how I didn't appreciate what was going on around me because all I cared about was making money."

Marlee dipped her gaze. "I spoke harshly."

"Not too many people in this town will tell me when I'm doing something wrong," Carson said, remembering what he'd thought about during the musical performance. "So I decided

I owed you an explanation. You see, my pa had a good head for business but he never tended to it like he should. He was always taking time away to visit a friend, go fishing, or some such nonsense. Finally, when he realized he'd let things go too far, he was nearly penniless. The strain got to him. His heart gave out."

"Oh, Carson, that's so sad," Marlee said.

"It didn't have to be that way," Carson said, the familiar anger growing in him every time he recalled how foolish his father had been. "My mama suffered because he wasn't taking care of his business. We all suffered."

"So you wanted to make certain that never happened to you," Marlee said.

"That's for damn sure," he said. "But lately…well, it occurred to me that I could let myself have a few pleasures and still manage my business."

"That sounds reasonable," she agreed.

"Take, for instance, decorating this house," Carson said. He caught her hand and pulled her to the parlor doorway. "While you were busy in the dining room, I took it upon myself to do a little decorating right here on this spot. I hung some mistletoe."

A breathy little sigh slipped from her lips, causing Carson to angle closer. He slid his arm around her and pulled her against him. A charge went through him as her soft curves met his chest. He leaned down and kissed her on the lips.

She moaned. He groaned and deepened their kiss. Carson tightened his hold on her, pulled her tighter against him. She parted her lips ever so slightly and he slid inside, then raised his hand and cupped her breast.

Marlee gasped but didn't pull away. Instead she pushed closer, melding their bodies together. Their kiss became frantic. Carson's knees nearly gave out from the sheer delight of the feel of her. He wanted her, as he'd never wanted another woman. He wanted her now.

But Marlee wasn't the kind of woman he would bed, then allow to walk out of his life. He had to know she would stay with him always.

Slowly he lifted his head, ending their kiss. Her breath was hot, her lips moist. He gazed at her feeling the unfulfilled expectation between them.

"I'd better take you home," he whispered.

She nodded and backed away.

Carson walked her home.

Chapter Eleven

"Lucy will be here soon," Audrey said as she entered the kitchen at Carson's house.

Marlee said a silent prayer of thanks. Carson had gone to the train station to pick up the businessmen he expected, and if Lucy didn't arrive soon to prepare their meal Marlee had no idea what she'd serve them.

"You look happy," Marlee said. "Things going well at the store?"

"Busy," she said, with a broad smile. "Even busier than yesterday."

Marlee gave her a closer look. "Somehow, I don't think a second successful day of the Christmas festival is what's got you smiling so much."

Audrey giggled. "Chord is back."

Marlee hadn't heard the news. She'd been at Carson's house almost all day preparing for his company.

"His papa is much improved," Audrey reported. "The family is still there, but Chord came back because he couldn't be away from his job any longer."

"Or away from you?" Marlee asked.

"We missed each other," she admitted. Then her expression changed. "You won't believe what Chord heard while he was in Colorado. It's about Lucy."

She glanced at the door that led out of the kitchen, then sidled closer to Marlee and lowered her voice.

"Chord had to change trains in the town of Marlow, so he stopped by the sheriff's office to pass the time," Audrey said. "Chord mentioned that Lucy and Ian were living here in Harmony. The sheriff assumed they were married, and was shocked to learn they weren't. Did you know that Lucy was married when she lived in Marlow? And that she and her husband divorced? According to the sheriff in Marlow, that husband of hers wasn't well liked. He was lazy and just plain mean. He treated Lucy terribly."

"I'd say Lucy was lucky to be rid of him," Marlee said. "Good thing he wanted to divorce her."

"No, no," Audrey said. "It was the other way around. In fact, when Lucy asked him for a divorce and he wouldn't grant her one, Lucy set fire to his belongings, then held him at gunpoint until he signed the official papers."

"Oh, my goodness," Marlee gasped. She could only imagine how desperate Lucy must have been to get out of that abusive marriage, and she admired the strength Lucy had shown.

"She's got herself a wonderful man in Ian," Audrey said. "Oh, and speaking of wonderful men, everybody is talking about what Carson has done for Christmas this year. Or were you behind the toy donation?"

"Toys?"

"Didn't you know?" Audrey asked. "He bought toys from all the merchants in Harmony and sent them to the orphans' asylum."

So that was the reason he'd left her at the Harmony General Store yesterday, Marlee realized.

A quick knock sounded on the back door and Lucy walked inside carrying two large baskets. Marlee and Audrey helped her get them onto the sideboard.

"Thank goodness you're here," Marlee said. "You're a life-saver."

Lucy smiled. "Honestly, I've had my fill of baking cookies, pies and cakes for a while. Flora can handle things at the bake shop for a change."

"I can lend a hand," Audrey said. "Mama and Papa can do without me at the store for a bit."

Marlee was relieved to have the extra help. This afternoon Carson had told her that he wanted her to act as hostess at tonight's dinner, which left her no time to assist Lucy in the kitchen.

Voices sounded in the house.

"That must be them," Marlee said, smoothing down the skirt of her dark blue dress. It was the best one she owned.

"You look fantastic," Audrey assured her. "Run along. We'll handle everything."

Marlee walked through the dining room and into the entryway where she found Carson and three other men hanging their coats and hats on the rack beside the door. She couldn't help but smile at the sight of Carson dressed in a white shirt, string tie and black vest. He looked considerably younger and stronger than his guests, all of them with graying hair and widening middles.

Carson made introductions and Marlee greeted them, feeling much more at ease here than in the kitchen preparing their meal.

"Let's go into the parlor, shall we?" she said, and led the way inside.

A roaring fire burned in the fireplace and the mantel was decorated with evergreen boughs, red bows and angels, giving the room a warm, cozy feel. As she'd seen Mrs. Montgomery do dozens of times, Marlee directed the conversation, asking the men about their families and their plans for Christmas.

"We're heading east on the last train out tonight," Mr. Ayers said and smiled. "We'll make it home for Christmas Day."

"There's nothing more important than family on Christmas," Marlee agreed. "If you'll excuse me, I'll go check on our supper."

As she left the parlor, Carson gave her a tiny smile of approval.

The supper of fried chicken, ham, potatoes, three kinds of vegetables and hot buttery biscuits was delicious. Marlee had set the table with the china Carson's mother and sisters had sent, and used a white candle surrounded by pine and holly as a centerpiece. The table sparkled under the lamplight. The conversation concerned the town of Harmony, mostly, and Marlee made a point to mention all its good points. But she also detected an undertone of business. Carson shrewdly worked favorable information into the discussion with an ease that made Marlee realize why he was such a successful businessman.

"You gentlemen go into the parlor and enjoy your cigars," Marlee said, after they'd finished their coffee and dessert.

Mr. Powell patted his belly. "I think I'll invest in Harmony just so I can come back for more of that pie."

The men chuckled as they left the dining room. Carson hung back.

"Everything was perfect." His gaze darkened. "You were perfect."

Marlee couldn't hide her smile, or stop the flush of pride that swept through her.

Carson left the dining room. Marlee gathered the dessert plates and went into the kitchen. Lucy and Audrey were washing dishes.

"You two did a wonderful job," Marlee said. "When that weaving mill gets built in Harmony, they ought to name it the 'Lucy and Audrey' mill."

"Do you think they'll invest their money here?" Lucy asked.

"I certainly do," Marlee said. After seeing the way Carson handled things, she didn't doubt it for a minute.

By the time they'd cleared the dining room, washed the dishes and put everything away in the kitchen, Carson returned.

"The meal was delicious," he said. "Thank you."

Lucy and Audrey gave him a grateful smile.

"The men are leaving now," Carson said. "I'll take them to the station."

Marlee took the package of food she'd set aside for them and followed Carson into the entryway.

"So you won't get hungry on your trip home," she said.

As they left the house, Carson said, "I'll be back soon. Wait for me."

Marlee returned to the kitchen just as Audrey opened the back door and Ian and Chord came inside. She figured they must have been waiting outside for Carson's guests to leave.

"I know there's some apple pie in this kitchen," Chord said. "I smelled it clear across town."

"You're too late," Audrey told him with a teasing grin. "We've already put everything away."

"No matter," Ian said. "We'll serve ourselves."

"Don't you dare," Lucy said, cutting in front of him. "You'll just make a mess. I'll serve it."

"Yes, ma'am," Ian said, and smiled at Lucy with such love that it made Marlee's heart ache.

Lucy served the pie while Audrey poured coffee for them. Laughter and conversation grew as they talked about the goings-on in Harmony. A short while later, the door to the dining room opened and Carson walked in.

His eyebrows shot up. "Am I hosting another party?"

"No," Ian told him. "We're just eating your food, then leaving."

Everybody chuckled, and Carson laughed along.

"I'll take another slice of that pie," he said.

"How did it go with those investors?" Chord asked. "Are they going to go in on the weaving mill with you?"

"Thanks to these ladies," Carson said, saluting them with the slice of pie Lucy had just handed him, "Harmony will have its weaving mill come spring."

The night was chilly and damp when they all left Carson's house. Along Main Street the last of the bonfires burned low and golden lantern light shone in the windows. Warmth settled around Marlee. She couldn't remember enjoying an evening so much. She glanced up at Carson.

How could she ever return to Philadelphia after Christmas?

"I can't believe the town is still so busy," Marlee remarked as she joined Audrey near a display of knives at the front of the Harmony General Store. Today was the last day of the festival and folks were still pouring into Harmony.

"Is it? Audrey asked, glancing out the window. "Oh, yes, I guess it is."

Becky joined them. "You haven't noticed the crowds on Main Street because all you're looking at is one man."

Audrey blushed. Marlee had noticed that all morning long Audrey had positioned herself near the store's windows, and that Chord seemed to be patrolling this section of Main Street far more than necessary. Marlee couldn't blame her. She hadn't seen Carson since last night, and she missed him.

"Having Chord back is the best Christmas gift I could get," Audrey said.

"And what about next Christmas?" Becky asked, nodding wisely. "You'll be a married woman presenting him with a son for Christmas."

Audrey gasped and her cheeks turned bright red, but she smiled gently and nodded. "That would make for a wonderful Christmas," she admitted.

"I can't wait to have a nephew or a niece," Becky declared,

and threw her arms around her sister. "Won't it be wonderful, Marlee? A baby by next Christmas!"

Marlee reeled back, as if she'd been slapped. She'd never been so stunned by anything anyone had said to her. Audrey married? With a baby? By next Christmas? Audrey and Chord were so much in love, and marrying and having children seemed like the best thing that could happen to them.

But what about her? What would she be doing next Christmas?

The thought sped through Marlee's mind like a runaway train. Next Christmas, what would she have? The same tiny quarters in Mrs. Montgomery's house? Alone? Hoping she might get to see her mother for an hour or so that day? Or would she return to Marlow, visit Audrey and Chord in their nice home filled with the laughter of the baby they were destined to have?

Marlee's heart seemed to skip a beat as another thought jolted her. What about Carson? Would next year find him married—to someone from Harmony? A man like him wasn't likely to stay single much longer. Would he be happily wed with a child of his own on the way?

All morning Marlee had thought about her time spent at Carson's house last night. How warm and welcoming it was. How delightful it had been to spend time with him, see how he worked, and to have been involved in bringing a prosperous new industry to Harmony. Marlee couldn't remember ever feeling as if she were such a part of something, as she felt here in this town with its people, its problems, its bright future... and with Carson.

Yet all of that could end?

She couldn't bear the thought.

Marlee rushed out of the store. She had to talk to Lucy.

Chapter Twelve

"That's it," Uncle Willard announced as he walked through the curtained doorway into the kitchen. He smiled broadly. "The festival is over, our doors are locked and today is going to be our best Christmas Eve ever."

Aunt Viola turned from the cookstove, wiped her hands on her apron and gave him a hug, as Audrey and Becky cheered and clapped. Marlee's spirits lifted, as she was swept up in the family's joy.

"We've made more money than I ever imagined," he said.

Marlee had heard the same from the other merchants in Harmony. The Christmas Festival had delivered even better than expected prosperity.

"I'm sure the town will want to do it again next year," Aunt Viola declared.

"And every year after," Becky said.

"All right, girls," Aunt Viola said, heading back to the cookstove and the turkey she was preparing for their Christmas Eve supper, "let's get going. We've got a lot to do before the church service tonight."

Laughter and chatter filled the kitchen, along with the smell of the pecan pies Audrey had baked earlier and the fresh Christmas tree Uncle Willard put up in the corner. Marlee pitched in stringing popcorn and berries for the tree.

"Look at these," Becky declared, as she opened a small wooden crate Uncle Willard had brought in from the storage room. Inside were tinsel and ornaments for the tree. She lifted out two red stockings that were a bit worn and frayed. "We've had them since we were children."

"Wait," Audrey said. She dashed up the stairs to the family's living quarters, then back down again. She held up a stocking, this one brand-new.

"For you, Marlee," she said.

Her heart rose in her throat. "For—for me?"

"Of course," Becky said. "You're part of our family."

Tears stung Marlee's eyes as she and her cousins hung their stockings on the mantel. Since yesterday when she'd run out of the store, she'd been overwhelmed with thoughts of leaving Harmony. Christmas Day was tomorrow, and the day after that she'd be gone. How could she leave this wonderful place?

Yet did she have a reason to stay?

She could possibly find some sort of job, but the skills she'd learned at school weren't in demand here. Uncle Willard would let her live in the store, but it wasn't right to impose on the family indefinitely. And what about her mother? If Marlee stayed in Harmony she'd see her on the very rarest of occasions.

Carson flew into her mind, and her heart ached anew. How could she bear never seeing him again? She supposed she'd have to find a way, since Carson had given her no reasons to stay.

Marlee chocked back her tears and forced a smile. If today was to be among her last few in Harmony, she'd put aside her troubles and enjoy it.

They sang Christmas carols as they put the decorations on the tree, and shared memories of past holidays, plans for the coming year, and a little town gossip. Just as Uncle Willard placed a gold star on the top of the tree a knock sounded on the back door. Audrey opened it, and with a gust of cold air, Lucy and Ian came inside.

"Merry Christmas," Aunt Viola said. "Come on in. Have some hot coffee?"

Ian stood firm and looped his arm around Lucy's shoulders.

"I know this is Christmas Eve," he said, "but it would bring great pleasure to Lucy and me if you'd come to the church. We're getting married."

"You are?" Becky exclaimed.

"Today?" Audrey asked. "Now?"

"She's made me the happiest man alive by agreeing to marry me," Ian said and tightened his hold on Lucy. Then he smiled. "I'm doing it quick before she changes her mind."

Everyone laughed and surrounded the couple, offering congratulations.

Marlee gave Lucy a hug. "I'm so happy for you, truly I am."

"After we talked yesterday, I couldn't think about anything else," Lucy said. "I don't want next Christmas to get here and find me still living alone, too afraid to take a chance on love."

When Marlee had left the store yesterday she'd gone to Flora's Bake Shop and talked to Lucy. She'd poured out her heart, telling how she planned to return to Philadelphia to face a lonely future. Even though her own destiny hadn't changed, Marlee was glad Lucy's had.

"You're doing the right thing," Marlee said, and genuinely meant it.

"Reverend Conroy has agreed to marry us today, just before the evening service starts," Ian said. "We're keeping the ceremony small—and quick—so we're only inviting a few folks."

As soon as Ian and Lucy left, everyone scrambled to put on warm clothing, and headed for the church. Few people were on the streets since most everyone was home with their family. Businesses were closed. The town seemed especially quiet, especially after the hustle and bustle of the Christmas Festival. Marlee's heart was heavy, thinking how much she'd miss Harmony.

Her spirits lifted as they approached the church and she spotted Carson and Chord waiting on the front steps. Even wearing heavy coats and hats, with their breath freezing in the cold, damp air, they looked strong and solid. Marlee wished she could throw herself into Carson's arms and stay there forever.

Carson escorted her into the church and they sat on a pew with the rest of the family. Candles were lit and greenery festooned the altar. Miss Marshall, who accompanied the choir on piano every Sunday, played a hymn, then Ian and Lucy rose from their seats.

As Reverend Conroy's ceremony began, tears pooled in Marlee's eyes. Carson glanced down at her. She thought he might be uncomfortable seeing this emotional side of her, but instead he closed his big warm hand over hers and held it securely.

The reverend's ceremony was short, a few simple words, then vows were exchanged.

"I now pronounce you man and wife," he said. "You may kiss your bride."

Ian gave Lucy a chaste kiss, then turned to the gathering with the biggest smile Marlee had ever seen on a man. Lucy was a radiant bride. It was obvious she knew she'd made the right decision in marrying Ian. Everyone circled the happy couple offering congratulations, hugs and handshakes.

They left the church with Aunt Viola, Becky and Audrey all sniffling. Marlee tried to hold back her emotions, but couldn't. She burst into tears.

"You all go on," Carson said. "I'll bring her home in a while."

Uncle Willard nodded and escorted Aunt Viola and Becky. Chord hooked his arm through Audrey's and followed.

"Your tears will freeze if we stand out here too long," Carson said.

He took her to his house. Inside, Carson helped her with her cloak, then left his coat beside the front door. He laid a fire in the parlor hearth. Warmth filled the room quickly.

"Sit down," Carson said, indicating the settee.

Marlee sat, gulping back her tears. Although she knew it wasn't exactly proper for the two of them to be alone in his house like this, and they'd done the same when she'd come to decorate and prepare for his investors, this time it seemed different. More intimate, more secluded. Yet Marlee didn't want to leave. Not when her departure to Philadelphia was but days away, and these few moments might be the only ones left to share with Carson.

He sat beside her. His warmth spread over her, hotter than the flames in the fireplace.

"Now," he said softly, "tell me what's got you so upset."

Marlee turned her head away. "I'm—I'm just happy for Ian and Lucy."

Carson leaned around until he caught her eye. "You're sure that's all?"

"Yes," she said softly.

But it wasn't, and she couldn't contain her feelings any longer. She sprang to her feet and burst out crying again.

"No," she wailed. "I have to leave—and I don't want to leave. But I can't stay here without a job and a place to live. And if I stay I'll never see my mother again. And—and I adore Becky and Audrey, and Audrey will surely get married soon, and have a baby, and Aunt Viola and Uncle Willard have been wonderful to me, but Mrs. Montgomery needs me, and I spent all that time in school learning to be a personal secretary, and—and—and I love you."

Marlee gasped, choking off her tears, realizing what she'd just blurted out. She whirled away. She couldn't face Carson.

Bad enough that he knew the deepest, longest-held secrets of her past, now he knew that she loved him.

She felt his hands on her shoulders as he stood behind her, then his breath against her cheek.

"I'm glad to hear you say that," he said softly. "Because I love you, too."

She spun around. "You—you do?"

"I fell in love with you somewhere between you threatening to shoot me, and learning that you can't cook, and seeing how hard you worked on the Christmas Festival and the supper for those investors," he said.

Marlee wiped away the rest of her tears. "But you don't really know me."

"I know enough. I know you've felt unwanted and unaccepted in the past," Carson said. "But not now. Not with me. I love you."

Hearing those words made her heart beat faster, but she was still afraid to believe them.

"How do you know you love me?" Marlee asked.

"You make me want to slow down," he said. "You made see me that by giving something away—that hundred dollars—I could get something even better in return. Can't say that I ever walked the streets of Harmony looking in store windows, taking the time to shop, talk to people or go to a musical performance before you came along."

"Really?" she asked, pleased with herself. "So you don't mind that I'm really not much of a homemaker?"

"We'll figure things out...together," Carson said. "For now, let's just enjoy knowing we love each other."

Marlee's heart rose in her throat, as the most wonderful sense of contentment came over her. "I'd like that," she said.

Carson gazed into her eyes, then lowered his head and kissed her. Marlee rose on her toes and looped her arms around his neck. He deepened their kiss. She moaned and kissed him back.

He lifted her into his arms and carried her up the stairs. At the entrance to his bedroom, he paused.

"If you're not ready for this, just say so," he said.

For Marlee, nothing had ever seemed so right. "I love you," she said.

He carried her inside and placed her on the bed. They kissed as their hands sought and found buttons and fasteners, and finally discovered each other's most intimate secrets.

Stretched out on the bed beside her, Carson kissed his way down the length of her. Marlee gasped at his touch, and moved closer, exploring him in the same way.

She welcomed him as he moved above her, locking her in his arms and whispering into her ear. She caught his rhythm, joined as one, until pleasure burst inside her. She held him tight as he called her name and followed.

Marlee roused from a light sleep contented in Carson's arms. She saw that he was already awake and smiling at her.

"I love you," he said, and kissed her softly.

"I love you, too," she said. "I fell in love with you the minute I stepped off the train in Harmony and saw you."

They lay together, content in each other's arms for a long moment.

"I have a Christmas gift for you," Carson said.

Of all the things that had happened between them so far, this one took Marlee by surprise.

"I don't have a gift for you," she said.

"You already gave me the best gift I could ever get."

"What gift? I didn't give you anything."

"Oh, but you did," he said in a deep, husky voice.

Marlee realized what he meant and felt her cheeks grow warm.

"In fact, that's one gift I'll always be happy with," Carson told her. "But don't feel like you have to wait for a special occasion or holiday to give it."

She giggled and swatted him playfully on the chest. "Just tell me what your gift is."

Carson pushed himself up on one elbow and took her hand in his. He gazed deep into her eyes.

"My gift is my promise," he told her. "I promise that you'll never feel alone or unaccepted again. I'll be here for you, at your side, whenever you need me. Forever."

Tears came to Marlee's eyes. A wonderful, warm glow filled her.

A little smile pulled at his lips. "Marlee Carrington, would you do me the honor of being my wife?"

"Yes!"

Carson pulled her into his arms. She'd never felt so happy, so alive in her life. He gave her a long, lingering kiss, then pulled away.

"How about we get married right now?" he asked.

"I thought you said I made you want to slow down?" she said.

"Okay," he told her. "How about an hour from now?"

Marlee giggled. "Tempting as that is, I need time to plan a wedding."

Carson considered her words, then said, "Just don't take too long—after your mama gets here."

Disappointment threaded through Marlee's happiness.

"I don't know that she'll be able to come," she said. "She gets so little time off, and it's a long trip out here."

Carson shook his head. "I want her to come here to live. Permanently."

Marlee's eyes flew open and she gasped. "You do? Oh, Carson, that would be wonderful. I'm sure she could find some sort of job here. Maybe she could work for Dorrie Markham at her dress shop."

"Your mama isn't going to have to get a job," Carson told her. "I'll take care of her. I'll build her a house or, if you'd rather, she can live with us. Whatever makes you happy."

"*You* make me happy," Marlee said. "And so does my family, and Harmony, and especially the Christmas festival. It's what really got me involved with everyone here."

Carson pulled her into his arms.

"I can't wait to see what happens next Christmas," he said. "And the one after that, and the one after that."

Marlee snuggled closer. She couldn't wait for next Christmas, either.

* * * * *

HIS CHRISTMAS WISH

Lauri Robinson

Dear Reader,

I've always loved the holiday season, so the opportunity to write a Christmas story was truly a dream come true. In *His Christmas Wish,* Cora and Morgan discover not just the gift of love, but how to share that gift.

We all share the gift of love in many ways, and we all have special holiday memories we hold close. I'd like to share one with you.

We moved to Kansas when I was nine. I don't remember thinking how different things were from Minnesota, but I do remember the December day a delivery driver knocked on the door and asked for help unloading a package.

Wrapped in burlap was the largest Christmas tree ever—I was a child so it may have been smaller than I remember—which my grandfather had had cut down on his property in Northern Minnesota and shipped to us in Kansas. I still remember decorating that tree, and how it smelled like Minnesota. Like Grandpa. It wasn't until years later that I heard how much effort Grandpa had put into that package of love. Since he wasn't in the tree-farm business, he'd had to acquire special permits so the tree could cross state lines.

My grandfather died six years later, and to this day—decades later—when we arrive on the land up north which he originally purchased I step out of the car, take a deep breath and smell the pines. Smell Grandpa.

Merry Christmas, dear readers, and thank you.

Lauri

DEDICATION

To my grandfather, who has been gone many years, but remains in my heart as strong as ever.

Look for Lauri Robinson's UNCLAIMED BRIDE
available November 2012
from Harlequin® Historical

Chapter One

Central Nebraska, 1884

It was late, well past the time when most folks were sound asleep, but Cora Palmer was wide-awake, lying there in bed, listening to the December wind whistling outside the cabin. Snowflakes ticked against the window, a detour in their swirling, tumbling journey to the ground, where they would rest upon one another until they grew inches deep and as heavy as the weight on her shoulders. Melancholy was like that, heavy and thick, and though she normally didn't let it get to her, right now Cora was as powerless as the snowflakes. She was at a crossroads in life, had known that for a while, but tonight, witnessing Morgan once again huddled on the far side of the bed with his back to her, the ache in her chest had become suffocating and a thick stew brewed in her head.

If only she could turn back the clock of time. No, that was naive, and she was beyond that. A widow with a child to raise couldn't live in the past. Besides, these wants and needs she had—grown-woman wants and needs—wouldn't let her. Over the past few months, the depths of her emotions had entered uncharted territories, which left her more confused—her anguish more severe. A sigh escaped her lips, one that threatened to take her heart with it.

She'd been jubilant the day Morgan had asked her to marry him, and even more so a week later when they traveled to Central City in his sturdy buckboard with little Nathan perched on her lap. Their wedding had been a simple affair, just she and Morgan, Reverend Davis and his wife, Edna, who held Nathan during the service. Even though her son hadn't yet had his second birthday that day, Nathan had sat quietly and listened to the service as if it was a story to behold.

Cora's misery, so thick and strong, had her eyes and throat burning. At the end of the ceremony, Morgan had brushed his lips over hers. The kiss had been so reverent and sweet she didn't need to close her eyes to remember the contact. Even now, two long months later, her lips still quivered and tingled, wanting it to happen again, and more. She wanted to be Morgan's wife in every way. Some days the desires were so severe they all but crippled her, and other times, like this very moment, they left her close to tears.

On the outside, there was nothing to cry about. Her family was happy enough. They had plenty of food, wood and supplies for the animals to last the long, cold months winter bestowed.

She turned again, to the outline of her husband. *We've been married two months, yet we're miles apart, farther now than before our wedding. How can we lie in this bed, together, night after night, yet have such a distance between us?*

Morgan shifted and Cora stiffened as a surge of guilt raced through her. He worked sunup to sundown and certainly didn't deserve her musings to disturb his sleep.

"Are you cold?" he asked.

It didn't take much more than that. The simple sound of his voice sent delicious sensations swirling inside her, along with a hint of a mysterious satisfaction she dually craved to experience. If only all she had to do was say yes, and he'd roll over and wrap his arms around her. Since that was about as likely to happen as the petals from a daisy falling instead of snowflakes outside the window, she answered, "No."

He flipped the covers back. "The fire's almost out. I'll stoke it and check on Nathan. That storm's really howling. I suspect we'll see a foot of snow on the ground by morning."

"I suspect," she murmured, not really caring if there was a foot or a mountain of snow.

She'd been here before, this crossroads muddling her mind—several times. When Orville had asked her to marry him. When they packed up and left Ohio for the Nebraska plains. When Nathan was born in their tiny cabin not two miles from where she now lay. When Orville died.

This time was different. Each of those times, even though they hadn't been clear and she'd been nervous, she'd known which route to take. Right now. Tonight. She didn't.

There were choices. She could stay on the trail she was on—*they* were on—where she and Morgan were courteous and respectful to one another and most likely would have a simple, platonic life on the outside while miserable on the inside. Or she could pack up and return to Ohio. Not that there was much there for her, but when you love someone you want them to be happy, and Morgan wasn't happy. A double-edged saw blade seemed to be cutting her in half. Because she loved Morgan so dearly, leaving wasn't the choice she wanted to make. Traveling with a child in the dead of winter would be foolish, dangerous even. Furthermore, if she were to leave, people would blame Morgan. She couldn't abide that. A finer man didn't exist, which made the third option calling to her stronger—it was the one that led straight to Morgan's heart. An odd sensation said that path could be rocky, dangerous even, but something deep in her core told her that when she reached the end of the journey, she wouldn't be disappointed. The trouble was, that appeared to be what Morgan didn't want, which threatened to tear her heart right out of her chest, for ultimately, his love was her greatest desire.

Across the room, the smoldering coals leaped to life as Morgan stirred them and added logs. Crouched in the glow, his dark hair rumpled and wearing the long underdrawers that highlighted his thickly muscled frame, he looked so fine Cora had to bite her lip to keep from moaning aloud. She wanted him, as a wife wants her husband, but it was stronger than that even, bolder and more primitive. It was as if she wanted him to live inside her.

She'd grown to love Orville, bless his soul—as people do when life throws them together—but she'd fallen in love with Morgan, and there was a big difference. For as devoted as Orville had been she'd never wanted him like this. Deep in her heart, the spot that held the secret to happiness, promised that life with Morgan would be a wondrous adventure. Beyond anything she could imagine. Thrilling, and divine, and worthy.

This time it was a dreamy sigh that escaped her lips, created by those inner possibilities she couldn't ignore.

Morgan rose and moved toward the small bed he'd constructed to fit in the small alcove beside the fireplace so Nathan would be warm even on the coldest nights. His stride was sleek and powerful, yet she'd never seen him be anything other than kind and gentle with both her and her son. Her longings— the sweet, luscious stirrings inside her—intensified as he bent down and tucked the covers close around Nathan's little body.

The fire snapped and crackled, and Cora closed her eyes, imagining the warmth it spewed into the room was Morgan's love radiating into her heart, filling her with joy. Right then, somewhere between dreams and reality, a revelation presented itself. Love was a gift, meant to be given away, not harbored or kept hidden. She just had to discover how to present it to Morgan. He wouldn't have married her if he didn't have some feelings for her, she knew him well enough to know that.

A surge of strength or perhaps resolve filled her spirit, gave hope where moments ago despair had sat like flour and water mixed into a thick paste. A hint of a smile touched her lips. When sugar, a touch of flavoring and leavening is added to flour and water a cake is created. A sweet dessert most people can't refuse.

Cora's excitement grew, and she sat up in bed. She just needed a recipe—a plan. No one sets out on a journey without a plan. Even a child, when learning to walk, has a plan—an intuition that tells them what to do—and soon they're running as if they'd always been able to. She had intuition. Morgan produced a great number of them inside her every day.

"He's forever kicking off the covers."

Morgan Palmer flinched at how Cora's whisper made his heart jolt. It shouldn't have surprised him, he knew she was awake, but that's just how his heart reacted to her. It hadn't been his own for some time, and that had him spooked. "I know," he answered, keeping his voice low and tucking the blanket beneath Nathan's tiny chin. "He's fine, go back to sleep."

"Aren't you coming back to bed?" she asked.

"In a minute," he replied, needing time before crawling in next to her again. Lying there was one thing while she slept—a whole other when she was awake. Morgan ran a hand over Nathan's soft hair, in hopes of diverting his attention. Reminding himself of why she and little Nathan were here was the only solace he had. Yet, even that—lamenting over the pain he'd caused her—was no longer working. The wall he'd built around himself was crumbling. No, he recanted, silently and perceptively. It had already crumbled. Fallen down and reduced to nothing but dust. They'd done that months ago, shattered his barrier, Cora and her tiny son.

It was a funny thing, how a child could affect a man. There was a special shine in Nathan's eyes that dang near choked

Morgan up, and when Nathan talked his gibberish, Morgan wished he could understand what the child was saying, for it filled him with a unique sense of wonder.

He found pride, too, in little Nathan, and had grown anxious for the day he could tuck the child in the saddle and ride the range, showing the boy everything that would someday be his. Morgan had never imagined he'd become a father. But he had, and loved Nathan as much as if he'd been the one to sire him.

A stinging sensation spread across his chest, as if he'd just been stabbed with a dull knife. The pain was almost enough to double him over. Loving Nathan didn't change the fact the child wasn't his. He hadn't been the one to sample Cora's delectable body, to couple with her to bring a new life into the world. Orville had. And Orville had been a fine man. One who hadn't done anything to deserve the lot he'd been given—dying from pneumonia before his son was old enough to remember him.

Morgan welcomed the remorse seeping in. It made him remember it was his fault—that he was responsible for Cora and Nathan. Providing for them was his duty. Orville had caught pneumonia rescuing cattle hosting the Palmer brand from the swollen river. It had been a shock, to say the least, when Cora showed up at his doorstep a week after the rainstorm, asking for assistance to bury her husband.

Morgan moved away from Nathan's bed to stand in front of the fire as chilling, razor-sharp fingers gripped the underside of his spine. It should have been him that died. His death wouldn't have left a woman and child on their own.

He'd dug Orville's grave, stood by Cora's side during the well-attended service and in the weeks that followed, tried to convince her to go back to Ohio. She'd refused, most likely because she was too distraught with the thought of leaving her husband behind. Then as the weeks turned into months and her refusals continued, Morgan assumed it was because she had no one to return to in Ohio. No family, no friends.

Six months later, when October rolled around and Morgan realized Cora had no choice but to stay through the winter, he'd proposed. It had been an impulsive, foolish thing to do—him, a bachelor pushing thirty, asking a sweet, youthful woman to marry him. But he'd had no choice. She was strong, and resourceful, but the winters here were long and hard, and the thought of her and Nathan struggling through the months had torn him in two.

The flames bit at Morgan's hands and he pulled them away from the fire, rubbing the heated palms over his thighs. The Fisher place was two miles west of his cattle ranch. Orville had built their cabin right next to what some called the Mormon Trail due to the migration of thousands who followed the footsteps of Brigham Young—the first to lead the worshippers across the plains to Utah and their land of Milk and Honey. Morgan and most locals called it the Overland Trail because more than just religious groups traveled the well-beaten path.

Orville, a wheelwright from Ohio, had thought by building a few miles outside town, he'd catch customers before they arrived in Central City. It had worked, Orville had sold plenty of wheels—when he'd been alive. It was after his death the dangers of a lone woman and her baby living alongside the trail let themselves be known.

Morgan had spent many nights bedded down in Cora's barn while a train camped nearby, and more than once persuaded a roaming visitor from going any closer to her little cabin. Keeping up the vigil come winter would have been impossible. Furthermore he'd witnessed other men willing to take over his sentinel. The thought of her marrying one of them had been harder to swallow than the fact he'd killed her husband, so with his hat in his hands and his heart practically pounding out of his chest, he'd proposed.

A fall off a bucking horse couldn't have knocked the air

from his chest any faster than her outright delighted answer had, and a week later, they were married.

Morgan stepped away from the fire, keeping his back to the bed where Cora lay. Not that it would help. Nothing did. The overwhelming longing he had for her couldn't be quelled that easy. Steamy, intense desires of how badly he wanted to sample her charming body lived inside him twenty-four hours a day. A kinder, gentler woman didn't exist. Nor was there one lovelier. The way her eyes sparkled when she smiled had the power to drop him to his knees, inside leastwise, where it mattered.

The consequences of his proposal hadn't hit him until after the ceremony, when he'd tasted the sweetest lips on earth. Brigham Young was wrong, leastwise in Morgan's eyes— Utah wasn't the land of Milk and Honey, Cora was. She was the closest thing to heaven on earth imaginable.

"Morgan," she whispered from across the room. "Aren't you coming back to bed?"

"Yes," he lied, half choking at the way his heart took to strangling him. "When the fire dies down a bit."

He threw himself into the rocking chair near the fireplace and stopped the sways by planting both feet on the floor, wishing he could control his feelings as easily. It had been two months since he'd moved her from her little cabin into his. At first it wasn't too bad. He'd spent most of his nights on the range bringing the cattle closer to the homestead for the winter months, or he slept in the bunkhouse, claiming to be too dirty to grace the sheets of her bed. But now that the ranch and weather had settled into winter, those excuses no longer existed and the attraction he felt for her had only intensified. He didn't quite know what it meant—this invisible draw inside him—other than it was driving him as crazy as a blind bull. He couldn't make it through half a thought without thinking of her.

He should go back to bed. She needed her rest. The woman never sat still, she was up before the sun and busy long after it set. But lying there, fighting the desires reeling inside him as her sweet scent drifted around was so difficult. At some point he'd break, that was a given, but he couldn't let that happen—not yet. Resting his head against the back of the chair, he let the hard wood irritate his neck. Maybe the pain would drive some sense into him. He should never have married her. It was bad enough he'd killed her husband, he couldn't—no, wouldn't—dishonor Orville more by sleeping with her. It wasn't right. A year of mourning was customary. Even in the untamed fields of Nebraska.

Leaning forward, he pressed his forehead into his palm, frustrated with his own justification. A year—when had he decided that was all it would take? Cora had said that amount of time was customary when Wes Barkley had approached her after Orville's funeral, but she'd been distraught that day. She may love Orville until the end of time, and Morgan couldn't blame her. Nor could he impress his emotions upon her.

There'd been a time or two when he may not have been the most respectable man on earth, but he always considered himself smart. Knew right from wrong, and for the most part was successful in all his endeavors, his decisions. Why, then, couldn't he get a handle on this situation? A silent moan rumbled his chest. He didn't seem to have a lick of sense when it came to Cora.

"Morgan?"

Unaware she'd left their bed and now stood before him, he leaped to his feet. When she wobbled, Morgan grasped her arms to steady her, and damned himself at the same time. The firelight danced in her hair and made the gown she wore translucent. He fought to keep his eyes from dipping to her breasts, but the almost mischievous glimmer in her silver-hued eyes was just as stimulating.

"Can I get something for you? Are you hungry? Thirsty?" she whispered.

"No," Morgan answered, teeth clenched and muscles as stiff as if he were wrestling a steer to the ground.

Glancing toward the fire, giving him a view of her graceful neck and profile, she rubbed her arms, shivered beneath his touch. "It must really be cold out. It's never been this chilly in here before."

He barely caught a moan before it slipped out. "Come on." Fighting himself, yet acknowledging he couldn't have her standing here shivering, he led her across the room. "Let's go back to bed."

She crawled beneath the covers, held them up for him.

Morgan swallowed the lump in his throat, and then, knowing he shouldn't, he climbed in next to her.

Chapter Two

As usual, Morgan was gone when Cora woke, causing another exasperated sigh to float over her lips. A smile followed, though, and a breeze of contentment fluttered around her. When he'd crawled into bed last night, he'd slipped one arm around her, shared the heat of his body with her.

She huddled beneath the covers for a moment longer, relishing how wonderful it had been to rest her head upon his shoulder, snuggle against the length of his body. The memorable bliss made her mind tumble. If only she knew what she'd done, why he loathed her so, then she'd be able to apologize—over and over until she found a way to make up for it, so they could sleep like that every night.

No, Cora reflected, burrowed beneath thick covers with his scent lingering on the pillow. Morgan didn't loathe her. He'd never made her feel that way. It was more like he was afraid of her, which was just as ridiculous. Morgan didn't show fear in any circumstance. His demeanor was steadfast, coupled with a thoughtful intelligence others valued and respected. It was a distinguishing characteristic that had intrigued her since their first meeting. It was all so baffling. Downright perplexing, the way he kept his distance, for Morgan Palmer wasn't a shy man, either. He was the epitome of grit and determination in so many ways.

Cora threw back the covers. Lying here—no matter how wonderful the memory—wouldn't give any more answers than it had yesterday morning, or the morning before that.

As always, Morgan had fueled the fire and built one in the cookstove before leaving. She stepped behind the screen partitioning off a private area and dressed quickly, for even with the fires blazing a chill hovered in the far corners of the cabin.

Pausing near Nathan's bed, she kissed her son's tousled blond hair before moving to the kitchen area to prepare breakfast. Morgan rarely joined them for a meal. He usually ate in the bunkhouse, but she always made plenty, unable to quell the hope one day he might. For months now the leftovers had been used for her and Nathan's lunch.

An hour later Nathan was awake, sitting in the high chair Morgan had built for him, when the door opened, filling the cabin with a blast of wintry air. Cora's heart leaped to her throat, pulsing joy through her bloodstream as Morgan hurried inside and closed the door with a solid thump.

"Moga!" Nathan screeched while clapping jelly-encrusted hands.

"Hi, buddy." Morgan's handsome face, red from the weather, lit up with a smile. "Brrr," he said to Nathan as he removed his hat. "It's cold out there."

"Brrr!" Nathan repeated.

Morgan chuckled and Cora wished with all her heart she could copy Nathan's enthusiasm, demonstrate the happiness jumping inside her, but the sixth sense that appeared just as swiftly as her joy had told her Morgan wouldn't appreciate such actions. Holding her silence and contemplating her lack of understanding, she rose to gather a cup and the coffee from the stove.

"Stay there," Morgan insisted, "I'll get it."

She slumped back onto the chair, dejected. It seemed he didn't want, nor need, anything from her.

No matter how heavy her heart hung in her chest, her eyes couldn't resist following him as he not only filled a cup with coffee, but piled a plate with bacon and scrambled eggs from the pans on the stove. Every simple movement he made had her remembering the feel of his arm around her, the rise and fall of his chest below her cheek, and caused the longing in her to grow until she ached.

He sat then, across the table from her but next to Nathan. A fleeting, disgusting thought shot across her mind. She was jealous of her own child—jealous that he could garner attention and affection from Morgan while she couldn't. She bowed her head, but only for a second because her eyes refused to stop watching him.

"Good stuff," Morgan stated, pointing his fork at Nathan's plate.

"Goo uff," Nathan repeated, nodding his head.

Again, Morgan chuckled, and again Cora felt a knife nick at her heart. She was extremely thankful Morgan enjoyed Nathan so much. Fact was, no matter how much she liked a man, or realized how important it was for Nathan to have a father figure, she could never tolerate one who didn't care for the boy. She just wished Morgan cared the tiniest bit for her.

A frown pulled on her brows. Why was she wallowing in self-pity? She'd made a decision last night, decided which path she'd take. Eyeing Morgan's handsome profile, she squared her shoulders. It was time to start traveling.

Morgan glanced over just then, caught her staring at him. Cora couldn't pull her eyes away, even when warmth pooled in her womb, as if it was preparing to carry his child as she had Nathan. Morgan frowned, not angrily, but confused, almost as if he sensed something. He broke the connection by lowering his head, and a spark of life seeped out of Cora.

The trail before her seemed longer and more burden-filled than the journey from Ohio had. The pitiful thought made her want to kick herself. She'd never shied away from hard work and wasn't about to start. Determination caught her spine. She'd survived the trek from Ohio, and would this one, too, even though it was different in so many ways and left a piece of her vulnerable in a place she'd never been before. What she needed was a bit of faith.

Folding her hands in her lap, Cora closed her eyes. *Please Lord, I know You have already given me so much and I'm extremely thankful for all Your bounty, but if I have one wish left, if there is one miracle You can perform for me, let it be for Morgan to learn to love me. Even just a portion as much as I love him will suffice.*

"Cora?"

Morgan's tone was soft, and reminded her of last night, when he'd led her back to their bed. A great warmth flooded her, as brilliant as the summer sun. "Yes?"

The slight frown furrowing the brows above the blue eyes looking upon her so tenderly would have made her swoon had she been standing. "Are you feeling all right?" he asked. "Perhaps you should go lie down. I know the storm kept you up last night."

His concern was genuine, and she balled her fingers to keep them from sneaking across the table to touch his arm. It was an obsession she had—touching him—and last night increased it severely. "I'm fine," she assured.

"You were—"

"I was praying," she cut him off.

A red hue appeared on his cheeks. "Oh." He glanced down at his food. "I guess I forgot to say grace."

A giggle slipped out. Whether it was due to his sheepish statement or his blush, she really didn't know, nor mind. He cared about her, and that's all that mattered. "I wasn't saying grace for you, nor reprimanding you for not." Cora rose and went to gather the pitcher of milk. *Prayers aren't answered im-*

mediately, she knew that, understood it would take work on her part. Bringing the milk and a glass back to the table, she refilled Nathan's small cup and then filled the glass for Morgan.

"I was making a wish," she answered, resolute. She was more than willing to do anything it took.

"A wish?" Morgan asked, glancing at the hand she rested upon his shoulder—her fingers had settled there of their own accord—and then up at her.

The scent of wintry air wafted from his broad frame. A shiver tickled her at the thought of rubbing his shoulders, massaging the bulk beneath his shirt. Someday she'd be able to do that, and that knowledge was enough for now. "Yes," she answered, smiling. "A wish." She gave his shoulder a slight squeeze before carrying the pitcher back to the counter, giddy at the prospect of the day she'd be able to touch him, kiss him, whenever she wished.

"I hope it wasn't a Christmas wish." His tone was light, or maybe sounded that way because she was more than a bit giddy.

"Oh, why's that?" she asked.

He nodded toward the door. "Because snow is falling by the bucket out there, I highly doubt it's going to let up all day."

White flakes still clung to the hat and coat he'd hung next to the door. She'd been inside, snug and warm, and fretting, while he'd been outside for hours, seeing to their livelihoods. "Are the cattle…"

"They're fine. They're close enough to the ranch for the boys to get feed to them. Hopefully the wind won't pick up again." He drank his milk, set the empty glass down. "But traveling to town anytime soon will be out of the question."

"Oh, well, as long as the cattle are fine, the rest doesn't matter. We have everything we need right here."

Morgan gathered the empty dishes in front of Nathan and slid them across the table. "So your wish wasn't for something in the window at Rieser's?"

She carried the dishes to the sink. "No, what I wished for can't be bought at the general store. It can't be bought anywhere."

His gaze once again captured hers, and the way his eyes grew cloudy and his face took on a pained appearance threatened to stop her heart. "I'm sorry, Cora," he whispered so softly she wondered if he'd actually spoken.

A chill rippled through her as if she'd just stepped outside and tumbled into an oversize snowbank.

"Down," Nathan said, squirming in his seat.

Unable to move, her gaze danced for a moment, between her son and Morgan's extremely sorrowful face. He hadn't done anything, not to her nor anyone else that she knew of. He certainly couldn't take responsibility for the weather. Yet his apology was so sincere she sought for a response that might ease his distress.

"Down," Nathan repeated.

"I'll get you, buddy," Morgan said, turning to the child.

"Wait," she said so loud both Morgan and Nathan held stunned expressions. Her mind was still a blank, unable to come up with a way to comfort her husband. Yes, her husband, she repeated silently. Sighing, she turned to the sink. "I'll get a cloth and wash the jelly from his fingers."

The tasty breakfast had turned to a glob in Morgan's gut. He hadn't noticed Nathan's hands were covered in jelly, not with the amount of remorse flaring inside him.

Nathan started to lick the fingers clean before Cora arrived with the cloth. The sight would have been enough to make Morgan laugh, had he not been so depressed. "As long as the cattle are fine," she'd said. Why hadn't he thought of that before opening his mouth? The cattle were what caused her husband's demise, and here he was carrying on about them. And of course her wish couldn't be bought in town, there was no doubt it was that Orville wasn't dead. He should have stayed in the barn; at least there his foot wasn't planted in his mouth and his heart wasn't on his sleeve—well, maybe it was, but the cowboys wouldn't notice.

After she cleaned Nathan's fingers, the child held up his arms. "Moga!"

Morgan lifted Nathan from his chair, and extracted giggles as he jostled the child in the air while carrying him across the room, to where they sat down on the rug in front of the fireplace. A bit of separation from Cora would do him good. His insides were swirling, remembering how she'd snuggled up against him last night. Holding her like that, he'd slept more soundly than he had in a long time. Months even. Yet, the simple action had made him want things he couldn't have even more. He'd been itching to get back inside since he'd walked out the door before the sun rose, and the weather hadn't had a thing to do with it.

"Pay!" Nathan grabbed a ball and shoved it across the small space.

Morgan picked up the toy and rolled it in his hands. Another one of Cora's handiworks. She'd wrapped scraps of cloth into a ball shape. The woman was amazing in so many ways.

"Mama," Nathan said, pointing across the room.

"Yes," Morgan agreed, rolling the ball toward Nathan. "That's your mama."

The boy scowled, little lines covered his forehead, and he pointed a chubby finger at Morgan. "Papa?"

A tiny gasp echoed across the room. Morgan swung around in time to see the ashen look on Cora's face before she spun to face the sink along the far wall. The invisible knife lodged in his chest all but gutted him.

Morgan retrieved the ball. "Here, buddy, catch."

The ball rolled over Nathan's legs. The child giggled and scrambled to catch the toy. Easily diverted, soon the child's giggles were nonstop as they rolled the toy to and fro. However, Morgan's depressed mind couldn't be sidetracked and he wondered what the hell he was doing. He couldn't play ball with Nathan all day. The child would soon tire of the game. The cowboys—the four men who worked for him—were hunkered down in the bunkhouse. He could join them, but being cooped up in a room half the size of the cabin with four men playing cards and smoking cigars held no appeal. Besides, a man would have to have a death wish to wander in the raging blizzard outside.

He'd downplayed the storm for Cora's sake. In all actuality, a person could get lost going to the outhouse, which was why he came to the cabin, to make sure she didn't attempt going outside for anything. When he built their house, the one he'd ordered plans for last month, they'd have a water closet. Then he wouldn't have to worry about such things. His justifications played havoc on him again. When had he gotten so good at making up excuses, lying to himself? He'd worry about her no matter how many water closets their house boasted.

As he'd predicted, Nathan grew bored with the ball. Morgan stood, scooping the child into his arms. "Should we bring the Christmas tree in the house?" he asked, glad he'd thought of something that might offer a distraction.

"Christmas Eve isn't until tomorrow," Cora said from where she stood at the counter, elbow deep in flour.

While riding fence lines a few days ago, Morgan had noticed the perfect little pine and had gone back out that evening to cut it down. It now stood under the porch awning near the front door. He'd never given the holiday much thought in the past, but this year it held a special appeal. Celebrating the day with Cora and Nathan had filled his mind as he'd hauled the little tree home. "I know," he said. They were his family now, and though he couldn't bring Orville back, he could provide them a holiday complete with a Christmas tree and gifts beneath it. "An extra day won't bother that little tree none at all." He nodded to Nathan sitting in the crook of his arm. "Or him."

She smiled, and his stomach flipped, tried to climb up his throat where his heart had already planted itself. Her hazel eyes had more tiny streaks of colors than a summer sunset. A certain glow always radiated off her and today was no different. Her chestnut-colored hair was tied at her nape with a piece of ribbon, and her blue gingham dress, all but hidden by the white apron tied around her waist, hugged her womanly curves delightfully. His heart increased its choke hold. No matter what she was doing, how she was dressed, she was beyond beautiful, and there wasn't a moment that passed where he didn't wish he could hold her in his arms, love her as she deserved to be loved.

Just one kiss, he thought, as rationally as he could right now. If he could steal just one kiss, maybe then some of these desires would calm down.

Chapter Three

~~~~

Cora, as calmly as possible, wiped the flour from her hands with her apron and walked across the room. Morgan watched as she approached, staring at her thoughtfully. An almost private smile had one corner of his mouth turning up, and that thrilled her as much as having his arm around her last night had. There was reluctance there, too, she noticed, in his hesitant grin, but she chose to overlook it. "I don't think it'll bother you one little bit, either," she said, delighted with the opportunity to tease him. "Here, I'll take Nathan while you get the tree."

It was a stare-down for a moment, like two animals eyeing each other up, looking for trust or kin or whatever it is they look for. She held her ground, even when the charge between the two of them grew to the point she imagined created lightning. Instead of a winter blizzard, summer thunderheads should be descending from the sky. Leastwise that's how her body felt—hot and sultry. She licked her lips, needing moisture of some kind.

Morgan shifted his gaze and stance, and held Nathan out for her to grasp.

"No," Nathan insisted, wrapping his arms around Morgan's neck.

Cora, half dizzy from fanciful thoughts leaping into her mind, reached up to unhook Nathan's hands. The pads of her fingers brushed the skin of Morgan's neck. The simple connection struck her insides, made her wonder if there was a thunderstorm brewing, but it was the way Morgan sucked in air that caused her to quickly pull the child from his arms. "Come here, so Morgan can get the tree," she said, attempting to hide the disappointment now rushing from the floor up. Stopping the indignation before it overpowered her by reminding herself she needed to take baby steps—she couldn't expect Morgan to simply pull her into his arms and kiss the daylights out of her simply because of a look—she stepped back.

"Tee," Nathan said excitedly.

Very conscious that the air between them was still charged, she kept her eyes on Morgan. "Yes, a Christmas tree," she said, shifting Nathan onto her hip. As Morgan moved, ready to fly out the door, she stopped him with her free hand. "Aren't you going to put on your coat?"

His gaze went from her fingers on his arm to her face. That persuasive little grin was back on his face, surprising her in a heart-skittering way. "There's no need," he said. "It's right beside the door." He patted her fingers. "I'll be right back."

Her breath stalled in her chest. His touch—so innocent and gentle—rendered her speechless, while instincts soared inside her. Morgan wanted to kiss her. It wasn't just her imagination. It was there, in his eyes. She swallowed, forcing her animated heart back into her chest, and nodded.

Still smiling, Morgan pulled open the door.

Cora wanted to fall to her knees, thank the heavens above for the glimmer she'd seen in Morgan's eyes, but the blast of icy air screaming its way into the cabin hit her like an awakening. The door closed as swiftly as it had opened, and she gave her head a clearing shake. She'd seen the blizzard out the window above the sink, but through the open doorway, she hadn't even been able to make out the barn, which was only a few yards from the cabin.

Her breathing, still far from normal, quickened even more as she stared at the door. The weather could play in her favor. Since they'd married, Morgan had never stayed a full day in the cabin. With the storm outside chores were limited. A spell of nervousness washed over her. She didn't know much about seduction, how a woman went about enticing a man.

"Moga, tee," Nathan said, interrupting her thoughts.

A joyful wave washed over her. Instincts, she suspected, would tell her what to do. After all, they hadn't failed her so far. Smiling she kissed Nathan's nose. "Yes, Morgan is getting the tree." She no sooner said the words when the door flew open again. Wind and large flakes of snow swirled in as a tree, as wide as the door, seemed to walk itself forward.

Cora set Nathan in his high chair and pushed it up to the table. "You wait here," she instructed, rushing to help Morgan, who was now dragging the pine inside by its trunk. "It's huge," she speculated as the bottom boughs caught on the door frame.

"Yeah, I guess it's bigger than I thought," Morgan said, giving the tree a hard tug.

The branches let loose of the door frame, spraying a shower of snow. She let out a screech and then laughed at the flakes floating in the air. Morgan held out an arm, as if to protect her as other branches swiped the door and spewed snow into the room.

"Bigger than you thought." She repeated his answer while moving to the door, ready to close it when the top crossed the threshold. "I'd say it's the biggest tree I've ever seen." Catching the hesitancy in his eyes, she added, "And the most perfect."

She was defenseless against the all-out smile that appeared on his face then, not that she'd had any intention of fighting the happiness welling inside her—now or anytime he chose to flash such a gaze upon her.

"Watch out while I swing it around," he warned.

By the time the tree was inside and the door shut, she and

Morgan, as well as the floor, were covered with wet, cold snow-flakes and bits of ice.

He propped the tree against the wall, the rest of the room now hidden behind its width, and shook his hand, flaying droplets. She squealed as bits of ice landed upon her cheeks, and stepped aside. Letting out a low laugh, he caught her arm. "Come here, you're covered with snow."

Before she could react, his hands were working, knocking the snow off her hair, shoulders and dress sleeves. She stood before him, soaking up the bliss every touch instilled. Thrilled at the thought of touching him, she reached out, brushing the now melting flakes from his chest and shoulders. Much too soon, the snow was gone.

The air around them stilled, and the lightning-bolt charge was back. The rest of the world faded away, leaving nothing but her and Morgan at this particular moment in time. His hands settled on her hips and her palms drew to a rest on the bulk of his upper arms as their gazes locked together with a click that vibrated the length of her body as if someone had turned a key in an age-old lock.

There was an unmistakable want in his blue eyes—one that set a blazing fire in her very core. Cora's lips tingled and she moistened them with the tip of her tongue. The movement brought his gaze downward, which made the tingle mature into a full-fledged ache.

Morgan went ramrod stiff. Cora felt it, saw it and ignored it. The moment had presented itself, and she wasn't going to let it slip away. Stretching onto the tips of her toes she placed one hand on his jaw to keep his head from moving, and taking the chance he'd completely reject her, touched her lips to his.

At first he didn't move, stood there like a mighty oak with mile-long roots as their breaths mingled in a gentle, poignant connection that was heavy with prospect, but when she stepped forward, wrapped her other hand around his back and pressed her breasts against the hardness of his chest, he shifted so their bodies aligned.

It was as if the lightning she'd sensed earlier struck, sizzling along every inch that touched him and shook the floor beneath them. Cora cupped his cheek firmer, and pressed her lips against his again, longer and harder this time.

"Cora," he whispered, his lips vibrating against hers.

Her reply, "Morgan," was more of a plea than anything, and she caught his bottom lip between hers as she begged, "Kiss me, please."

He moaned, creating a stimulating reverberation to race over her, and then folded his arms around her so tightly she wondered if she'd be crushed to death.

Oh, what a heavenly death it would be, she decided as his lips maneuvered over hers in a kiss that held no reservations. It was a claiming of sorts, his and hers, a union that was much more than their wedding kiss. The overwhelming delight and harmony the connection created made her weak and powerful at the same time. She clung to him, not just to continue the kiss, but to keep from joining the melting snow covering the floor.

When the kiss ended, Cora had to blink several times to clear her vision. Morgan's dear handsome face came into focus and a herd of stampeding cattle couldn't have chased away the smile that landed on her lips.

With a tender touch, he brushed her hair from her temple. "Cora, I..."

She refused to let anything, especially unease on his part, tarnish the moment. "I've wanted you to kiss me like that for some time, Morgan."

"You have?" he asked, somewhat skeptical.

The thought of convincing him tickled her, inside and out. "Yes, I have." She kissed him, quickly, softly. "For months."

"Cora."

There was such emotion in the way he said her name, she

gasped, and was still holding the air in when his lips landed upon hers a second time. The first kiss had been a reconstruction of her spirit, confirming her wants and desires, whereas this one was more of a passage, a ritual that opened a new world and gave newfound awareness to the array of undercurrents leaping to life beneath her skin.

His hands rubbed her back, flowed down her sides and back up to gently brush the sides of her breasts, leaving a trail of feverish tingles that spread across her body, making every piece of her beg to be touched, caressed.

Cora had waited so long for this, loved him so much, the desires she'd forced to remain buried thrust to the surface with such energy she clung harder to Morgan. The passion, obsession she had for him, charged forward, leading her actions and stealing all coherent thoughts. Her body was throbbing, climbing some sort of invisible ladder, and she pressed against the length of him, from hip to chest. The echoes of her gasps filled her ears, and she searched, tried to catch his lips as they raced across her cheeks, down the side of her face and neck.

"Morgan," she begged when his lips eluded hers.

The sound of his chuckle made her smile in spite of all that was happening. And his lips, as they snagged onto the corner of hers, were smiling as well.

"Are you going to kiss me?" she asked, amazed she had the wherewithal to do so.

"I think I am kissing you," he said, tugging on her bottom lip with both of his.

"Maybe you are," she answered, swaying her hips across his.

"Maybe?" he asked.

"Hmm…maybe," she teased, completely enchanted by the playfulness that had developed between them.

With a growl that sent a wave of excitement right to her center, Morgan's tongue entered her mouth and bred an outpouring of hunger she'd never fathomed. Matching the way he explored her mouth, she twirled her tongue with his. The dance was mystical and fueled the flame growing between her thighs. She'd known it would be like this. That once Morgan kissed her she'd want it all. It was the speed that surprised her. The demand rapidly overtaking her was like a wildfire racing across an August field of buffalo grass.

As if he knew exactly what she needed, Morgan reached down and grasped her behind one knee. Hooking her leg around his thigh, his fingers ran along the underside of her leg, from her knee to the curve of her bottom. Arching into the touch, she grasped a fistful of his shirt.

It was heavenly, yet hellish. The heat of his roaming hand penetrated her dress and pantaloons, but it wasn't enough. Desperation, hot and raw, swirled out of control, and Cora lifted her leg higher, wrapping it more firmly around him.

"Cora—"

Before he could whisper another word, she captured his mouth and swirled her tongue deep inside. His hold compressed her harder against him. The pressure infused her heavy, aching breasts with such a sweet, agonizing pain, Cora wanted to weep with pleasure. His hand found its way inside the hem of her pantaloons. Hot, divine fingers raced along her skin, scorching and tempting as they worked their way up from her knee, closer and closer to the heat at her core.

Throbbing with excitement, and aching for more, she shifted, giving his fingers an open invitation to find her center.

It was her turn to moan, and she did as his fingers traveled along her inner thigh. Her nails dug into his shoulders as she pleaded, "Morgan—Morgan—" She trailed a line of kisses along his chin and down the side of his neck.

He nibbled on her earlobe, suckled on the sensitive skin below it. "Cora, sweet, sweet Cora," he whispered as his fingers reached their destination.

Her moan of pleasure was so long, so intense, it left her

throat raw. Nothing had ever been sweeter. His touch was perfection, gliding along, teasing her to heights that made her squeeze her eyes shut. Cora could have stayed there forever, absorbing him, living him, but with suddenness that left her reeling, Morgan scooped her into both arms and bolted across the room.

The cabin spun before her eyes and, startled by a thunderous commotion, Cora tightened her hold around Morgan's neck. She blinked, gaping at the tree bouncing off the floor in the exact spot they'd been standing. It was shocking, but nothing in comparison to the miniature burst that let loose in her core. The wild sensations Morgan had coaxed to a peak erupted with such sweet release she let out a tiny whimper and tightened her thigh muscles in harmony with the pleasure. At the same time, a snow shower spewed from the tree's stiff branches and clumps of icicles bounced across the floor as the tree fluttered to a rest with a final swish.

Cora, reveling in the unexpected satisfaction sweeping across her body, let out a sigh and laid her head on Morgan's shoulder. She should be mortified—at least embarrassed by her complete act of abandonment, but there was no room for any such feelings.

It may have been seconds later, or a much longer length of time, since time held no place in her mind, when Nathan's shout of glee penetrated her contentment.

Clapping his little hands from the safety of his chair on the far side of the table, her son gurgled excitedly. Happier than she'd felt in months, perhaps years, Cora giggled and glanced to the man holding her.

"Are you all right?" Morgan asked.

She nodded, not sure if her vocal cords would work yet. The way he grinned and brushed the tip of his nose against hers was all the reassurance she needed. "Actually, Morgan Palmer, I'm better than I've been in a very long time."

He cocked a brow, but before he could respond, Nathan shouted, "Do 'gain, Moga, do 'gain!"

Cora wanted to say the same thing. Not trusting the shout wouldn't come out on its own, she bit her lips together.

"I can't right now, buddy," Morgan answered, but his eyes were on her.

Her heart, already full, swelled even more at the promises in his gaze. Cora buried her face against Morgan's neck, kissing the skin right where his pulse raced. His arms tightened as he continued to hold her high above the floor and he nestled his chin against the top of her head.

Though she wanted to, she knew she couldn't stay in his arms forever. Cora drew in a fortifying breath that was filled with his amazing scent, and lifted her head. "I best get the broom."

There was no doubt what he saw when he looked at her with those smoldering blue eyes. The happiness in her heart couldn't be contained. It flowed through her body with every beat of her pulse. Therefore, it was in her eyes, on her face. And there wasn't a thing she was going to do about it. She loved this man, and wanted him to know it. He just wasn't ready to hear it, even with what had just happened, she understood that.

Morgan brushed a kiss to her forehead as he lowered her to the floor. Her toes touched, yet still, gently, he held her until her feet were firmly planted beneath her and her legs steadied. Lacking the desire to, but knowing she should, she took a step.

One of Morgan's hands caught hers.

She squeezed his fingers, and while still gazing into those glorious eyes, she sought a way to express all she felt. "Thank you, Morgan. For marrying me. For bringing us here. For being such a wonderful man."

His face went lax, as if her words shocked him.

Her smile grew, and she gave his fingers a final squeeze before slipping away to retrieve the broom. Walking was a chore with her body quaking from the commotion he'd cultivated, but at the same time, she felt as if she fluttered like a spring butterfly on its way to a flower.

By the time she found the broom and a few rags to wipe the floor, Morgan, with the help of Nathan, if you could call the efforts of a two-year-old help, carried the tree across the room to stand in front of the window opposite the fireplace.

Morgan glanced her way and though his gaze left a million other things vying for the number-one spot in her thoughts, she nodded. It was the perfect place for the tree.

He laid the tree on the floor and knelt in front of Nathan. "You stay here. I'm going to get some boards to nail to the trunk so it won't tip over again."

Cora didn't need to look to know the child nodded in agreement. He'd agree with anything Morgan asked—as would she. Cleaning up the mess of water and ice and frozen pine needles, she watched Morgan cross the room to the door on the back side of the kitchen that led to the lean-to. It was a small addition he'd built after she'd arrived, where he stacked cords of firewood so she wouldn't have to traipse through the snow. It was thoughtful on his part, she knew, but also not necessary since he always made sure the log bins were full.

After disposing of the wet rags and pile of needles, Cora rinsed her hands and went back to the sugar cookies she'd been mixing when Morgan decided to carry in the tree. She'd planned on cutting the cookies into star, bell and heart shapes to hang on the branches, and now the idea seemed even more pleasing. Nathan would help frost them, and so would Morgan. She could almost envision the three of them sitting around the table, tying ribbons on the cookies, and laughing, talking and maybe feeding each other icing off the tips of their fingers.

While Cora stood in the kitchen, dreaming about cookies, Morgan was in the lean-to, reliving the nightmare he'd created in the kitchen. Pressing both hands to his temples, he sat down on the upturned tub, the one they used for bathing. A fiery sting bit into his backside and he leaped to his feet. It wasn't the cold metal, but the thought of Cora, naked in the object, that made him lean against the woodpile instead.

What had come over him? Why had he kissed her like that? Why had he touched... Damn if it wasn't all he'd known it would be—and more. She lit a fire in him that not even a spring flood could dowse.

If that tree hadn't fallen over he'd have carried her to the bed. Still wanted to. The blood in his veins pounded, hot and swirling like a swollen river, and Cora's fascinating, divine scent lingered in his nostrils. His loins, throbbing painfully, ached to feel her hips pressed against his again—but without the barrier of clothes.

He was split right down the middle and didn't like it. For one, he'd never been here before. His entire life he'd known right from wrong. The pit of his stomach grew heavy. What had just happened was wrong. Yet, he had to admit, nothing had felt more right. A blazing six-shooter couldn't have stopped him from kissing her when she'd looked up at him with all the want of the world glimmering in her eyes. No man could have denied her.

He punched the wall. She better not look at other men the way she looked at him. Nor touch them the way she touched him. Even the most innocent touch of her hand had his insides sparking like dry kindling. A whole other surge of frustration rolled in his stomach. It wasn't her fault, none of it. He was the only one to blame. Cora probably thought that's what he expected—most men did, expected their wives to take care of all their needs, to bear their children. His body started humming again, imagining Cora round and plump with his child. Now, that would be something. He pondered the thought, imagined it fully before he let out a heavy sigh. When had he let his guard down, the one he'd erected years ago, about never letting a woman get inside him? It had been there for years, shortly after he'd witnessed one man steal another man's wife.

Morgan spun around, trying to reroute wandering thoughts that wouldn't solve anything, and his toe caught on something. He reached for the woodpile, but the log his hand landed on flipped, knocking others aside as it rolled. He stumbled, trying to catch his fall as logs knocked into one another. What happened next was a colossal run of events. That one log, awkwardly flipping about, unbalanced half the structure, knocking his feet out from beneath him in the process.

When the ruckus ended, after the last log found a place to land, painfully bouncing off his inner thigh first, Morgan lifted his arms away from his face. Cora stood over him. The first thought he had was the lantern she'd brought into the dark space turned her hair a golden-red and gave her an overall angelic glow. The second thought was he loved her. Loved every bit of her sunshining face, glorious tempting body and sweet, loving soul. And would until the day he died, or longer.

"Morgan?" She knelt down beside him and started tossing logs aside. "Morgan, are you all right?"

A third thought came then, one that wasn't as welcome as the other two. He was a scoundrel. A low-down, dirty, mud-sucking scalawag for coveting another man's wife. Lying on the frozen dirt, covered in a cord of wood, the truth hit him. He'd been in love with Cora Fisher since the moment he saw her, over three years ago when she and Orville moved onto the forty next to his land. And that day, he'd become the man he'd always claimed he'd never become—just like Matthew Stone, the man who'd taken his mother away and left his father with four young boys to raise.

"Morgan, talk to me." Cora patted his cheeks. "Please, Morgan, talk to me."

"Mama? Moga?"

Morgan rolled his head, glanced to the doorway. His saving

grace—the child. The only barrier he had against his lust for Cora. "Hey, buddy," he said to Nathan. "Go check on the tree."

The child spun around and ran back into the kitchen.

"You," Cora started, her face inches from his, "scared the dickens out of me." A frown twisted her petal-shaped mouth. She patted his cheeks, then shoulders and arms. "Are you all right? Nothing's broken?"

He stopped her hands before they went to his waist. His back could be broken and still her nearness made him grow hard. "Yes, I'm fine," he half growled. The want to kiss her again was gutting him. It was a strong emotion that she'd opened up inside him—this love he'd never known—and it left him helpless. He had no control when it came to her. None. Not over his heart, nor his body. An urge to put some distance between them had him shoving aside a few stray logs. "The, uh, woodpile fell over."

"I know that." She planted both hands on his chest, kept him from rising. His muscles were much greater than hers, but her simple hold rendered him weak, and the glimmer in her unique smoky eyes made his breath sit in the back of his throat as if someone had slid a lynching rope over his head.

For a split second, Morgan thought she was going to kiss him. His body froze and blazed with heat at the same time.

Her head fell onto his chest. "Oh, Morgan," she whispered. "I'd die if anything happened to you."

Shame flooded his system, and he draped his arms around her, pressed a kiss to the softness of her hair. He was such a fool. So worried about his own feelings, his wants and desires, he hadn't thought about hers. She'd already lost one husband. He certainly didn't want to bring that type of pain upon her or Nathan.

"I'm fine," he offered. "And I'm not going anywhere. I won't leave you and Nathan to fend for yourselves again."

She stiffened and sat up, stared at him with a perplexing gaze. "What?" Shaking her head, she asked, "Why?"

His mind went blank. "Why?"

Leaning back farther, eyeing him warily, she braced both hands on her hips. "Yes, why won't you leave me and Nathan?"

His tongue had grown thick and heavy, didn't seem to want to work right. "Well, because."

"Because why?" she insisted stubbornly.

The coldness of the space entered his bones, threatened to freeze his blood right where it had stopped in his veins. There was no way he could tell her the truth, but lying wasn't an option, either. He pushed the remaining logs away, careful of Cora and the lantern she'd set on the ground beside him, and rose before offering her a hand.

She stood, pointedly ignoring his proffered hand, and picked up the lantern so swiftly the little flame fluttered inside the glass globe. "Why, Morgan?"

He used the pretense of brushing bark and dirt from his clothes, and then flexed as if to make sure nothing had been injured. "Because," he answered, feeling a bit annoyed since he had no idea what she expected him to say. At that moment he felt, well, vulnerable. Leastwise that's the only word he could use to describe the sinking in the pit of his stomach. No matter what he said, it was going to be wrong.

"Because…" she said, giving him no extra time to find an answer.

"Because you're my wife, Cora. Nathan's my son." Her intake of breath had him sputtering, "Well, my adopted son."

Cora's eyes had turned dark gray, like a storm brewed in them—one that made the blizzard outside look like a simple skiff of snow. "Why did you ask me to marry you, Morgan?"

Her freezing tone made his tongue stick to the roof of his mouth as if it were a frost-covered flagpole.

Chapter Four

A massive wave of tears pressed at the back of her eyes. Cora blinked, refusing them permission to come forward. Morgan's face had gone ashen and his Adam's apple quivered in his neck. She took a deep breath, pulling strength from the very core of her being, and turned, gallantly putting one foot in front of the other.

"Because I killed your husband."

The words echoed off the ceiling, the walls, her inner ears, yet she shook her head, questioned her hearing. "What?" She spun around. "What did you say?"

He appeared to be ten feet tall in the dark, tiny space. "I married you because I killed Orville. You became my responsibility."

Anguish burst forth. All this time she'd been wrong. Morgan didn't care for her—leastwise not in the way she wanted, the way she dreamed. "Responsibility?"

He gave a single head nod.

The tears could no longer be suppressed, not with the way her heart wrenched as if someone had just grasped it with a hard fist. She squeezed her eyes shut as a single tear slipped out, singed her cheek as it trickled downward. A thousand thoughts jumbled her mind, but one held precedence over all the rest. Responsibility, the way Morgan said it, meant burden.

"Moga?"

"Come here, buddy," Morgan said, kneeling down to catch Nathan as he rushed past her. "Cora—"

She shook her head. "I—" Her throat constricted, plugged too tight to speak. She flipped around and, holding in a sob that threatened to tear her apart, she left the lean-to, took refuge in the only private space the cabin offered—behind the dressing screen. There she slumped to the floor and let the tears flow freely, but silently, refusing to let even the tiniest sob escape. That might shatter her, and she was broken enough.

All along she'd been fooling herself. Morgan would never love her.

Guilt. Responsibility. Oh, they were fine qualities, but not what a wife wants her husband to feel toward her.

She'd also been wrong in thinking she'd done something to turn Morgan away from her. He'd never been attracted to her in the first place. Who could be attracted to a yoke around their neck? Covering her mouth to muffle the increasing, painful sobs racking her chest, she expected a wave of humiliation to engulf her, to join the rest of her depressing realizations. He must think her a shameless hussy.

Memories of their earlier encounter flooded warmth where pain sat, quieting her sobs. She hadn't been embarrassed when it happened, and she wasn't now. Had she honestly thought it would be that easy? One kiss and the world would be all she ever wanted. That was flat-out foolish. In all actuality, things weren't any different than they'd been this morning, except now she knew why Morgan kept his distance. Wiping the tears aside with the backs of her hands, she leaned against the wall and pondered this new route her thoughts took.

It was sometime later when noise filtered through to her— the sound of a hammer striking a nail, Morgan's voice, Nathan's giggles. She'd thought, wondered and gone to that place within where the outside world ceases to exist. It was peaceful there and grounded her, made her see reason when her conscious thoughts found none.

Pushing off the floor, Cora moved to the washstand. She'd known Morgan didn't love her, that's why she'd wished he'd learn to. The water she dunked the cloth in was chilly, but refreshing as she wiped her face. What concerned her now was that if Morgan took the blame for Orville's death upon himself, did he believe she blamed him, too?

Empathy was a strong emotion, hurting for someone else, and when it came to Morgan, her entire being ached for him.

After patting her face dry, she glanced in the tiny mirror. Her eyes were red-rimmed and puffy. She lifted her chin, squared her shoulders. There wasn't anything she could do about her looks, but there was something she could do for Morgan. If he'd let her.

Twisting, she glanced to the screen, listening to Morgan's and Nathan's hushed chatter. She'd known that it might be a precarious trail she took, the one that led to Morgan's heart. Determination lifted her shoulders. She was halfway there and nothing would stop her now. Morgan was worth fighting for, even if it meant fighting him.

Cora hung the towel over the bar on the side of the stand, and feeling almost reborn, walked around the screen.

"Mama, tee." Nathan jumped to his feet and scrambled across the room.

She bent and lifted him into her arms. "Yes, I see it." Kissing the top of Nathan's head, she eyed Morgan squarely. "It's beautiful. You and Morgan did a wonderful job."

Morgan, shifting from leg to leg, stared at her as if he wanted to say something, but didn't know where to start. The feeling was mutual, and that, too, gave her courage. Accepting his unease, she glanced to the tree.

The pine, its trunk now nailed to a set of cross boards so it couldn't topple, stood taller than him. The top branch almost touched the ceiling and the entire structure glistened in the light filtering through the window. "It is a beautiful tree, Morgan. Thank you."

He opened his mouth as if to speak and then closed it. His gaze went to the floor. Half of her wanted to wrap her arms around him and smother him as she did Nathan when he was unsure of himself, and the other half wanted to shake him, to tell him no one was responsible for Orville's death—least of all him. But she couldn't, not yet.

She set Nathan on the floor. "I think we should decorate our tree. Don't you?"

The child nodded. "Yup."

"First," she said, glancing at the mantel clock which proved more time had lapsed since breakfast than she'd imagined, "we need to have some lunch and you need to take a nap."

Nathan's face puckered. "No nap."

"Lunch first," she said, tackling one battle at a time. "Aren't you hungry?"

"I'm hungry," Morgan said. "Aren't you, buddy?"

If possible, she loved Morgan more at that moment, when, whether he realized it or not, he supported her. "Morgan's hungry," she told Nathan. "We better feed him."

"Ya! Feed Moga!" Nathan took off for the kitchen.

She started to follow but when the path led her past Morgan he laid a hand on her arm. "Cora," he said, swallowing. "I—I'm sorry."

"Not now, Morgan," she replied softly. "But when Nathan is napping, I'd like to talk—I'd like us to talk."

He nodded. His expression was so forlorn she couldn't help but reach up to pat his cheek.

Her fingers were warm and tender, and Morgan tipped his jaw, absorbing the feel of her against him no matter how simple. Then, as if a stick of dynamite had detonated in his chest, his heart exploded. He reached out and pulled her close, enveloping her with his arms and body.

The quiet, muffled sounds of her tears had eaten at him the whole time she was behind the screen, worse than if she'd been sobbing aloud. He wanted to go to her, hold her close, but he hadn't. Couldn't—he'd had no idea how to ease her pain. A hell of a thing for a man to admit, even to himself. It had been torture, carrying on as if nothing was wrong. He'd restacked the wood, and played with Nathan, all the while she'd cried alone. Morgan tightened his hold, wishing he could take all her hurting away, all her worries. He'd gladly carry them for her—from now until the end of time. "I'm so sorry, Cora."

She wrapped both arms around him, held on tight while resting her cheek on his chest. "Oh, Morgan," she whispered.

Perhaps in time when Orville's name was mentioned, she wouldn't grieve so. At least he hoped so. He kissed the top of her hair. She smelled so wonderful, always did, and he wondered how. It was light, sweet yet spicy, and wholesome and fresh all at the same time. There were nights when she'd be sound asleep that he'd lain on his side, his nose near her pillow, just luxuriating in the heady scent.

"Mama. Moga. Eat."

Morgan opened his eyes and smiled at Nathan standing next to the table. What he'd said in the lean-to had been the truth. Nathan was his son—if for no other reason than he loved both Cora and the boy beyond life, and always would. "We're coming, buddy."

Cora twisted, but kept one arm around his back. He kept one around her shoulders, wanting to offer any comfort he could, and side by side they walked to the kitchen. Once there, she rubbed his side for a moment before removing her hand. Like a flower petal falling from a blossom, quiet and graceful, she slipped out from under his arm and walked to the stove.

He bent down and picked up Nathan. After setting the child

in the high chair, Morgan pushed the chair up to the table. The woman was amazing. In the small amount of time it took him to settle the child and retrieve plates, silverware and glasses from the neatly stacked cupboards, she had filled the room with the wondrous smell of food cooking to perfection.

It was astounding how some people knew just what to do. He'd been cooking for years and had never figured out what went with what to make it mouthwatering and filling. His fare had been life sustaining, but that was about it. Whereas her meals made eating a pleasurable experience and not just something that had to be done in order to live.

Morgan's mind continued down this path, and he let it, not wanting to think of the anguish he'd caused. That would come later—when they talked.

As she busied herself, he took in the cabin she'd turned from a shell to a home. In two months, she'd sewn curtains and cushions, pillows and quilts, and even braided rugs to cover the floor near the door, in front of the hearth and beside the beds. She'd also canned the few vegetables his little garden had produced, which was nothing compared to the jars of things she'd brought over from her place. Of course he'd acknowledged all this before, but today it seemed more prominent than ever, making him conscious of the fact he didn't want to live without any of it. Namely, because it all was a part of her.

The meal was consumed with little fanfare, and only one glass of spilled milk, which Morgan sopped up with Nathan's napkin, assuring the child no harm had been done. While Cora washed the dishes and cleaned the kitchen, he carried Nathan to the bed tucked in the tiny alcove beside the fireplace. He sat on the edge while Nathan squirmed and fidgeted. When the child was settled, Morgan began to tell him a tale of a little bunny who stole carrots every day. It was a simple, silly story, one he'd heard Cora share when tucking the child in one evening. The child soon dozed, but Morgan continued the tale, hoping to avoid the anxiety creeping in over the upcoming talk with Cora. In all actuality, he was afraid of what she would say to him. Would she leave him? Admit living with the man that killed her husband was too difficult? He couldn't blame her.

Virginia Fisher lent rooms in her big house on the edge of town. He could pay for several months in advance, give Cora time to mourn Orville properly, without all the worries she'd had at her place. A wicked quickening happened inside him. What if she wanted to return to Ohio? He'd have to let her go. The thought caused his blood to drain.

Her touch, though soft and gentle on his shoulder, made him all but leap off the bed. A man heading to the gallows couldn't feel more remorse than he did right now. He stood and followed her across the room to the chairs in front of the fireplace. His gaze took in the room for a moment. Their bed was on the far wall, along with the screen partition. Then there were the two rocking chairs, a small settee and now a large tree in the center of the room. He turned, glancing over his shoulder. The kitchen, with several cupboards, the cookstove, table and chairs, filled the other end, along with the door that led to the lean-to, and opposite that was the little alcove that held Nathan's bed and trunk. He'd built this place for a single man. She deserved so much more, which was why he'd ordered plans for a larger one, had the ad wrapped up in shiny paper for her to open Christmas morning.

"Morgan," Cora said. "Please sit down."

She was in one of the rockers, so he took the other one, after he added a log to the fire.

"I've ordered plans for a larger house," he said abruptly. So much for the shiny little package hidden in his saddlebag out in the barn's tack room.

"Oh?"

That's it, oh? He didn't quite know what to say, had envisioned she'd be excited about a new house, maybe even start planning where things should be. Then again, this wasn't Christmas morning, and hardly the time to bring up such a discussion. "Yes," he said. "I plan on building it this spring."

"Really?"

"Mmm-hmm," he answered, trying to keep any emotion out of his voice. "We can add on as many bedrooms as you want." His cheeks blazed like a prairie fire. He should just shut up. Remember what his father always said, "don't speak unless spoken to." That was good advice.

"That's wonderful, Morgan," she said, but he didn't look up—couldn't take the chance of seeing what was truly reflected in her eyes. "And yes," she continued softly, "we can add on as many bedrooms as you want."

"As I want?" Dread hit his chest, spread through him like a stampede. She was leaving him. "Cora—" Thoughts hung in the back of his mind like icicles on the porch eaves, but he couldn't find anything to say. If he started offering reasons as to why she shouldn't leave he may never stop.

"Morgan, can I ask you a question?"

Half-afraid to open his mouth, he nodded.

"If that cord of firewood had injured you when it fell, would that have been my fault?"

Every ounce inside him snapped to attention. "Of course not. Why would you even think such a thing?"

"Because you built the lean-to so I wouldn't have to go outside to fetch firewood. If I hadn't moved in here, you wouldn't have built it and the wood would never have fallen on you."

"That doesn't make it your fault," he replied. She was not a dense woman, had more common sense and quick-wittedness than most men he knew, so why was she acting so foolish about the woodpile?

"Good," she said with unequivocal satisfaction.

"Good?" A queer sensation tickled his spine—and brain.

"Good," she repeated. "Then I know you know how fault works."

"Uh?" Was he the dim-witted one?

Sitting there as calm as a little peach hanging on a tree, gently swaying back and forth in the high-backed rocking chair, she cocked her head slightly and looked at him as if she was perplexed. "You said the woodpile falling on you wasn't my fault."

"Of course it wasn't your fault," he said slowly, making sure she understood. "It was an accident." He searched for more of an answer, but came up short. "Accidents just happen, that's why they're called accidents."

She gave a little nod. He let out a sigh of relief—glad she finally understood.

"So, if I and Nathan were outside and a storm came up, and we ran as fast as we could to get to the cabin, but lightning struck a tree, knocked it on top of us, would that be my fault?"

Fear shot him to his feet. The edge of the seat knocked against the back of his knees as the chair rocked haphazardly behind him. "Damn, Cora. Don't say such things."

Cora—quite calm compared to all that was going on inside him—sitting in the chair, rocking to and fro, stared up at him. "I didn't say it was going to happen," she said. "I asked, if it did, would it be my fault?"

"Hell, no, it wouldn't be your fault!" He paced the rug in front of the fire, his body quivering at the thought of such danger befalling his family. "Lightning is an act of God. A freak of nature. It's nobody's fault."

Cora stood and took a step, blocking Morgan's path. The idea of Nathan being injured formed a thick glob in her stomach, tore at her heart, but she had to find a way for Morgan to relate to what she was about to say. He was clearly agitated, and that, too, had her insides balling. She drew a fortifying breath, willing her voice to remain calm, and rested a hand on his forearm. "Morgan." Waiting until his eyes met hers, she bit her lip, needing his full attention. "Lightning spooked Orville's horse. That's why he fell in the river. It wasn't your fault, it wasn't my fault and it wasn't Orville's fault. It just happened."

Morgan's face, flawless in every way, except for the deep scowl, held statue-still as he gazed down at her. She was in too deep now; it was either sink or swim. Stepping forward, she placed a hand on his chest, imagined she could feel the steady beat of his heart beneath her palm. "Orville was a good man, Morgan, a very good man. And I'm sorry he died, I miss him in many ways." She caught his arm, stopping him from moving away. "I would have stayed married to him for the rest of my life and never regretted it, but that's not what happened."

He broke away, turning his back on her. She followed, taking a hold of his elbow. "Please, Morgan, let me say the rest."

The muscles beneath her fingers tightened, and she clasped on harder. He turned to face her, and she took the movement, no matter how he meant it, affirmatively. Leading him a few steps she lowered onto the settee and tugged him down beside her.

A million thoughts swirled in her mind, twice as fast and strong as the blizzard whistling outside the cabin. There was no guarantee this would work, that he would understand or that his guilt would dissolve, but it was all she had. This was the only way her wish could come true. She glanced to the tree, standing straight and tall, filling the air with the fresh scent of pine, and in a deep and sacred way, hope. It fueled her will. Straightening the story in her mind, Cora began, "I was eighteen when I married Orville. He was twenty-nine. My grandmother and I lived next door to his family. I used to watch their children once in a while."

Looking as if he was about to spring off the sofa at any given moment, Morgan frowned, seemed to back even farther away if that was possible. "Their children?"

"Yes," she explained. Orville never spoke of all he left behind in Ohio, and respecting his silence, neither had she. "Orville was married before," she continued. "He and Roxanne had two children, a girl named Ada and a boy named Adam."

"What happened to them?"

The pain of the past was still there, a bruise on her heart as was Orville's death, but she'd come to terms with it, understood how life went on despite great losses. "They died," she answered solemnly, clearly recalling how fast most of the community took ill.

"My grandmother did, too. A smallpox epidemic all but wiped the entire town off the face of the earth." She paused, remembering chaos-filled days. "Homes and businesses were burned trying to contain the disease and, well, in the end, Orville and I packed up a few remaining provisions and left with several others. Eventually Orville came across a newspaper article about the wagon trains traveling west and said Nebraska would be a good place to go. We married before joining the train, and along the route we chose Central City because it was right in the middle of the state."

Another remembrance formed clearly, but Cora chose not to mention it—at this time anyway—for it was the first time she'd seen Morgan. She'd been in the wagon and Morgan had ridden up on a large roan, stopping to talk with Orville. It had been the only time in her marriage she'd regretted her impromptu wedding for at that moment something had flared inside her. She'd seen him countless times afterward, since Morgan had helped build their tiny cabin and larger barn, but by then she'd scolded herself out of overly admiring his fine physique and quiet demeanor. Though, now, she had to wonder if she'd ever truly buried the lust the sight of him instigated.

At some time, while she'd been talking, Morgan had reached over and laid a hand upon hers, a gesture of sympathy. No matter how sincere, pity had no place in their conversation. She rolled her hand, gently rubbed the calluses along the top of his palm. "Orville was good to me, Morgan, and I loved him for it. But that's who he was. He was good and kind to everyone he met. You couldn't have stopped him from going after your cattle any more than I could have. He was already ill before he went out. For some time after he died I wondered if he did it on purpose, so he could be with Roxanne and their children, but I soon realized that was just grief talking. Orville never put himself before anyone."

"Cora—"

She pressed a finger to his lips. "Let me finish."

Chapter Five

Cora waited until Morgan nodded before she removed her finger from his lips. The touch had lit a fire in the pit of her stomach. Even while she shared how much she cared about Orville, Morgan's irresistible magnetism drew her and made her want him above all else. A deep sense told her what she'd experienced earlier was a mere snippet of the pleasure Morgan would provide. Yet, the weight of a heavy truth welled inside her, overrode the intensity of the love she held for him. Pride could break a person, she understood that, but also knew a person had to respect themselves.

"Before Orville died," she started, "he asked me to get you when the event happened. He told me you were a good man and would take care of Nathan and me." She bit on her bottom lip, hoping the next statement came out right. "He also said if you asked me to marry you, I should say yes."

Morgan drew in air so quickly he wheezed. His gaze was on her, but she couldn't read his expression or, unfortunately, his mind.

Her nerves were on the outside of her skin, and she drew a breath, trying to quell the trembles that threatened to overcome every limb. She wrapped both hands around one of Morgan's and lifted it to hold near her breast. Of all she'd lived through, nothing compared to this moment. This baring of soul. "But, Morgan, that's not why I said yes when you asked."

He was quiet for so long the silence stung her ears. She wanted to go on, but had to know he wanted the information.

"Why did you say yes?" he finally asked.

She met his gaze eye for eye. "Because I love you."

He looked away, as if unable or unwilling to admit he'd heard her. Determined, Cora reached up and caught his chin, turned him back to face her. "I married one man because he felt responsible for me. I was young and naive. Didn't believe I could take care of myself. I've grown since then, Morgan, and things were different this time. I had money in the bank. Had the land Orville and I homesteaded. I could have sold out at any time, packed up and moved. But I didn't want to." Her emotions joined her nerves on the surface. A dangerous place, but surrendering her love was all she had left. "I wanted to marry you, Morgan. I wanted to live with you, as husband and wife. And I still do."

Something tight and fierce clutched her heart as Morgan shook his head. "Cora," he started, "Orville—"

"No, Morgan," she interrupted. "This is no longer about Orville. It's about you and me."

A sudden blast of cold air filled the room, along with the crash of the door flying open. Morgan leaped to his feet as Russ Barber, the ranch foreman, entered the cabin.

"Boss, you gotta come. That big old cottonwood lost its top. It crashed through the barn roof." Russ paused then, as if just recalling his manners and shut the door while looking at her. "Sorry for the intrusion, ma'am."

Cora rose as she nodded toward the man. Morgan's hand still held hers and his fingers tightened as he glanced between her and his hired man. Their conversation wasn't over; she knew that as well as he did, but she'd said her piece, had no more to add. The next move was his.

He opened his mouth, but closed it just as quickly. The frustration that overcame his face touched her heart. Offering a consoling smile, she gestured toward the door where Russ stood with bright red cheeks and snow-covered clothes.

"I don't know if it was the wind or the weight of snow on its branches," Russ said in the silence that had fallen upon the room. "The top half of the tree broke right off. I can't believe you folks didn't hear it. It damn near rattled the roof right off the bunkhouse." He nodded to her again. "Excuse me, ma'am," he apologized, quickly rewording his statement. "It pert near rattled the roof off the bunkhouse."

"Mama?" Nathan said, drawing her attention as he sat up in his bed.

"I'll be right out," Morgan told Russ, barely taking his eyes off Cora. To hell with the barn, he wanted to shout. To hell with the world. It would all be there tomorrow, and the next day, and the day after that. Right now all he wanted to do was pull Cora into his arms and comfort her for all she'd been through.

Morgan would have gathered her into an embrace, right then and there, but with a gentle squeeze on his hand, she was gone, crossing the room to gather Nathan from his bed. Morgan glanced to the door, where Russ stood staring at him, and then back to Cora. The room seemed to swirl as fast as the thoughts in his head. Had she said she loved him? That she'd wanted to marry him. Be his wife.

Nathan spoke in his garbled language, and Cora said something reassuring as she carried the child toward the screen. Passing by, she smiled and gave another nod toward the door. Only then did the air in Morgan's lungs release—with a gush. He turned and asked Barber, "How bad is it?"

"We got a mess, that's for sure," Barber said.

"Morgan, don't forget your gloves. It's cold out there," Cora said from behind the screen where Nathan was most likely using the small chamber pot.

Barber grinned, but was smart enough to hold his tongue. Morgan couldn't help but grin himself and moved toward the door. He grabbed his hat, coat and gloves. "Cora, you stay inside."

"We will," she responded.

Barber pulled the door open and, still buttoning his coat, Morgan followed the man out into the elements to assess the damage, though his mind was still in the house. She'd had choices, just like she'd said. Could've packed up and left, sold her acreage. He'd pointed most of those out to her, and as long as he was being honest—maybe the cold wind stealing his breath away was also clearing his mind—there'd always been a part of him that hoped she wouldn't take his advice.

The wind hadn't let up, was still acting like a tornado's first cousin, and the ice-cold bits of snow finding a way to sweep inside his upturned coat collar and bite his neck made him think of the little cabin Cora and Nathan would still be in if he hadn't married her. It was sturdy, he and his men had helped Orville build it, as well as the barn, and she'd have gotten along just fine. That's the type of person she was. Capable and strong-willed. Resourceful, too. Several of the cows in his barn were hers. The ones she'd milked, and sold butter and cream to the wagon trains as they passed. Truth was, she hadn't had to marry him.

Barber, shouting to be heard above the whistling wind, tapped his shoulder. "See what I was talking about?" The man pointed to the barn roof where half a tree stuck up like a cross on a church steeple. Morgan had no choice but to push all other thoughts aside and start issuing orders. The sooner he dealt with the tree, the sooner he could deal with Cora.

Morgan wasn't sure how long it took, four or maybe five hours, before he found himself standing inside the barn, alone, gently rocking the little wooden horse he'd made Nathan for Christmas. Tomorrow night, after the child was asleep, he'd sneak out here to retrieve it and place it under the pine—along with the locket he'd purchased for Cora. He was dually glad now he'd bought her something besides the house plans. His heart rate increased, and he took a moment to contemplate exactly what that meant.

He'd thought of her the entire time he'd been working, removing the top half of the cottonwood that had snapped off like a twig and planted itself in the roof of the barn, but now he was pondering things deeper. Like how he'd taken extra precautions when he'd climbed through the ice-crusted branches to get a rope around the top of the tree. It hadn't been fear for himself, but fear for her. He didn't want her to become a widow—again. That now held more weight than before and the implications of that had clung to him all the while he worked.

The job was done now. They'd needed the help of a plow horse to get the tree out of the roof and safely to the ground without doing much more damage, and as soon as the storm broke they'd begun the repairs. He was thankful how minor the destruction had been. No stud walls or support beams had been damaged, so once the roof foundation and new shingles were nailed in place, the barn would be as good as new. It really had been nothing more than a minor accident.

His fingers stalled on the rope mane of the toy. A minor accident, his mind repeated. Some things in life were just that, mishaps or even disasters that were no one's fault. He twisted slightly and leaned a hand against the top of a stall, staring at the barn door as if he could see through it and the one on the cabin. Guilt was an odd thing, the longer you carried it, the heavier and larger it became.

If the storm hadn't spooked his cattle that night, if Orville had just come down sick and died, would things be different? A chill, not induced by the weather, shot through him, hit Morgan's bones. He certainly wouldn't have allowed Cora to take the blame, to feel she somehow had caused such a calamity.

His sigh caused a swirl of steam in the air. So where had this burden come from? Why had it set root in his core? He'd known other men who'd died and left widows. Was it because he didn't believe he deserved a woman as pure and beautiful as Cora?

Morgan pondered the thought for a moment, but it didn't take root. He was a God-fearing, hardworking man who believed everybody gets what they deserve, good, bad or indifferent. His gaze went back to the rocking horse. He'd had one similar as a child. Pa had made it. His stomach churned as if the simple thought had the ability to open the old, festering wound he'd believed had long-ago healed.

It had been over ten years since he'd learned of his mother's death in a saloon down in Kansas. He'd visited her resting spot, even laid a few flowers near the wooden cross marking her grave. His older brother, Vince, had been there, too. The memories flowed before his eyes as clearly as the day they'd stood in the cemetery.

The hot summer sun had beat on their heads to the point his temples had pounded. After they'd set down the flowers, Vince had laid a hand on Morgan's shoulder, and said, "The old man always said, 'you can't change the past, only the future.' So that's what we gotta do, Morgan, change our futures."

They'd ridden out then, their quest of finding their mother over. Vince had gone to Colorado, found himself a good gold vein, and Morgan had gone to Nebraska. Tad and Telly, his two younger brothers, had stayed in Missouri, on the family farm. They wrote once in a while, and from what the letters said, they were all doing well. A frown pulled on his brows as if he had just comprehended something. They'd all—every one of them, Vince, Tad and Telly—married. He had a passel of nieces and nephews. And from what Tad and Telly said, Pa was happier than a pig in a poke with all the young ones back in Missouri.

The cold got to him then, made him shiver from the inside

out. He blew into cupped hands and rubbed them together before picking the lantern off the shelf. Absently he checked the animals that long-ago had been fed and watered, and made his way to the door. When the wintry air attempted to steal his breath, his heart jumped. Cora had told him what she wanted—without mincing a word. She wanted to be here. Wanted to be his wife. That's what he'd wanted, too. He'd just been too stubborn to admit it.

Turning, his gaze landed on the rocking horse again. Had his childhood left a belief any woman he loved would leave him for another man? Cora already had a chance to marry practically every single man in the territory. Yet, she'd held out for him. Married him because she loved him, which was exactly why he'd married her. He pushed the door closed—on the barn and his past.

He'd been a damn fool, that's what he'd been. Blaming Orville, blaming himself, blaming his past, when all along life had given him exactly what he wanted. All he'd had to do was open his eyes and see it. Afraid was what he'd been. Terrified that if he admitted the truth, told Cora how he felt, she'd run for the hills, or Ohio.

The snow let up just then, gave a clear picture of the house. Lights flickered in the windows and smoke twirled out of the chimney, giving it a welcoming, homey glow that seemed to brighten in the twilight. His footsteps picked up speed. He had a lot of making up to do.

Mere seconds later, warm air stung his cheeks and the smell of fresh baked cookies filled his nose as he pushed open the cabin door. Cora, a vision of pure loveliness that filled his heart with unadulterated joy—now that he let himself acknowledge exactly what she meant to him—rushed across the room. The sight alone warmed him twenty degrees.

"I was getting worried," she said, closing the door behind him. Her hands went to his shoulders, brushing the snow off while he pulled the frozen gloves off his fingers. "I saw the men go to the bunkhouse a long time ago. How bad is the damage?"

He'd started to undo the buttons of his coat, but his stiff fingers weren't cooperating. She swept his hands aside and deftly unfastened his coat. "How bad is it, Morgan?"

Worry touched her eyes, but they held something else. His heart slammed into his rib cage. Love. How had he not recognized it before now? He framed her face and used the tips of his fingers to smooth away the little worry lines crinkling her skin. "It's not bad, Cora," he managed to whisper. His lips were on top of hers as he added, "It's not bad at all."

Her hands slipped inside his coat. Warm and tender, they massaged his sides and then his back. "Good," she whispered.

His hands slid down her arms, then around her back. He kissed her again, briefly. Her response told him she wasn't thinking any more about the barn than he was. She caught his lower lip between her teeth, gave it a little nip. "You did have me worried," she said.

"I'm sorry," he answered, though remorse was the last thing he felt right now. "Forgive me?"

She let out a little giggle that was more than charming. Husky and low, it sent his blood zipping through his veins. "Of course," she whispered.

His smile was so broad he could barely pull his lips together to brush over hers again. She came to him so willingly, so affectionately his heart swelled three times its normal size. He'd certainly been a fool. All the while he'd had this perfect, loving woman here at home, but his stupidity had had him out chasing cows and sleeping on the hard ground. Well, that was over starting today. He had men he paid to work the cows, and from now on, he'd make sure he was home every night.

They kissed several times, teasing nips that had them both grinning and his spirits soaring. When her lips parted, Morgan plunged fully into the kiss, savoring her sweet nectar. They could have been on top of the world for all he knew.

Heated now, well beyond normal, he accepted the arousal filling his britches as something that would happen every time he held his wife. He tugged her closer, luxuriating in how her breasts kissed his chest. The thought of caressing those mounds, of tasting the peaks, made him wish the conversation they had to have was already far behind them.

As insightful as she was beautiful, her fingers slid under his shirt, scorching his back with enchanting heat as she shifted a leg between his, and used it to tease him completely by running her knee along the inside of his thigh. He broke the kiss, grasped her shoulders. "We need to talk, Cora."

"I know," she said, without losing an ounce of glimmer in her eyes. "But this is more fun, isn't it?"

He kissed the tip of her nose. "You know it is."

"Yes, I do," she answered, running a finger over the top button of his shirt. "I was just wondering if you do."

"I know lots of things, Cora." He winked and kissed her nose again.

She giggled and laid her head on his chest, sighing with what sounded like extreme satisfaction. He chuckled and then nuzzled the top of her head with his chin. As they stood like that, the elation simmering inside Morgan said it was right to love her. All his past doubts were gone now, completely, along with the fears, guilt and resentment he'd hoarded. Damn, it felt good to be on the right trail again.

He gave her a good, solid hug that lifted her off her feet.

She leaned her head back to look him in the eye. "So," she asked, "how bad is not bad?"

Morgan wondered how she had the state of mind to remember their earlier conversation. His mind was still off in some foreign, wonderful land. He set her down, kissed her forehead. "Not bad," he replied. "The boys will have the damage repaired in no time. Probably tomorrow. The storm feels like it's running out of steam."

"Well," she said, stepping out of his embrace. "Get out of this cold coat. I have hot coffee ready and supper is almost done."

He glanced down. He did still have his coat on, and normally hot coffee would sound good, but right now, nothing compared to holding her—perhaps never would again. His gaze went back to her.

Tucked in those sparkling eyes with all the colors of the rainbow was a promise of making his dreams come true. She kissed the tip of her finger and then pressed it to his lips before turning to walk to the table. Morgan shrugged out of his coat and hung it on the hook, then leaned against the wall, taking in the room with new appreciation.

She'd been busy. The pine was covered with bows of shiny ribbons and heart, star and bell–shaped decorations. He glanced to Cora, who was at the stove, pouring steaming coffee into a cup. She was amazing, this wife of his.

"Tookie!" Nathan took a bite out of one of the ornaments.

"Those are for after supper, young man," Cora said, arriving at Morgan's side.

He took the cup she held out and wrapped his other arm around her. "I don't think he wants to wait," Morgan offered, nodding his head toward Nathan while taking a sip of the hot brew. He could understand. He didn't want to wait, either.

Nathan took another bite of the cookie. "Dood!"

Morgan laughed. "I'm sure they are good, buddy." He looked down at Cora. "Life is good."

She wrapped both arms around him and snuggled in under the crook of his arm. "Yes, Morgan. Life is good."

A kettle boiling over interrupted the embrace and soon the table was set for the meal they consumed while talking about insignificant things and laughing together at Nathan's gibberish. After the dishes were done, Cora announced it was bath night, which sent Nathan running across the room as though a band of braves chased him. In some ways that was exactly how Morgan's heart reacted.

"I'll get the tub," he told Cora, walking toward the lean-to, "while you catch him."

"Thank you," she said, stepping in his path.

It was obvious she wanted a kiss. He wanted one, too, but the next time he started kissing her, he wasn't going to stop, not for a very long time. He flicked a finger against her chin. "Catch Nathan," he said. "I'll get the tub."

They'd lived as a family for two months, but Morgan, wallowing in his old dreary world, had stayed away, never partook in the little everyday things that went on around him. After positioning the tub behind the screen, he carried over hot and cold water while Cora wrestled the giggling Nathan out of his clothes. "Need any help?" he asked.

She tugged Nathan's chubby arms out of the sleeves of his shirt. "No," she said, glancing his way, "but you can watch."

All of a sudden Morgan had an image of her sitting in the tub. It was all he could do not to close his eyes and imagine the vision completely.

"Baf, Moga."

"You could get me his nightshirt," Cora said. "I laid it on the foot of his bed."

Morgan took the opportunity to escape. He was worse than a buck in rut. Every thought he had ended at the exact same spot. He'd gone from dreading the act of lying down beside her to counting the minutes until he could, in less than a day. The nightshirt was where she said it would be, but Morgan took his time retrieving it. He walked to the pine tree and examined the decorations.

With icing she'd painted their names on some of the cookies. Near the top, four large hearts hung. Morgan. Cora. Nathan.

The final one had 1884 painted on it. A warmth touched him in a unique and foreign way. He'd never experienced anything quite like it, and liked it. Matter of fact, he was not only prepared to accept this happiness, but to cherish it in all the days ahead. He turned then and moved to deliver the nightshirt.

Once Nathan was shiny clean, grinning from ear to ear and dressed in his flannel nightshirt, Morgan picked the child off the bed.

"Morgan." A blush covered Cora's cheeks as she folded Nathan's used clothing and laid them on the bed.

"Yes?" he answered, smiling at the sudden shyness she displayed.

"Could we wait a short time before our discussion?" She gestured toward the tub. "I'd like to take a quick bath."

Excitement quivered in the pit of his stomach. "Sure, no sense wasting hot water," he answered while wondering how fast he could convince the child to fall asleep. The wide-eyed happy grin on Nathan's face said that wasn't about to happen anytime soon. "I'll keep this guy busy, take your time."

"Thank you," she answered, already on the way to the stove to retrieve the steaming water kettle. Moments later, the swish of her skirts sounded before water sloshed against the tub's sides.

After five minutes of staring at the screen, imagining he could see faint shadows, Morgan shook his head. He stood, scooping Nathan up with him. There was a pair of tin snips in the lean-to and had to be an old can in there as well. "Come on, buddy," he said. "Let's make a star for the top of our tree."

"Tar!"

"Yes, a star."

Chapter Six

Cora heard Morgan and Nathan playing and talking, but didn't let it interfere with her bath. Something had happened while Morgan was outside. He'd released his guilt, she saw that in the way he looked at her, and that had her heart singing.

Tonight, when they crawled into bed, nothing would come between them.

A giggle slipped between her lips before she pressed her hand to her mouth, muffling the sound. The happiness filling her was delightful, as was the warm water swishing around her, but the sizzling anticipation of bedding down with Morgan was what had her soaring through the clouds as if she were an eagle in flight.

The thought of his hands roaming over her skin, his lips kissing her and the heavy, awesome weight of his body pressing upon hers... The soap in her fingers slipped out, hit the water with a splash that sent droplets flying. She leaned her head against the tub's rim, wondering when she'd ever felt such intensity.

Never. Never had her body felt so in tune to what was to come, to what she needed.

A clatter or thud made her ears perk. Nathan's gibberish and Morgan's deep tone both sounded happy, playful. She wasn't concerned, but curious, since they were almost too quiet, too secretive. Quickly rinsing away the soap from her skin, she climbed out. After combing her hair and leaving it uncontained to dry, she donned her best nightdress, a white chiffon with pink ribbons she hadn't worn for years. She'd probably freeze without a housecoat, but only until she and Morgan retired. Death wouldn't befall her before then, and she didn't plan on that being too far away.

She dipped the empty bucket into the tub and carried it around the screen to dispose the bathwater down the kitchen drain, thankful she wouldn't need to go outside for the chore.

From the table, Morgan and Nathan looked her way, Nathan grinning ear to ear, Morgan gaping.

She smiled, utterly satisfied with the effect the gown had on Morgan. "What are you two doing?"

"Tar!"

"W-we, uh—" Morgan closed his eyes for a moment. When he opened them he said, "We're making a star for the tree."

She dumped the bucket and paused at the table before going to refill it from the tub. "I see that," she said, standing near his shoulder. Several cans, with their tops and bottoms cut away, sat on the table. Three quite disfigured star shapes sat amongst the rubbish. A fourth one, lying in front of Morgan, was perfectly formed. "That's a beautiful star," she said earnestly, and reached down to brush a finger over its shine.

Morgan stopped her by placing a hand over hers, sending a firelike sting up her arm, like a string of lit fuse line. "Careful," he warned, "the edges are sharp."

She couldn't tug her eyes away as he gazed up at her. Time couldn't move fast enough for her. She wanted to be in bed with him now so badly her knees wobbled. He tightened the hold he had on her hand. It wasn't as if he tugged her downward, but yet it felt that way. Slowly, watching his expression, her face lowered. As did her lids when their lips met.

It was pure magic, the soft gentle merging of their mouths.

The tip of his tongue, sweetly, leisurely, glided from one corner of her mouth to the other and back again.

She dropped the bucket.

Morgan chuckled and kissed her cheek as he bent to retrieve the pail. She grasped the handle and as off-kilter as a three-legged kitten, maneuvered across the room to the screen. Lowering the bucket in the water, she grasped the edge of the tub to regain her balance.

Never, not once since the moment she knew she carried a baby, had she wished Nathan was anywhere but at her side, but right now, at this minute in time, she dearly wished the child was sound asleep in his bed.

When able, after several deep breaths and a slight mind scolding, she rose and carried the bucket back to the kitchen to empty it once again. Morgan now held Nathan over his head as the child awkwardly hooked the piece of wire twisted on a peak of the star onto the single top branch of the tree.

Cora dumped the pail and went to stand beside them. "That looks perfect."

"Tar," Nathan whispered reverently.

"Yes, it's a star, buddy," Morgan said, drawing her in with one arm. "And it is perfect."

"Christmas Eve isn't until tomorrow night," she said, wondering if she had her dates mixed up. The moment certainly felt miraculous.

Morgan looked her way. "Maybe Christmas came early this year."

"Maybe it did," she whispered, barely able to breathe.

His gaze never wavered as a slight frown tugged his brows closer together. "I've been a fool, Cora."

She bit the tip of her tongue, took a moment to remind herself all wasn't settled between them. "Oh," she said, "how's that?" A groan tried to escape her lips. She hadn't meant to sound flip or nonchalant, but lucid, serious thinking seemed to be miles away.

A fleeting grin tugged at one side of Morgan's mouth, but disappeared as quickly as it had formed. "I'm sorry, Cora," he said. "I…"

In the moment he paused, her insides clenched, tremendous spikes of fear flew straight into her heart.

"I never thought of what you wanted," he continued. "I told myself everything I did was for you, what you needed, but it wasn't."

She was shaking her head, trying to understand, yet not able to grasp what he was saying.

"I was thinking of myself," Morgan said, glancing toward Nathan still sitting in the crook of his arm. "Of what I wanted."

"And what was that, Morgan?" she managed to ask.

He steered her to the sofa, waited until she'd sat before he set Nathan down on the floor near the basket of wooden blocks and rag balls. While she held her breath, Morgan's gaze went from the tree to Nathan before it landed on her. "This," he said. "This is what I wanted. You. Nathan." He shook his head. "I was just afraid to admit it."

"Morgan." Cora didn't realize she was holding one hand out to him until he took it, folded his fingers around hers and sat down next to her.

"I was ten when my mother left," Morgan said, glancing toward Nathan knocking over the small tower of blocks he'd built.

Cora already loved Morgan, but nonetheless imagined her heart expanding. "Left?" she asked softly, knowing he had to tell her in order for him to love her as freely as she loved him.

He nodded. "We lived down in Missouri. Tad and Telly, my younger brothers, and my father still live there. Vince, he's my older brother, lives in Colorado. I'm sure there was more behind it all now, but then it seemed like Ma was there one day and gone the next." Morgan turned then, looked at her. His gaze wasn't cloudy with pain, just crystal clear and sincere. "She left with the neighbor man, Matthew Stone. Of course, I didn't know that at first. He left behind a couple kids, too, and a wife. Pa sent Vince and me over there to do chores for her, but she chased us away, said she didn't want any help from the likes of us."

Cora kept herself from gasping, thinking of two small boys being blamed for something they had no control over. The wheels of understanding started turning in her head. Cora laid her free hand upon his knee. "She said more than that, didn't she?"

"Yes," Morgan answered with a shake of his head. "She certainly did. And Vince and I, as kids do, couldn't believe our mother would have done anything wrong. We figured it was all Matthew Stone's fault—that he stole her from us. We vowed then and there we'd find our mother and bring her back."

"Did you?" Cora asked. "Find her and bring her back?"

Morgan made an expression that was half grimace, half grin. "Our father didn't think much of our plan, so it was several years before we took off looking for her. We did find her grave about ten years ago, down in a small cow town in Kansas. People there knew her, but they'd never heard of Matthew Stone."

"Morgan, I'm so sorry," she whispered, clutching both his hand and his knee firmer.

"Don't be," he said. "You have no reason to be."

"I—"

Morgan shook his head. "I'm no longer sorry, Cora." He reached up and ran his fingers through a mass of her hair resting on her shoulder. "Actually I don't know what compelled me to tell you all this."

He had the ability to touch her deeply in so many ways Cora couldn't stop the sigh that escaped her lungs. "I think I know."

"You do?"

She nodded. "Sometimes we can't surrender to love until

we understand it. And we can't understand it until we're free from the confines it's placed inside us."

Silent, combing his fingers through her hair, he seemed to study her face for some time before he said, "You are a very intelligent woman."

"No," she said. "Just an honest one." She waited a brief moment before adding, "That loves you."

The hand infused in her hair slid up her neck, cupped the back of her head and pulled her forward. "I love you, too, Cora."

"I know," she whispered, leaning forward to meet his lips. "And I'm so very happy about that." The kiss was slow, an undemanding merger that touched her significantly. More so than the heated urgent ones of earlier in the day. When they separated, both smiling, she had to ask, "You imagined yourself as Matthew Stone, didn't you?"

His smile faded, making her continue. "You even went so far as to blame yourself for Orville's death."

"Yes," he answered, "I did. But how do you know all that?"

"Because I was in your shoes at one time, Morgan. I knew Orville didn't love me when we married, just as I knew I didn't love him. He asked me because he felt responsible for me, and I said yes because it seemed to be the right thing to do. It wasn't until after I gave birth to Nathan that I understood love. Knew its all-consuming joy. That's also when I knew I had to let my fears go, and—" Cora kissed his chin "—accept that I had fallen in love with you."

Morgan leaned back, stared at her intently.

Slightly shaken herself by how clear everything now was in her mind, Cora blinked, but then smiled. "I tried to convince myself I wasn't, but it was a lie. I even wondered, if I'd loved Orville the way I loved you, maybe he wouldn't have died."

"You can't blame yourself for his death," Morgan insisted, grasping both of her shoulders. "Even Doc—"

"I know Dr. Braun said I did everything I could have, and I know love couldn't have prevented Orville's death." She turned to the tree, looked at the little decorations she'd made while Morgan was out in the barn. "Maybe it's the magic of the season, a time of miracles, but it wasn't until last night that I realized what a gift love is, and how it can arrive when a person least expects it."

Morgan, though his mind was tumbling, could barely resist the urge to pull her into his arms and kiss her until she couldn't be kissed anymore—which, now that he thought about it, he hoped never happened. He'd never tire of kissing her. Nor looking at her. Right now, the firelight turning the thin sparkling material of her nightgown transparent, his imagination was running wild. Catching the thought, he tucked it aside for a moment and went back to their conversation. "So you understand you weren't responsible for Orville's death?" He might be beating a dead horse, but he had to know she didn't blame herself.

"Yes, Morgan. The question is, do you?"

"I never thought you were."

"Not me," she said. "You. You no longer blame yourself, do you?"

Morgan took a moment to examine his heart in a way he'd never done before. "No, Orville's death was an accident. No different than the barn." He spoke the truth, and had to admit, he no longer harbored animosity for Matthew Stone, either. Cora had been right, he'd needed to clear things aside in order to let new emotions in. Like this full-to-the-rim love he had for her and Nathan.

"Are you ready to start over, Cora?" he asked, somewhat surprising himself with the question, but the past was over and he wanted to keep it that way.

The gentle smile on her face faltered. "What do you mean?"

He ran a hand along the length of her hair. The tresses had dried as they sat, and were soft and silky beneath his touch. She was beautiful, this wife of his, and thoughts of sharing his life, living with her at his side for years to come was quite humbling. "This whole marriage thing. I think we should start over. See if we can get it right this time." He leaned forward, kissed her in a leisurely way that had sparks igniting inside him.

When he lifted his lips, her eyes were closed, and remained that way for some time. He didn't doubt her love, yet an urgency rose in him. "Cora," he whispered, kissing one eyebrow. "If I can't love you soon, lie with you in my arms in that bed of ours, I don't think I'll live to see tomorrow. Christmas or not."

Her eyes opened, and the bedazzled brilliance in the rainbow of colors struck him dead center, as did her whisper. "Yes, Morgan, let's start over." She giggled then, and pressed a hand to her breast, making him wonder if her heart was taking flight as his was. "Oh, goodness," she said breathlessly as a crimson blush appeared on her cheeks. "This must be how a bride feels."

That, too, struck Morgan. She'd been married twice, and though he didn't know what her wedding night with Orville had been like, the one she'd experienced with him wasn't what it should have been. Second chances were hard to come by, and he was going to treasure this one.

Nathan let out a loud yawn as he toddled toward them, leaving a scattering of blocks across the carpet in his wake. He laid his head on Morgan's knee and looked up at Cora with glassy eyes. "Teepy," he murmured.

"You're sleepy?" Cora asked, ruffling the child's hair.

"Mmm-hmm," Nathan said.

Morgan shifted, lifted the child off the floor. "You mind putting him to bed?" he asked. Heat crept into his neck, along with a bit of bride-groom nervousness he never knew existed. "I...uh...should take a bath myself." He nodded toward the stove. "I heated more water."

She stood, took Nathan in her arms. "No, I don't mind putting him to bed."

Morgan stood as well and reached down to retrieve the bucket she'd set near the tree earlier.

"Morgan," she said from behind him. "Holler if you want some help."

The bucket clattered across the floor. Morgan raced after it, wondering for a moment if the tree would hit the floor for a second time today. Bucket in hand, and tree still standing, he turned around. The air held the snap and crackle of excitement, anticipation. She lifted both brows, smiled coyly and shrugged.

The laugh that burst inside him had him tossing his head back. Life with her was going to be something. That was sure. And he didn't want to miss a moment of it. Ever. When he arrived at the stove, he set the bucket on the counter, next to the remnants of his star making. The crude cut tin of his first few attempts shimmered in the lamplight, as if they too held a spark of holiday cheer, even as cast-asides, and that touched him, deeply, like something infinitely precious. Very few things were perfect the first time around. His gaze instantly went across the room. Cora was at Nathan's bed, but facing him, watching him closely.

He grinned, and winked. "I do believe Christmas has arrived early, Mrs. Palmer."

The ranch hands as well as folks in town had called her Mrs. Palmer, but Morgan never had. The sound, the way he said it, made Cora so giddy she almost dropped Nathan. Lowering the child onto his bed, she grinned as her heart went right on tumbling end over end. It was when she straightened that she realized the weight on her shoulders was gone, not even a residue remained. Add that to the fact she no longer needed to conceal her feelings for her husband, and the world took on a whole new wonder for her. Gazing across the room, knowing her eyes were full of what some might declare worship, she nodded. "I do believe you're right, Mr. Palmer."

While Morgan carried fresh water to the tub, Cora tucked

Nathan between the covers, and after picking up the blocks scattered across the room, she settled herself on the edge of the bed to tell him a story. Since most of her attention was on the sounds behind the screen, she lost her place in the bedtime tale and, having no idea what she'd said last, had to start over more than once.

Her lack of concentration didn't seem to faze Nathan, and she really had no idea when he fell asleep because her eyes were on the screen, irritated they couldn't see through the partition. It was the child's slow, even breathing that made her glance his way. Excited beyond belief—it usually took two or three stories before her son gave in—she kissed his forehead and rose from the bed.

As if they had glue on the bottom, her feet remained where she stood. How forward could she be? She really had no experience in such things, widowed or not. Orville had always initiated their mating, and she'd complied. Not only had it been her duty, she'd owed Orville for his kindness, his generosity. This—what she felt for Morgan—was completely different. She wanted to give herself to Morgan. Wanted to share their love. She pressed a hand against her midriff, where vibrations stirred hungrily. The overwhelming sense of passion rearing itself within her was like some sort of primal beast.

A smile lifted the corners of her mouth. Sweet, sensible Orville would have ducked for cover if she'd attacked him the way she wanted to attack Morgan. The splash of water sounded and her smile grew. Morgan was definitely not Orville, and she highly doubted anything would make him turn and run.

She blew out the lamp on the table and added logs to the fire before she moved to the tree, staring a moment at how the fireplace flames reflected off the tin star. "Merry Christmas," she whispered.

A tinkle, far off in the recesses of the world, sounded. Most likely it was her imagination, as was the equally soft, equally magical answering, *Merry Christmas*.

A tremble caught her, not of chill or fear, but of exhilaration. She spun, her feet barely touching the floor. It was as if they moved a few inches above the boards as she drifted around the partition wall.

With both hands Morgan scrubbed his face, splaying water this way and that. She took advantage of his blindness and scooted around to the back side of the tub. Water dripped from the ends of his hair and made tiny trails down his broad back. Cora knelt down and placed both hands on his shoulders, near the base of his neck. He stiffened for a second and then relaxed. The tenseness of his muscles seemed to melt beneath her fingers, and she began to gently massage the bulk of his shoulders and upper back.

"Mmm," he moaned, "that feels wonderful."

"Yes, it does," she agreed. Her fingertips pressed deeper into his skin, as if they could somehow absorb him. After thoroughly kneading the muscles, she moved her hands along his shoulders to his upper arms, rubbing and caressing every inch. He was as hard and solid as rock, yet as supple and pliable as bread dough.

He leaned his head back and the water from his wet hair penetrated the thin material of her gown. The action awoke the skin covering her breasts. They tingled and her nipples throbbed as they tightened. She bent forward, drawing his head against her cleavage, and ran a line of kisses down the side of his face. Her arms wrapped around him and her fingers combed through the curls on his chest. He was massive, strong and powerful, yet underneath, he was flesh and blood, no different from her. Leastwise, she hoped her touch had his skin tingling as much as hers was.

"Maybe," she whispered between kisses, "I should check you for scrapes and bruises from when the woodpile toppled."

He twisted, kissed the underside of her jaw. "I don't have any cuts or bruises."

"Are you sure?" She plunged her hands beneath the water, caressing the tight muscles of his stomach. "I could kiss them for you."

He caught her hands before they slipped lower. "Cora." His voice was husky and hushed, and sent a delightful thrill clear to her toes. "Do you want to torture me?"

She nipped his shoulder with her teeth and then slid her tongue over the skin. "You know what I want, Morgan Palmer."

With remarkable swiftness, he rose from the water, twisted and lifted her off the floor all at the same time. She let out a squeal and grabbed his shoulders. His hands were on her hips, where his firm but gentle grasp held her suspended. "Now, how would I know what you want, unless you've told me?" he asked, touching the end of her nose with his.

She stared into the blue eyes level with hers, wondering for a split second if he was serious. After all, her experience in such things was limited. A teasing, somewhat taunting grin appeared on his face. She took it as a challenge. Eager and more than willing to play along, she wrapped both arms around his neck. "Then I'll have to tell you, won't I?"

His brows arched.

Stopping her lips before they touched his, she whispered, "I want you, Morgan." Encouraged by his swift intake of breath, she kissed his upper lip. "Every bit of you." Her tongue ran over his bottom lip, pulling back before he could catch it. "Inside me. On top of me. Loving me." She drove home her last statement by lifting her legs and wrapping them around his torso. The skirt of her gown bunched up near her hips, and his hands caught her bottom, holding her against him, allowing his skin to fuse with hers.

"You want me, do you?" he asked, pulling her closer. His

arousal touched her inner thigh and she pressed against it, seeing the pleasure in his face.

There was no doubt bliss was on her face as well. The friction was wonderful, had delicious flames scorching her skin. "Yes, I want you, Morgan Palmer," she admitted freely, with no sense of shyness. "Like I've never wanted anything in my life."

A desire-filled groan sounded between them, and Cora didn't know if it was hers or his. Not that it mattered. She could feel his passion, knew it was as strong as hers.

"Aw, Cora, darling," Morgan said, stepping over the tub. "I want you, too."

Quivering, she tightened her thigh muscles, keeping their connection as he moved.

"I want you now. Today," he said, kissing her forehead as he walked across the room. "Tomorrow." His lips trailed down her nose. "Next week." His kisses continued, catching her lips, brushing her neck and the tip of her chin. "Next year, and the next, and the next." He had her very bones aching with want. "And every moment in between," he said as her back touched the cabin wall.

Divinely trapped between him and the wall, her parted legs cloaked his shaft, presenting a sweet mayhem she'd never guessed existed. "You do?" she asked, wondering if she'd survive much longer. The heat consuming her was vast and propelled her hips forward in a newly unearthed fashion.

His hips reacted, moving his shaft up and down her, the tip of him gliding through her patch of hair and touching the bottom of her stomach. "Oh, yes, I do," he answered, kissing her once again.

The excitement and overwhelming stimulation made her gasp before she fixed her lips onto his. She drank his moisture as if dehydrated and devoured the inner recesses of his mouth with her tongue until she became breathless.

His lips slipped away, covering the sides of her face and

neck with sweet, tender kisses that were almost her undoing. "Cora," he whispered over and over again.

She understood. No word could form in her mind other than his name. "Morgan," she whimpered several times while kissing his temple, his eyes and forehead. An indescribable desperation was building inside her, creating an unfathomable havoc.

Just when she thought she might burst, he pulled her away from the wall, and without disrupting how she rode, carried her across the room. When they arrived at the bed, he bent, gently lowering her onto the mattress. Her body bucked as his slipped away, and she grabbed his shoulders.

He kissed her mouth again. "I'm not going anywhere, sweetheart, ever."

A sudden wave of fear rippled her chest, and she dug her nails into his skin. She needed him so badly. Not just right now, but forever. All the miracles in the world couldn't replace him. "Please, Morgan, promise you'll never leave me, never, ever."

The world stopped for a moment, hung there like a single star in the sky, as he took her by the waist with one arm and lifted her. He tossed the covers to the far side of the bed with his other hand, and then laid her back down. Morgan then knelt beside her. His eyes glimmered brilliantly, showered love as he gazed upon her, vowing, "I promise, Cora, I'll never leave you." He kissed her cheek. "Never." While kissing the other cheek, he added, "Ever."

The world was back on its axis, spinning so fast she grew dizzy. Tears of sweet joy pooled in her eyes. "I love you, Morgan." Unable to control or understand the intensity of her emotions, she added, "I love you with a love I didn't know could exist. It's so deep, so..." Words couldn't describe how she felt.

"So powerful you feel it in every inch of your body," he finished for her.

"Yes. That's it. How do you know?"

"Because it's how I feel about you."

Her heart threatened to explode. It simply couldn't hold anymore. How many nights had she lain in this bed, shed tears into her pillow, wishing he loved her? To know he did was nothing shy of a miracle. No, he, this man, her husband, was the miracle. She placed a palm over his cheek. "Oh, Morgan, you make all my dreams come true."

"I love you, Cora Palmer, and I always, always will," he said seriously, but then his gaze went to her breasts and a teasing grin appeared on his face.

She loved it. It made her feel young and carefree. The want to taunt him in return couldn't be contained. "Even when I'm old and gray and wrinkled and—"

"I'll love you even more," he whispered ardently, as he brushed a fingertip over one nipple straining against the thin chiffon material.

The touch reignited the fire inside her that settled into a smoldering heat when he laid her on the bed. "You will?"

His hands went to the hem of the gown twisted around her hips. He unwound it, inching it upward. Anticipation of lying next to him, unclothed, overtook her mind, had her wiggling, aiding him as he relieved her of the nightdress.

"I will," he said.

Somewhat mindless, she asked, "Will what?"

"Love you even more."

Incapable of waiting, she sat up, raising her arms for him to lift the gown over her head. "And I'll love you even more," she whispered. "I'll love you even more."

Chapter Seven

~~~~~~~~~~~~~~

Morgan tossed the gown aside, oblivious to where it landed. Life literally surged through his body. He'd never been more alive, more driven to participate in existence.

Cora's hands touched his shoulders, and she pulled him forward. "Kiss me, Morgan," she implored, "kiss me until I can't be kissed anymore."

"Now, how'd you know I wanted to do that?" he asked, loving how she rose to his teasing.

"I read your mind," she quipped.

More than willing and able to comply, he kissed the tip of her nose. "Then you know I plan on kissing you for years to come." He captured her mouth, and drank until he was dizzy and burning with a desire so strong it had to be deadly.

Easing her backward, he kissed her chin. "I intend to kiss you here," he said as the ability to speak returned. "And here," he added, kissing her cheek.

"Oh," she cooed, sinking deep into the mattress.

He chuckled, running kisses along her chin and neck. "Definitely here," he said, nibbling on her ear. He ran his hands over the sleek, ultrafine skin covering her collarbone and lower until the marvelous mounds of her breasts filled his palms. "And here," he said, kissing the span of her shoulder while the pads of his thumbs played with her nipples.

She trembled beneath the touch and moaned a sigh he deduced came from extreme pleasure. "Aw, yes," he whispered, "I must kiss you here." He took one of the rosy peaks into his mouth. She gasped and stiffened a touch.

Her back arched, thrusting the mound deeper into his mouth, even though she said, "But, Morgan, you shouldn't kiss—"

"Yes, I should," he assured, gliding his lips across her breasts. "I'm kissing away your bumps and bruises."

A tiny giggle floated in the air. "I don't have any bumps and bruises."

"You don't?" he asked, twirling his tongue around one nipple.

"No." Her fingers combed through his hair, massaging his scalp.

"Do you want me to stop?"

"No."

With his lips he pinched the tip of the breast, and Cora let out a charming moan. Arching her back again, her hands pressed his head downward.

Morgan continued suckling and kissing, introducing her to all the pleasures awaiting them as man and wife. While his hands roamed her sides and her belly, the insides of her thighs, he whispered to her, fully enjoying in her delight, how she encouraged his every movement. Her excitement, enthusiasm and downright eagerness heightened the nuances of every touch, every kiss.

As his fingers fluttered to the channel where her thighs met, she spread her legs, giving him sweet permission to continue his exploration. He used his fingers, stroking and cajoling her hot, wet core until she was writhing and quaking.

"Morgan," she pleaded, "I—I... Oh, goodness, you—"

"I love you," he stated as he lifted his mouth from her breasts and used his tongue to blaze a trail to where his fingers played.

She bucked when his mouth took over for his fingers. He

caught her hips, lifting her for more access. A feverish delirium overtook when she shuddered and quivered as he tasted her core. Immersed in her essence, completely occupied with her pleasure, he slipped his arms under her legs and lifted them until her knees fell over his shoulders.

The muscles in her thighs squeezed against his head and he snuck his thumb near the base of her folds, stroking while still suckling. Her body bucked and strained, yet he continued, increasing his speed and pressure with every thrust of her hips. He could feel her climbing and climbing, and when she reached the summit, the peak he'd wanted her to find, she leaned forward, dug her hands into his hair.

"Morgan!" she cried as her body convulsed. Seconds later, still quivering and trembling, she groaned sweetly, "Oh, Morgan."

Smiling, he kissed his way back up her body, stalling at her glorious, glistening breasts for a few moments. Her cheeks were flushed and her lips curled into a satisfied grin. "You told me to kiss you until you couldn't be kissed anymore," he teased.

She lifted her lids and her smile grew as her eyes fluttered shut again. "I did, didn't I?"

It took every ounce of discipline he had to stretch out beside her on the mattress and do nothing more than run a finger down the side of her face and under her chin. She was so beautiful, so wonderful. He'd never tire of looking at her, watching her. "Yes, you did."

She rolled her head, looking at him with what he'd call the gaze of worship. He called it that because it was the exact way he looked at her.

"I never knew…" She shook her head. "I never felt…"

He leaned down, kissed her lips gently. "Me, neither," he admitted.

"You, either?" A frown formed. "But you didn't—"

He winked. "Not yet. This is our wedding night, and that,

my dear, was just the beginning." He cupped one breast, teasing the nipple with his thumb.

Cora gasped. It was unbelievable that her body could leap into such a feverish want again after what it had just been through, but as Morgan fondled her breasts the lightning storm that had just played out took hold all over again. She rolled onto her side and pushed him onto his back.

Before he had a chance to move, she flipped on top of him, rubbing her breasts over the top of his chest and her hips against his. "Just the beginning?" she asked while kissing his jawline from ear to ear.

He clasped her hips, held her against him. "Yes."

She pulled her knees so they rested near his hips and rose, sitting on him. Pressing her center against him, she ran her fingernails down his chest. "That was quite a beginning," she said, tracing the ripples of his rib cage.

"Yes, it was," he agreed, as his stomach tightened while he sucked in air.

She smiled, excited her touch did that to him. Scooting until she sat on his thighs, a moment of shyness and insecurity clutched her mind. "Morgan?" she asked.

"Yes?" His eyes held hers, shimmering with a loving gaze.

She bit her bottom lip, hoping he would consent. "Can I touch you?"

His member jolted. "If you want." Then he quickly added, "You don't have to."

She folded her fingers around him. "I want to. I really want to." It was amazing, how his skin was velvet soft, yet the center rock hard. Touching him, stroking him, sent a river of pleasure rushing through her veins. She closed her eyes, relishing the moment, the connection.

Every movement, every touch, made her want more and she grew bolder. Her hold intensified, her strokes became more feverish and intense. A fire blazed in her, building and building. Morgan's body reared off the mattress, joining her in the race to the ultimate ending that was somewhere ahead of them.

"Cora." Morgan clasped her arms with both hands. "Come here, sweetheart."

A second later, she was flat on her back, the mattress soft beneath her, and he was hovering above her. Head swirling, she gasped for air. "I wasn't done."

"Yes, you were," he said, spreading her legs with one knee.

"But I wanted to kiss you, like you did me, until you couldn't be kissed anymore."

"You did, sweetheart," he said.

"No, I—"

With one easy, yet powerful thrust, he entered her. It was like an awakening, a new beginning as her body welcomed him fully and deeply.

"Another time, Cora," he said. "I can't wait any longer. Trust me."

Sighing with extreme pleasure, she wrapped her arms around his neck. "I do trust you, Morgan. With everything I am, everything I'll ever be, I trust you."

His mouth met hers in a merger so perfect she wanted to cry out with joy. Their bodies, joined as one, absorbing and withdrawing with unionized blessings, freed Cora of any inhibitions that might keep her from fully experiencing the ultimate, sacred ritual of loving Morgan.

Energy surged her forward, pitching her into glorious, extreme perfection. It took her breath away and then intensified to a point where she wondered if she'd met her earthly limits. If she had, Morgan was with her, soaring skyward and elevated beyond reality in a timeless realm as they journeyed as one.

His body tensed, as did hers, with a thunderous, amazing climax that couldn't be of this world, and a shattering release that left Cora incapable of doing anything except clinging to Morgan as a harmony of aftershocks spread through her system.

Slowly, effortlessly, she floated back to earth, landing on the bed as gently as spring blossoms fall from an apple tree. Morgan was still with her, his arms, full of strength, surrounding her and his wonderful weight, featherlight, protecting her.

He eased off her, rolling onto his side. His arms tucked her into a warm, loving embrace. She snuggled in, kissing his chest. They stayed there, not moving or talking, just existing in the world they'd created.

Sometime later, he kissed the top of her hair. "Cora," he whispered.

"Hmm?"

"Can I ask you a question?"

Curious, she wiggled a bit so she could look upon his face. The loving, intense gaze in his eyes made her heart skip a beat. "Of course you can ask me a question."

He swallowed, acting a bit unsure of himself.

"What is it, Morgan?" Growing a touch anxious, she insisted, "Ask me."

"This morning, at the table—" He shook his head and kissed the tip of her nose. "Never mind."

She stiffened. "Oh, no, you don't. You can't ask to ask a question and then not ask it."

"It was nothing."

She gave him a make-believe angry glare. "Morgan."

He sighed and rolled onto his back. Staring at the ceiling, he softly said, "I was just curious what you wished for today."

She bit her lips, but the smile couldn't be contained. It landed on her face with as much ferocity as she landed on Morgan's chest. Flattening her body atop his, she squirmed about until the length of her fit perfectly into his hills and valleys. "I wished," she stated with intent, "for you to love me as much as I love you."

The look in his eyes was a bit skeptical.

"All right," she admitted, "I wished for you to love me just a fraction of the amount I love you."

His hands roamed up and down her back. "Really?"

"Yes, really. That was my one wish. My only wish."

"I do love you," he said.

He'd already said as much, and showed her, but she still liked the sound of it. "I know." She kissed his chin. "But you can say it as often as you want."

"All right." He kissed the tip of her nose. "I will say I love you so often you'll get sick of hearing it."

"No, I won't," she admitted. And then because the thought had entered her mind, she asked, "What about you? If you had one wish, what would it be?"

"I'm holding it in my arms."

She smiled. "That was a very good answer, but try again."

"Honestly, there is nothing. I have you. We have Nathan. We have the ranch…" His voice trailed off then.

There was something more, she felt it. "Come on, tell me your wish. I know there's something."

His gaze locked on hers. "A daughter," he said, "who looks just like her mother, Mrs. Cora Palmer."

Her heart leaped to her throat, thudding erratically. She leaned down, kissing the hollow of his neck. "Can I share that wish?"

"Of course, I'll share everything I have with you. Forever," he whispered.

They did share the wish.

Emily Rebecca Palmer was born a year later, on December 23.

Christmas came early that year, too.

* * * * *

ONCE UPON A
FRONTIER CHRISTMAS

Debra Cowan

Dear Reader,

Christmas inspires a mix of emotions for me. While it's a time of celebration and excitement, it's also a time for remembering the past and those who are no longer with us.

Caroline Curtis doesn't want to remember—a choice that's taken out of her hands when her presumed-dead fiancé returns two Christmases after he disappeared. Smith Jennings wants to reclaim his life, and the woman whose memory got him through the past two years, but things are different now. She's different.

Doesn't matter. Smith came back for Caroline and he means to have her. Still, it will take a motherless boy and the spirit of Christmas for this couple to finally claim the future they thought was lost. I hope you enjoy their story.

May you all have a wonderful holiday season.

Debra

DEDICATION

To those who have given second chances.
And those who have taken them.

Chapter One

Indian Territory, 1872

Caroline Curtis hadn't always hated Christmas. Only for the last two years, since Smith Jennings had died during a frigid December on his way home to Mimosa Springs from a cattle sale. The holiday had lost its appeal even though Caroline had put the past behind her.

Knowing she and her first love couldn't be together even if he *were* alive sparked a melancholy that sometimes settled over her this time of year.

In another week, school would be dismissed for the holiday. She stacked up the last of her students' slates, refusing to let her thoughts go to that awful Christmas.

Pushing away thoughts of Smith and the last time she'd seen him, she focused on the bare corner at the back of the schoolroom. So far she'd held off on the tree the children wanted, but it wasn't fair to deny them based on her antipathy. Come Monday, she would probably have to relent.

Her gaze shifted to the small window on the wall adjacent to her desk. Though it didn't snow every winter in this very southeastern part of Indian Territory, it was snowing now. Just as her friend Della had predicted.

It wasn't heavy, but certainly enough to haze the day's remaining light. While Caroline had finished grading essays, dusk had settled and the stove fire had died out. She should get home before daylight was completely gone.

After draping a thick wool shawl over her head, she shrugged into her heavy wool cape and buttoned it to the throat. She stuffed the essays into a battered leather valise she'd inherited from her mother, doused the lanterns then tugged on her suede gloves. Bracing herself, she opened the door and her breath cut when a powerful gust of frigid air stung her face, nearly ripping the door from her hand.

Holding on for all she was worth, Caroline stepped out and managed to wrestle the door shut. She snuggled her face into her cape, carefully making her way down the schoolhouse's three wooden steps. Blasted by another surge of freezing air, she bowed her head against the sleet now mixing with fat snowflakes and angled down the side of the building.

The weather had been like this two years ago when Smith had sworn to return by Christmas Eve, but he hadn't. And he never would.

Sad and a little vexed that she couldn't get him out of her thoughts, she squinted through the swirling silver shadows, halting when she thought she saw someone.

A big man moved slowly out of the brittle twilight, making his way toward her, leading a horse.

He was bundled against the weather almost as heavily as she was and walked with a limp. Though Caroline didn't know anyone with a bad leg, something about him seemed familiar. Still, she didn't think it wise to be alone with him.

She stepped backward, intending to go through town so she wouldn't be on her own.

"No, stop." Though muffled, the deep, masculine voice was familiar and had her heart stuttering in a painful rhythm.

Beneath the rush of the wind, the man sounded like… No. That was impossible.

"Caroline?"

Her pulse jumped. Sleet pelting her cheeks, she peered into the winter haze, unable to get a clear picture through the frosty light. The man was very tall and big-framed, wearing a deer-hide coat with a low-crowned black hat pulled low over his eyes and a bandana protecting the lower half of his face from the elements. It wasn't her fiancé, Ethan Galloway. Ethan was nowhere near that tall. How did this stranger know her name?

"I can't see you." Her voice was muffled through the shawl around her head. "Who is it?"

The man reached her, his eyes slitted against the weather. Even with them narrowed, she felt the intensity of his regard. The heat. His dark gaze moved hungrily over her face as he tugged down the bandana to reveal a whiskered jaw, chiseled cheekbones and a mouth she knew all too well. "It's me."

Smith! Disbelief and grief exploded in her chest, making her knees weak. She hadn't had this dream in ages. Her entire body went numb.

"This can't be," she whispered. "You're dead."

"I'm not. See?" He reached out and folded her gloved hand in his.

Through the suede, she could feel the leather of his gloves, the hard strength of his hand. His touch felt so real.

Tears blurred her vision. She could barely speak around the lump in her throat. "Smith?"

"It's me, sweetheart," he said thickly.

Black spots danced in front of her eyes. She felt herself falling. Then…nothing.

Warm lips brushed hers. "C'mon, honey, wake up."

Caroline opened her eyes slowly, becoming aware of where she was.

Her house. The front room was warm, cozy with the scent of woodsmoke. Her gloves, shawl and cape had been removed. She was on the sofa and a big man—*Smith*—knelt on the floor next to her, stroking her hair. She began to shake.

He stayed very still, black eyes steady on hers.

"This isn't real," she whispered. "You aren't real."

"I know it's a shock, but I am," he said quietly, his concerned gaze locked on her face.

He no longer wore his coat, hat and gloves. The fire burning in the fireplace lit him from behind, outlining shoulders broad enough to block her view of the opposite wall. One large hand rested heavily, possessively on her hip. He was whipcord lean, his blue shirt hanging loosely on a pair of shoulders that used to fill out the garment.

"You caught me," she said faintly.

He nodded.

His thick black hair was cut short, much shorter than the ragged length it had been when he had left. Shadowed with beard stubble, his jaw was still strong, but his face was thin and haggard.

Joy so sharp it pierced her chest spread through her. "Smith?"

He smiled, the smile that always traveled straight through her and pooled hotly in her belly.

Teeth chattering, she reached out and laid a trembling hand against his chest. Warmth seeped through his shirt to her cold palm. Beneath her touch she felt the hard, deep thump of his heart. Tears stung her eyes.

His hand covered hers as he bent toward her. "I missed you." He kissed her, softly at first then harder. Desperately.

Her arms automatically went around him and she kissed him back. Afraid he might vanish like smoke, she tightened her hold on him. Elation then confusion tumbled through her. Her mind could hardly accept that he was here.

He lifted her against him, emotion tightening his chest. He drew in her soft vanilla scent. The feel of her against him, the slender warmth of her body in his arms blasted every thought out of his mind.

He angled her head, went deeper and slower. She tasted like heaven, honey-sweet and hot. During his time away, he'd held on to this memory, but his mind hadn't done it justice. Hadn't done *her* justice. She was here, really here and kissing him back just as feverishly as he was her.

He didn't want to stop. He wanted to touch her skin on skin. Run his mouth over every inch of her. But there would be time later. They needed to talk.

He drew away, his breathing rough. Hers was, too. Her ivory cheeks were flushed, her eyes a deep dreamy green. He helped her sit up, staring at her mouth.

She kept a hand on his chest, as if trying to catch her breath. Determine if this was really happening.

He'd gone too far, too fast. Smith hadn't been able to help himself. It took considerable effort to loosen his hold and he did, but he wasn't letting go. Never again.

"You're even more beautiful than when I left." His gaze traced her fine-boned features, her pert nose, pink kissable lips. Her silvery-blond hair was pulled back in a low ponytail, emphasizing her elegant neck, her high cheekbones.

"I don't understand." She stared hard at him. "Am I really seeing you? Your parents looked for you. So did your sister's husband. They all saw your name on a list of dead prisoners."

"Dead?" Why would they think that? Was that why no one had ever come for him? What had happened to the letters he'd sent to his folks and Caroline?

She still looked dazed. "They were led to a mass grave where you had supposedly been buried."

"I don't know why I was on that list, but I aim to find out. What were my parents told?"

"That you had died in the Fort Smith jail."

He cursed. "I was there, then transported to a Kansas prison."

She wiped at the damp tear tracks on her face and Smith wanted to hold her even tighter, but he didn't.

She shook her head, clearly bewildered. "Everyone thought you were dead."

That certainly explained why he had never been found. He rubbed her back. "On my way home from the sale in Kansas City, there was a train robbery. A gang of Indians and half-breeds robbed a train in Indian Territory. Cherokee country. Several U.S. Marshals were already patrolling the area for them.

"Because of the cattle sale, I was carrying a lot of money. Even though I had the bills of sale, the marshals didn't believe the cash was mine, but they couldn't prove it. They were ready to let me go until a train passenger identified me as one of the gang."

Caroline gasped. "What? Why?"

"I think because they thought I was an Indian."

"Your coloring and your hair," she said grimly.

Unable to keep from touching her, he ran a finger down her velvety cheek. That wasn't the first time he'd been mistaken for an Indian. "One of the marshals let me talk to the passenger who accused me, but she stuck to her story that I had robbed the train with the others. They wanted to turn me over to a tribal government, but I told them I didn't belong to any tribe. I gave them my name, told them to contact my folks at the Diamond J, but they didn't check into anything. They hauled me to Fort Smith with ten other men."

Horror darkened her eyes as Smith went on. "I was tried and convicted then shipped off to a prison in Kansas. Leavenworth County."

She covered her mouth with a shaking hand. "That's awful. Just as awful as everyone being told you were dead."

"I'll find out how that happened." He wanted to sit beside her, hold her, but he stayed where he was, giving her a chance to absorb what was happening. Still, he didn't release her, wasn't going to.

"But…if you were in prison, couldn't you have gotten word to your parents? Or me?"

"I tried. I sent out messages with guards and a couple of released inmates. Obviously none of my letters ever arrived."

Her gaze slid over him, making his skin go tight and hot. "Is that where you were hurt? Prison?"

He nodded, unsure of how much to tell her. "I had a broken leg that didn't heal right."

"How did that happen?"

"Sometimes there were fights." There was no reason to tell her he had been attacked simply because he was a new arrival. "But I'm fine, thanks to another prisoner. A friend."

She swallowed hard, sadness creasing her features. "You served your time so they released you?"

"They released me, but not because I'd done my time. An Indian was arrested recently for rustling. When they brought him in, he had most of the valuables from that train robbery on him."

"Then they knew it wasn't you."

"They weren't totally convinced until the outlaw said I wasn't part of his gang. The judge sent a marshal to Leavenworth straightaway and I was escorted over the Kansas border then released."

"Why didn't you send word to anyone?"

"I was afraid if I stopped to wire home, the marshal might decide a mistake had been made and I shouldn't have been released. I wasn't risking it. I rode hell-for-leather, getting as far from there as I could. I had to get home to you. Where I belong."

She stilled, her gaze sliding away from his. "Wh-when did you arrive?"

"When you saw me at the school. I came here first."

Something flickered in her eyes, but was gone so quickly he couldn't identify it. "Your parents have been visiting Ivy this week. They're supposed to be home tomorrow."

He didn't want to talk about his folks or his sister. He wanted to lay Caroline back on that sofa and make her his, the way he'd almost done before he left on the damned cattle trip that had cost him two years of his life. Two years of *their* lives.

He ran his thumb across her lower lip, drawing in her soft vanilla scent. "I don't want to waste any time."

She frowned.

"Our life was interrupted. I want us to get married soon, before Christmas, and start the family we'd planned."

In the flickering firelight, it looked as if she went pale. Slipping from his hold, she rose from the couch and stepped away.

He got to his feet, ignoring the throb in his bad leg. "Prison taught me to take advantage of the time we have and I've already missed out on too much time with you."

An odd look crossed her face. "You've only just returned."

"Yes, and I want my life back. *Our* life."

She reached into her skirt pocket then opened her hand. The engagement ring he'd given her glinted in the golden light.

"You've been carrying your ring." He smiled. "Now you can wear it again."

She stared down at the thin band.

He moved closer. "I don't want to spend another minute apart from you. Our life has been on hold long enough."

She closed her eyes, looking pained. "Don't you need time to settle in? Let your folks get used to you being here?"

"No," he answered slowly. "Do *you?*"

Tears welled in her eyes and she turned away.

"Caroline, what's wrong?" Uneasy, he cupped her shoulders.

After a long moment, she faced him. Her skin was waxy, her eyes hollow in her chalk-white face. A sense of foreboding dropped over him like a weight.

Visibly shaking, she held out the ring. "I can't marry you."

Even over the hammer of growing dread, he heard the stark, cutting words and they punched the breath right out of him. This was every bit as unexpected and vicious as the attack in prison that had nearly ended his life.

Chapter Two

Smith stared at Caroline then at the diamond ring in her tiny hand. "You mean you can't get married right now? Okay, when?"

"I mean get married, ever."

He was dimly aware of the hiss and crackle of the low-burning fire behind him, the scent of woodsmoke. Heavy silence hung between them.

It took long seconds before he could get a full breath. "What? We have plans."

Her mouth tightened. "Not…any longer."

"We're going to build a house near the river where our kids can swim and fish."

She just looked at him.

Heart thudding hard, he frowned. "When you fainted, I caught you before you fell, so I know you didn't hit your head."

But maybe *he* had because none of this made a lick of sense.

Caroline's green eyes were dark with wariness and what appeared to be pain.

"You're in shock from seeing me." It was as though he were watching this happen to someone else. "That's what this is."

"Smith."

"I love you, Caroline." He folded her hand over the ring and covered her hand with his. "I came out of that hellhole for you."

She winced. "Don't say things like that."

"It's true."

"But it shouldn't be."

What the hell? "I don't understand. What's going on here?"

"You've been through so much. You've only just returned home."

"And?"

Her eyes were bright with unshed tears. "I don't want to hurt you."

"Then let me put that ring back on your finger."

"I can't." Her face was ashen in the flickering light.

Frustrated, his voice rose. "Why not?"

She hesitated. "I'm keeping company with someone."

He froze for a moment. "Because you thought I was dead. Now that I'm here, you can call it off."

She shook her head.

His free hand curled around her waist and he eased her closer. She'd said "can't," not "won't." He was trying to understand even as his gut tangled like rusted barbed wire. "You belong with me and you know it."

"You've been gone two years, Smith."

"I know every damn minute of how long I've been gone," he gritted out, his hold tightening on her. "You still love me. You kissed me not ten minutes ago."

"I shouldn't have done that." She flushed and he knew she was turning that rosy-pink all over. "I'm thrilled and grateful that you're alive, that you're home, but I forgot myself."

His head started to pound. "Are you telling me that you've moved on?"

"Yes," she said raggedly. Her eyes were tortured. Bleak.

He could see she meant it. "This is crazy. What's gotten into you?"

"I'm trying to explain." She tugged at the hand he still held, but he refused to release her.

"Are you angry because I was gone so long? I told you I had no control over that. And I did try to get word to you."

"It's not that," she said hoarsely. "It's just that…there's someone else."

It was as if he'd been kicked in the head. He understood the words; they just didn't mean anything at first. Then realization sliced through him. "Are you in love with this other man?"

Her gaze skittered away and something sharp shoved up under his ribs. Another man? That couldn't be right. "Caroline, tell me."

She squared her shoulders and looked him in the eye. "Yes, I'm in love with someone else."

"You're lying." He just didn't know why. Expecting her to fumble around for a name, he challenged, "Who is it?"

Without hesitation, she said, "Ethan Galloway."

Galloway! Smith reared back. He knew Galloway, liked him! The cattleman was honest, hardworking and a damn good judge of stock.

Well, he couldn't have Caroline. "You're not in love with him. You can't be."

"I'm sorry, Smith," she said thickly.

The knot in his gut coiled tighter. Disbelief edged into anger. "We had plans for a life together."

"I'm not saying this to hurt you."

He uttered a curse she had never heard him use before.

"You deserve to move on, too."

"Like you have," he said bitterly. "You want me to fall in love with another woman?"

She looked down, tugging again to free her hand and this time he released her. She wrapped her arms around herself.

The walls of her small house closed in, suffocating him. "This is bull."

She shook her head. The anguish in her green eyes said she was telling the truth. He'd endured two damn years, wondered night after night if he would ever see her again, hold her. *Marry her.* Now he was here—finally—and she wanted to be with someone else.

His lips twisted. "How long did you wait before you decided to move on?"

"Just…this year."

"How long have you been seeing Galloway?" he demanded.

"About two months."

And this relationship was already strong enough that she no longer felt for Smith what he felt for her?

He wanted to hit something. "Did you ever want to marry me?"

Though she winced, she met his gaze. "Of course I did."

"Guess I'll just have to take your word for it." Furious and hurt, he jerked up his coat, gloves and hat, limped toward the door.

"Smith!"

He stopped, hoping she would say she had changed her mind, hoping she wouldn't let him walk out.

When she didn't speak, he looked over his shoulder. She held out the ring. The sight snapped the little restraint he had left. "I'm not taking your ring."

That she still wanted him to went through him like a spear. "You're not the woman I thought you were."

He yanked open the door and went out, slamming it behind him.

The icy winter air did nothing to cool his blood. He pulled on his coat, slammed his hat on his head then swung into the saddle, ignoring the bite in his bad leg and the sting of frigid leather on his backside. He paused, glancing at the window to see if she was watching, but she wasn't.

He turned his horse toward home. He wanted to hit something and keep hitting.

They had been the one thing he'd believed he could count

on. The thought of them had gotten him through endless nights of cold and sleeplessness and pain.

And now they were over.

You're not the woman I thought you were.

Two days later, Smith's words still circled around in Caroline's head. He had no idea how right he was. She wasn't the woman he had left behind. She wasn't even a whole woman and she never would be again.

She had barely managed to keep from running after him and confessing everything. Instead she had sunk down onto the sofa and sobbed. Her eyes still burned from all the crying she'd done since then.

Watching him walk out had been like losing him all over again. Even knowing she was putting his happiness ahead of hers didn't ease the searing ache in her heart.

She would never forget the look of betrayal in his eyes, the utter disbelief and hurt. Like she'd ripped off a strip of flesh.

And she hadn't even told him everything.

She had to stop thinking about him. What she'd done was the best thing for him and she couldn't second-guess herself.

Pushing away thoughts of him, she turned her attention to the conversation she and Ethan were having with her friend and former schoolteacher, Della Whitaker. The three of them stood between the church and schoolhouse. Distracted, she heard Ethan compliment Della on her newest hat.

Caroline fully expected Smith to attend church today with his family. Everyone in Mimosa Springs was champing at the bit to see him and she knew he would want to see them as well. The anxiety coiled the tension in her shoulders tighter. Restlessness sawed through her like a dull blade.

Now the owner of the town's general store, Della had children older than Caroline, yet her age was indeterminable. Slightly plump, the woman's dewy skin was unlined and smooth except for laugh lines around her mouth. Her hair was coal-black with no hint of gray.

The older woman's penchant for hats was well-known. Today, she wore a black velvet bonnet, ordered from New Orleans. It was decorated with loops of rose-colored ribbon that bunched together on the brim. A small decorative bird perched in the nest of ribbon.

Holding his flat-brimmed hat, Ethan grinned at her. His blue eyes twinkled. "I saw a raven circling your hat a while ago, looking for a place to light."

Della swatted at the brawny rancher. "You rascal."

Caroline laughed, her gaze skimming over the several inches of snow on the ground, blinding in the Sunday morning sunlight. The few bare patches around the school where people had scooped up snow and staged snowball fights were nearly covered by the snow that had continued to fall yesterday and last night. The hills and evergreen trees beyond were blanketed in white, which also coated the leafless oaks and maples.

Della glanced at Caroline. "Are the children behaving? I imagine they're itchin' for the holiday. This is their last week of school before Christmas, isn't it?"

"Yes. They're excited, but aren't causing mischief. Not yet anyway," she added.

The other woman lowered her voice. "How are you doing, dear?"

Beside her, Ethan stiffened. Caroline had known Della would ask about Smith's homecoming. She had expected Ethan to ask questions after she told him about Smith's visit, but he hadn't.

Caroline gave a small smile. "I'm all right although I admit I was overcome with shock when I first set eyes on him. If I hadn't seen him—" *or kissed him* "—I wouldn't believe he was alive."

The rattle of wagon wheels and jingle of harness announced

the arrival of more people for services. A crow squawked over-head as neighbor greeted neighbor.

"I want to see the boy for myself," Della said. "Everyone's talking about his return."

Word had spread though Caroline didn't know how because she had told only Ethan. Perhaps Smith himself had shared the news although she hadn't seen him in town.

"It sure beats all I've ever heard." Ethan ran a hand through his brown hair. "Locked up in prison for two years, for some-thing he didn't do."

Though his tone was neutral, there was a tension in his voice. Until now, Caroline had only focused on how Smith's return from the dead affected her. For the first time, she won-dered what the man beside her thought about it.

"In prison?" Della exclaimed. "Whatever for?"

Caroline explained quickly.

"Oh, no." The older woman shook her head. "When Em-mett and Viola return, they'll be over the moon to find him alive and home."

"Yes," Caroline said quietly.

An abrupt silence fell behind them. A sudden chill skipped down her spine and she went still inside. Smith had arrived. She knew it.

Her friend's brown eyes filled with tears. "There he is. I declare."

With a sniffle, the older woman moved past Caroline and Ethan as they turned.

While Smith looped the reins of his Appaloosa over the hitching post in front of Della's mercantile, people surged to-ward him. Everyone spoke at once, their voices rising and fall-ing in excitement.

Sheriff Newberry was the first to shake Smith's hand. Then Dr. Stephen Miller and his wife, Kate, greeted him.

Helpless to look away, Caroline kept her gaze locked on the man at the center of attention.

Yes, she'd already seen him, but she still felt a jolt of surprise and joy. And a familiar quiver low in her belly.

Though he had lost weight during his absence, his deerhide coat skimmed shoulders that were still as wide as a door and opened to reveal a white dress shirt flattened against a muscled chest. Dark trousers sleeked down long powerful legs. The memory of being held against his strong body sent a flush of heat through her.

He shook hands and spoke to everyone gathered around him.

Amid all the hugs and back slapping, someone tugged on her elbow. She looked down to see a sandy-haired boy.

"Good morning, Miz Curtis." Ten-year-old William Dorsett was one of her best students.

She smiled. "Hello, William."

The boy glanced across the street, his blue eyes growing wide as he watched Smith. Awe was plain on his thin features as he breathed, "Ben Wallace said Mr. Jennings was back from the dead, but I didn't believe him."

"Now you've seen him with your own eyes." Because Caroline had conjured up her former fiancé so many times, she wouldn't have believed only her eyes. But he had kissed her. The hard steel of his arms around her, the firm pressure of his mouth and the feel of his big body against hers had proven he was very real.

Favoring his right leg, Smith slowly worked his way through the crowd and reached his former schoolteacher. He swooped Della up in a bear hug.

"Smith Jennings, you really are alive!"

"I am." He carefully set the older woman on her feet. "And you're as pretty as ever."

She smiled, stepping back to give him the once-over. "Your parents were due back from Ivy's yesterday. Did they make it?"

"Not yet. I figure the snow held them up. It didn't stop until late last night."

She patted his cheek. "You need some fattening up."

He grinned, his attention shifting as Ethan walked up to him, extending a hand.

"Welcome back. It's good to see you, Jennings."

The men exchanged a friendly handshake. Caroline couldn't seem to move. Or stop looking at Smith. She could still feel his mouth on hers.

His gaze shifted to her and something dark flickered in his eyes. He tipped his hat. "Miss Curtis."

His formality underscored the distance between them and her throat tightened. Somehow she managed to speak around the lump there. "Hello, Smith."

The other night seemed like a dream, but he was standing right here in front of her. His beard stubble was gone. The square line of his jaw looked newly shaven and his black hair was trimmed above his collar. On the snow-touched chill of the wind, she caught his scent—male and dark and heady.

Thank goodness, he was paying her no mind as he spoke with the other man.

"How's your pa getting on, Galloway?" he asked.

"Fine. He's tough as an old boot."

"Is Lem showing any signs of slowing down?"

"Not a one, just like your pa."

"And the ranch?"

"Doing well," Ethan answered.

Smith's gaze slid to Caroline and sensation hummed beneath her skin. "And how's your pa, Miss Curtis?"

His polite tone scraped her nerves raw. She wanted to walk away from this torture. "He passed on about four months ago."

Galloway moved back beside her with a fond look. "My fiancée has been remarkably strong."

Smith's gaze snapped to Caroline. "Your fiancée!"

The boom of his voice drew the attention of those standing nearby. Caroline's face heated.

Ethan frowned, glancing at her.

"I didn't have a chance to tell you," she said hoarsely to Smith. She could barely keep from squirming under the smoldering fury in his black eyes.

He had every right to be angry, especially after being ambushed by Ethan's declaration.

A muscle flexed in Smith's jaw as his gaze bored into her. He was visibly trying to restrain himself.

Inwardly she winced. She hadn't wanted him to find out like this. In truth, she hadn't wanted him to find out at all even though that would have been impossible.

She should have told him the other night, but after the blow she'd dealt him concerning their future, she couldn't. It would have been like rubbing salt in the wound. Now Caroline saw that had been a mistake. It would've been more merciful coming from her when they were alone rather than hearing it from Ethan in front of half the town.

She held her breath, half expecting an explosion of temper or a barrage of questions from Smith. An awkward silence grew. When he finally spoke, he didn't ask what she expected.

He gave her a flat stare. "What happened to your pa?"

So, he wasn't going to congratulate them. And why should he? Caroline asked herself. The life he thought he'd left behind was gone. She said raggedly, "Stephen said his heart quit."

"I'm sorry for your loss."

"Thank you." Caroline couldn't tear her gaze from the knowing look in his black eyes.

Smith was well aware that she felt more relief and freedom at her parent's death than loss. Gil Curtis had resented his only child almost as much as he had resented her mother.

Standing so close to her first love had her on edge and relief washed through her when the bell for morning services clanged.

"Guess we'd better get inside." Ethan put a hand at the small of her back, guiding her across the snowy ground.

She smiled up at him, catching sight of Smith when she did. Caroline nearly faltered at the rage and fierce possessiveness radiating from him.

His gaze dropped to the other man's hand on her and his jaw went anvil-hard. The look in his eyes was piercing, dangerous enough that she drew in a breath.

For a brief moment, she thought he might order Ethan to take his hands off of her.

Eyes glittering, features like granite, Smith turned and started toward the small white church. Caroline shuddered. Despite his limp, he managed to get several feet ahead of them. William hurried up beside him and Smith slowed as the lad spoke to him.

Ethan leaned down to her, his voice low and tight. "Was there some reason you didn't tell Jennings about us?"

"I just couldn't. I'd already told him we had no future."

"He needed to know."

"Ethan." It vexed her in part because he was right. Her tone was curt. "It was too much at once."

Smith had thought things would be the same as when he left. They weren't. They would never be the same.

Her fiancé studied her hard, irritation flashing in his blue eyes. "I can see why it threw him."

So could she and she didn't need Ethan pointing that out to her. Still, it wasn't fair to blame him. She didn't want to talk about Smith anymore.

Ethan hesitated on the bottom step. She glanced up at him. "It's almost time for church to start. Shall we go in?"

After a long moment, he asked, "Are you okay?"

No, she wasn't. The raw hurt in Smith's eyes tortured her.

"Despite seeing him the other night," Ethan said, "I can't imagine running into him this morning was easy for you."

It hadn't been and not only because of the awkward declaration Ethan had made. Would she feel this jolt of shock every time she set eyes on Smith? This flood of relief and searing joy?

She had told her fiancé that Smith had come by her house to give her the news of his return in person. She hadn't told Ethan that the man had kissed her senseless. Or that she'd kissed him back just as enthusiastically.

Ethan's gaze went to Smith as the other man walked into the church with William. "I can take you home, if you'd like."

She was tempted, but this would never get easier. Best to get it over with. "I appreciate that, but it's not necessary."

After another search of her face, he nodded, saying nothing else until they stopped in the doorway. "Let's sit up there, by the Millers."

She nodded, her gaze skimming over the weathered pine floor. Wet boot prints, large and small, as well as little clumps of mud led up the aisle. A fire burned in a small stove in the corner to her right. On the cold air, she caught a mix of scents—horseflesh, leather and rosewater.

Ethan slid an arm around her waist and she stiffened reflexively. If he felt it, he gave no indication, continuing to hold her near as he guided her up the aisle. Past Smith.

Was Ethan doing that on purpose? Staking his claim? Showing Smith that she no longer belonged to him?

She could feel Smith's gaze on her, burning a hole through her. From the corner of her eye, she saw others looking from her to the recently returned rancher.

She wished she could disappear. Her chest tightened. If only she were the same woman he had left behind. But she wasn't.

Despite Smith's return, they couldn't be a couple anyway. She could no longer give him what he needed.

Throat aching, she settled on the pew beside the doctor and

his wife. Her first love took a seat three rows in front of them and squeezed William's shoulder as the boy scooted past him to sit on the same pew with his friend Ben. William said something that made Smith chuckle.

Pain streaked through her at the exchange between the two. She looked past her bronze silk skirts, fixing her gaze on her black button-up shoes as she tried to corral the emotions churning inside her.

Smith was a natural with kids. He deserved a family and the future he'd planned. He wouldn't be able to have that with her. It was just as well that she had moved on.

She hated herself for hurting him again. He'd been through enough pain in the past two years.

Still, she didn't want to second-guess her decision to move forward into a new relationship. It had taken too long for her to accept that Smith was never returning. That she could be happy with someone else even though she would never love anyone the way she had loved Smith.

She might be tempted to reconcile with him, but what they had was in the past. Over. And it had to stay that way.

Chapter Three

How could Caroline have fallen for someone else? Smith still couldn't believe it, but he'd seen it with his own eyes. Hell, he couldn't stop seeing it.

Galloway's hand on her, the way he looked at her. *His fiancée.*

Smith's chest felt hollow, just as it had since coming up on the two of them together at church.

Hours later, he was sprawled on one end of the long sofa in the Jenningses' large front room. His father sat at the opposite end and his ma was settled in her rocking chair to Smith's left. A fire burned in the massive stone fireplace, warming the airy space. A colorful woven rug was spread in front of the hearth.

Emmett and Viola Jennings had arrived home just before dark, delayed by the snow, as Smith had guessed. Whenever he glanced at his mother, she had tears in her eyes. His pa squeezed his shoulder every half hour. To make sure he was real, Emmett said. This was the homecoming Smith had wished for from Caroline. It had started out well enough then gone to hell.

After his parents' shock at seeing him alive had faded, they'd eaten supper and Smith had filled them in on what had happened to land him in prison. His parents agreed that he should try to determine why his name had been included on a list of dead prisoners.

So far, neither Emmett nor Viola had asked if he'd seen Caroline. Which suited Smith just fine. He didn't want to talk about her. The image of Galloway's hand on her still blistered him up.

Frustration had him getting to his feet and going to the stone fireplace to stoke the fire.

His mother studied the sock she was darning, asking casually, "Have you seen Caroline?"

So much for not talking about the woman who had ripped his heart out and stomped all over it with her tiny feet. He jabbed at the burning wood, sending ash and sparks flying.

His grip tightened painfully on the poker as he turned to face his parents. "Yes. And I know all about her engagement."

Just saying the word put a greasy knot in his gut.

"I'm sorry, son." Viola set aside her sewing and came to him, giving him a big hug. Her light rosewater scent was comfortingly familiar yet suffocating at the same time.

If his and Caroline's roles had been reversed, he wouldn't have forgotten her as quickly as she'd forgotten him. "I guess I shouldn't have expected her to wait for me."

Compassion burned in his father's dark eyes, the same black as Smith's. "Did she tell you the night you returned?"

"She didn't tell me at all. Galloway did."

Emmett frowned.

"Just before church this morning," Smith added bitterly.

His mother patted his arm, her blue eyes sad. "I'm so sorry, son."

Tension stretched across his shoulders. Thinking of Caroline with Galloway—with any man—made Smith feel empty and dark. The same way he'd felt in prison.

"This is the first time since your presumed death that she's let anyone court her," his father said.

"That doesn't make me feel better." He replaced the poker,

moving to one side of the fireplace and propping a booted foot on the wall behind him. "Why Galloway? What is it about him?"

"He's a good man," the older man offered.

Smith grunted. It didn't matter how good Galloway was. Caroline shouldn't be with him.

This morning, Smith had somehow kept from tearing Galloway's arm off and managed a civil tongue in his head. It was a good thing he'd left soon after services ended because he wanted to sweep Caroline up in his arms and carry her off somewhere.

"They've only ever been friends. When did things change?" *Why* had they changed? He just wanted to understand.

His mother shook her head. "I think they grew close when he helped out around her place after her surgery."

"Surgery?" Smith snapped to attention, his boot heel striking the wood floor with a loud thud. Ice-cold fear ripped through him. "What surgery? When? What was wrong with her?"

"She didn't tell you that, either?" Emmett frowned.

"No."

"It was over a year ago," Viola said. "She had an inflamed appendix."

"What's that?"

"An internal organ low on your left side." The older woman touched a spot just above her hipbone.

"Doc Miller said she could've died," Emmett put in.

Damn it! Why hadn't Caroline told Smith any of this? He glanced at his parents. "But she's okay now?"

"Yes," his mother answered. "She seems to have recovered fully although something has never quite been the same. She's different somehow."

Emmett leaned forward, resting his elbows on his knees and holding his coffee cup between both hands. "Galloway,

Della and one of Caroline's students took care of her until she got back on her feet."

Smith frowned. "Maybe that's why she thinks she's in love with him."

"You don't believe her?" his parents asked in unison.

He didn't want to believe it and he found he just couldn't. Still… "She's engaged to him. I guess I have to believe her."

He knew it wasn't fair to have expected Caroline to put her life on hold the way he'd had to, the way he had been forced to do to both of them, but right now fair didn't hold much sway with him.

Oh, he'd gotten her message loud and clear. She'd moved on and he should, too. Trying to think past the seething anger and violence inside him, Smith changed the subject.

"How are Ivy and Tom?"

After a sober silence, his mother spoke, her voice cracking, "Tom passed away about nine months after you disappeared."

"What?" Stunned, Smith could barely take in the fact that his brother-in-law was gone.

Emmett cleared his throat. "He was thrown from an over-turned wagon and broke his neck. He didn't suffer."

His sister was a widow. "Why hasn't Ivy moved back home?"

"You know how she is," his mother answered. "She wants to continue to run their stage stop."

"Alone?"

"She's doing a fine job of it," Emmett said.

Viola smiled. "She'll come home in a heartbeat when she hears you're alive."

Ivy lived two days' ride from Mimosa Springs, close to a small town that had no wire service. "I'll write her a letter and send it with the next stage going her direction. Does one still run that way on Tuesdays?"

"Yes." His mother's eyes softened. "I can do that if you'd rather avoid town for a while."

"Thanks, Ma, but I can do it." His sister wasn't the only woman Smith wanted to contact.

He should leave his former fiancée be, but he couldn't. Not yet. He had too many questions.

It was midafternoon the next day before he was able to get to Mimosa Springs. The air was still cold enough to freeze the horns off a steer and the snow had been packed down by feet, wagons and hooves.

Smith dismounted in front of Whitaker's and looped his gelding's reins over the hitching post. He glanced at the school just yards from him then turned away, shifting his attention to the north side of town. His gaze skimmed past the telegraph office that stood next to Whitaker's, touched on the jail then Doc Miller's house.

Hammer clanged on metal, drawing Smith's attention across the street to the blacksmithy and the livery. The saloon sat quiet next to the saddlemaker's shop, but the neighboring Sundown Restaurant was a hive of activity. Next to it stood Miss Millie's boardinghouse. Sunlight, blinding against the frozen snow, slanted across the pink painted frame house.

Smith entered Whitaker's, which also housed the post office, and wrote a short letter to his younger sister. He almost smiled as he imagined her reading the message that he was alive.

After he finished, he went next door to speak to Sheriff Newberry about the best way to discover why he'd been listed as dead. Some minutes later, he had agreed to let Bart make the queries. Smith stepped outside, waiting for school to be dismissed.

His eyes were gritty from lack of sleep and he'd worked like a demon all day trying not to think about Caroline—her surgery or her engagement—but it hadn't worked.

Suddenly the schoolhouse door flew open and a group of

noisy children clattered down the steps. He waited until the students had scattered and all was quiet before making his way there.

He stopped in the doorway, taking the chance to look at Caroline before she knew he was here. The sunlight turned her hair a molten gold. The thick silkiness was piled on her head, wisps of hair teasing her elegant neck and dainty ears. Thin black stripes threaded her deep gold dress.

Smith's gaze moved down the trim line of her back to the gentle flare of her hips as she swept the floor at the front of the room. She pushed the dirt onto a flat piece of tin and dumped it into the trash bin beside her desk.

There was no Christmas tree. Because some families didn't and couldn't celebrate Christmas, Mrs. Whitaker had always insisted on a small tree in the schoolhouse, well away from the stove. Had Caroline discontinued the tradition? He barely had time to wonder about it before she turned.

Her eyes, emerald-green in the afternoon light, widened. "Smith."

The way she breathed his name had his body going tight.

"Wh-what are you doing here?"

"I wanted to talk to you." He wanted more than that, but he knew he wouldn't get it.

"If this is about Ethan—"

"It's not," he interrupted. Not all of it anyway.

The bodice of her practical dress was snug, her lace collar neat and starched. The garment wasn't fancy, but she looked like a princess to him. All dainty and golden and beautiful. His attention lingered on the way the fabric molded to her full breasts.

When she rubbed her arms, Smith realized the door was still open. He reached back and shut it, dispelling some of the chill. Her gaze went to the door then back to him.

Stepping closer, he removed his hat. She stood motionless,

tension vibrating from her. Unable to help himself, his gaze did a slow glide down her body, pausing at her waist then dropping below. Where was her scar? How big was it?

The thought of anything marking her creamy ivory skin rattled him.

"Smith!"

He looked up at the command in her voice. A blush stained her cheeks. He'd embarrassed her. She had no idea why he was staring at her. As if her just standing there weren't reason enough.

"Sorry, hon—Caroline."

"What can I do for you?" she asked coolly.

Put my ring back on your finger. Smith pushed away the thought and came back to what he'd learned from his parents. She could've died.

He cleared his throat. "I heard you had surgery a year or so ago. Why didn't you tell me the other night?"

Wariness flickered in her eyes. She propped the broom against the wall and eased behind her desk, putting it between them. "It never crossed my mind. Seeing you, learning you were alive was the only thing I could take in."

He nodded, looking again below her waist. She'd needed him and he hadn't been here. But Galloway had, damn him. Smith's grip tightened on his hat. "What happened?"

Her eyes darkened with some unidentifiable emotion. "What do you mean?"

"I mean, were you sick? Did it come over you all of a sudden? Were you in pain? How did you know something was wrong?"

The blood drained from her face and Smith thought she swayed. She curled her hands over the back of her straight-back chair.

What had he said to make her look like that? Concerned, he took a step toward her. "Caroline?"

"One day, I was hit with a sharp pain." Her voice was low, shaky. "Stephen checked me and said something had burst."

"Your appendix?"

"What?" For an instant, she seemed startled. Almost as if she weren't sure what he was talking about. "Yes, my—that."

Her gaze dropped, a flush crawling up her neck. He figured her unease was due to talking about such things—ladies didn't—but he wanted to know.

"Stephen had to do surgery," she continued.

Smith was glad their friend since childhood had taken care of her, but her close call gnawed at him. "Ma and Pa said you almost died."

"Yes, but I didn't." She gave him a forced smile. "I'm fine now."

So why did she appear fearful? Surely she wasn't afraid of *him?*

Smith realized he was crushing his hat and relaxed his grip. "I heard Galloway helped you through it."

"Della, too. And William Dorsett."

"Is that when you fell in love with Galloway?" That bitter rage began to simmer again.

She studied him for a moment. "That's why you're really here, isn't it? To talk about Ethan."

"I'm here because I just found out you nearly died," he bit out.

"But you want to know about Ethan. You can't accept that I have feelings for him."

Feelings? She was supposed to love the man.

Smith moved closer. "After the way you kissed me, you can see why I have doubts."

"I explained about that." She held the chair to her as if it were a shield. Did she feel she needed to protect herself? "You took me by surprise. And besides it didn't even feel real."

"Felt real to me," he said flatly. "Every damn kiss."

She turned bright pink.

The question was out before Smith knew he was going to ask it. "Does it feel real when you kiss Galloway?"

"Smith."

"Does it?"

She looked down. "I think you should go."

Yeah, he probably should, but he couldn't. Especially now that one insidious thought popped into his mind.

Where all had Galloway put his mouth, his hands on Caroline?

Though the idea of it was sheer torture, Smith had to know. Just the possibility that she might have been intimate with the other man spurred a black viciousness inside him. Particularly because he and Caroline had come close a couple of times, but agreed to wait because their wedding was so near.

Well, that had never happened. Maybe he should've just taken her before he left on that damn cattle trip. If he had, she wouldn't have been able to move on so easily. So completely.

Searching her fine-boned features, Smith clenched his fists. The words felt dragged out of him. "I want to know if you've given yourself to him."

She drew in a sharp breath.

"Caroline?" he pressed sharply.

Her eyes narrowed. "That's none of your affair."

It should've been, though. Smith should've been her first, her *only*. Had thought he would be. He'd been so sure of her feelings for him and now it appeared he'd been mistaken.

Suddenly he felt weary and spent. Alone. "Did you ever love me?"

"Yes." She shifted, looking uncomfortable. There was no denying the agony in her green eyes. "Of course."

He moved forward until he stood at the corner of her desk. Close enough to feel her body heat, to draw in her soft vanilla scent. "I thought you'd always be mine."

"I thought you were dead." She sounded choked. "I had to move on."

"That's what I keep hearing."

"I didn't do it to hurt you." Eyeing him warily, she backed up a step. "You should try to move on, too."

"Why?" His voice lashed at her. "So you won't feel guilty about doing it yourself?"

"I have no reason to feel guilty." Her eyes didn't quite meet his and her chin quivered.

The anger that had been bubbling inside him boiled over. "I reckon it might take me a day or two longer to get over you than it took you to get over me."

Pain flared in her green eyes, hitting him with instant regret and that blistered him up, too.

"I've seen you with Galloway," he ground out. "You aren't in love with him."

"Smith—"

"You aren't. I just don't know why you're saying you are."

Her gaze lifted to his and she said in a trembling voice, "What matters is that I'm not in love with you."

The soft, ragged words bored right through him like a spike, cut off his breath. Had she really said that? She had. And she meant it, he realized with a sinking heart as she angled her chin at him and met his gaze.

Hell, he couldn't breathe for the crushing pain in his chest. Numb now, he settled his hat on his head and turned to leave.

"I won't bother you again."

She said his name, but he walked out and closed the door. On her, on the memories, on their past.

He stood for a moment on the landing, his head as fuzzy as if he'd had one too many at the Trail Dust Saloon, yet it was all due to Caroline.

He couldn't imagine being with anyone except her, but they

were finished. She was with someone else now. Someone she planned to marry.

Hell. He might not be convinced of her feelings for Galloway, but he was damn sure convinced of her feelings for him. There were none.

Caroline almost went after him.

What matters is that I'm not in love with you.

The brutal words made her wince. She didn't want to hurt him, but she had moved on. He should, too.

From the corner of her eye, she caught a movement out the window. Tears blurring her vision, she walked over. She couldn't help herself. Sunlight glittered on the icy ground and hit the glass. Smith limped past with William Dorsett.

Suddenly the two males stopped and William pointed to a spot behind the school.

Pulse jumping, she stepped to the side in case one or both of them turned around. William said something and Smith cocked his head toward the boy. His tall frame dwarfed the lad's, his dark hat casting a shadow over William's homespun brown cap.

What were they talking about?

After a few moments, the pair of them angled behind the school. William lived back there in a small house with his mother. Was that where he and Smith were going?

The need to find out was strong, as strong as the one urging her to go after her first love and tell him…what? That she hadn't meant what she'd said? She might wish she hadn't chosen the words she had, but she had meant them. Hadn't she?

She turned away from the window and gathered her things.

In the days that followed, Caroline put all her energy and attention on her students. It was a flat-out effort to erase the image of the raw hurt in his eyes, the heaviness in her chest.

She was so focused on not thinking about Smith that it took her a few days to register that there was a problem with William.

For the third time in as many days, she stood over his desk shaking him awake. Dark circles under the boy's eyes and his drawn features gave clear evidence that he was exhausted. Instead of eating lunch or roughhousing outside with the other boys during recess, he had fallen asleep at his desk.

She realized now this behavior had started at the start of the week. When she dismissed school that afternoon, he was out of the room before anyone else. She called him back, closing the door after the others had gone.

She walked to her desk and he followed. He yanked off his cap, his sandy hair sticking up in spikes. "Miz Curtis?"

"Is everything all right, William?"

Blue eyes watched her carefully and he seemed to brace himself. "Ma'am?"

"The lessons you've turned in this week have been sloppily written," she said gently. "And you did poorly on your history exam today. That has never happened."

His neck reddened. "I'm sorry, Teacher. I'll do better."

"You haven't been yourself. Your studies are suffering."

"Yes, ma'am."

"I'm concerned, William," she said in a soft voice.

He looked down at the floor, scuffing one worn boot across a crack in the planked floor.

She put a hand on his shoulder. "Things aren't fine with you. You look exhausted. Is there trouble at home?"

"No!" His head jerked up and tension coiled in his small body. "No, ma'am."

"I'm not scolding you." She eased down on the corner of her desk. "I want to help you."

"I'm doing some extra work," he mumbled, digging the toe of his boot into the pine floor. "To buy, uh, for Christmas."

Caroline smiled. "I admire that, but it's taking too much of a toll. I can't imagine your mother approves. Does she know?"

"No, ma'am." The words seemed startled out of him. "Um, I want to surprise her."

Caroline might have believed him if he hadn't sounded choked. Something was going on, but what? "What kind of work are you doing? Sweeping up at Whitaker's? Are you still feeding horses for Mr. Peterson at the livery?"

"Yes, ma'am, I'm still helping at the livery and I've been working for Mr. Jennings at the Diamond J."

She went still inside. "Smith or his father?"

"Smith. Well, sometimes his ma and pa, too. I do whatever needs to be done."

"I see." The boy was pale and he looked as though he'd lost weight. "How often? Every day after school?"

"Yes, ma'am."

"How long do you stay out there each day?"

He gave her an odd look. "Till the chores are finished."

"Is that usually after dark?"

He nodded.

She stiffened. Smith was working the poor kid into the ground. "That's too much."

"I really need the job." His voice cracked as he said earnestly, "I'll work harder at my studies, Miz Curtis."

"You're already working hard." Too hard. His mother needed to know what was going on.

Caroline rose and went over to bank the stove. "I'll walk you home."

He paled, his eyes huge in his elfin face. "Why?"

"To talk to your mother."

"You can't." At her sharp look, he amended, "I mean, please don't."

He crushed his hat in his hands and she noticed that the

sleeves of his coat were too short. They rode well above his wrists. "Please don't tell my ma."

"William, you've done nothing wrong, but you also shouldn't be working so many hours after school. Your mother should be made aware."

"But—"

"William." Caroline pulled on her cape and gloves. "Douse the lanterns, please."

Looking defeated, he extinguished the one hanging behind her desk then the one on the adjacent windowless wall. "I'll talk to her. I promise I will."

Caroline opened the door, waiting. As they walked down the steps, she asked, "Is there some reason you don't want me to speak with your mother?"

He hesitated a moment then said in a rush, "She's feeling poorly. I swear I'll do better. I swear, Teacher."

The boy was truly afraid he would get in trouble. They walked behind the school and toward his small frame house.

She smiled down at him and patted his shoulder. "It will be all right, William. Perhaps you can do some chores for me. I'll pay you."

"Yes, ma'am," he mumbled.

"I'm sure we can figure something out with your mother."

They reached the house. Leaves and clumps of dirt were scattered across a porch usually swept clean.

Just as Caroline raised her hand to knock, William jumped in front of her.

"Let me go in and see how she is."

She frowned. "Very well."

The boy opened the door only enough to slip inside. Before the door shut, she glimpsed dirty dishes on the table and an overturned basket of clothes on the floor.

He came right back out. "She's sleeping. I'm not supposed to wake her."

How sick was Helen? "Maybe we should get the doctor."

"No!" At Caroline's frown, he said, "I— We can't pay."

"Dr. Miller wouldn't charge you."

William's jaw set. "Ma wouldn't like it."

Was this a matter of pride or something else? Caroline wondered. She studied him for a moment, struck by how desperate he seemed to keep her from talking to his parent. She didn't want to embarrass the woman or her son, but the subject of William's extra work at the Diamond J needed to be addressed.

"Very well." Relief crossed his young face until she said, "Let's go talk to Smith—Mr. Jennings."

A look of horror flashed through William's blue eyes.

Caroline had only said that to gauge his reaction, but now she knew something was definitely going on. She was going to see Smith.

He was working the boy too hard and Mrs. Dorsett appeared in no shape to deal with the situation.

Smith wouldn't want to see her and for a moment, Caroline considered not going, but this wasn't about him.

Thirty minutes later, she had changed into her split skirt and ridden out with William. The boy's mule plodded alongside her so Caroline kept her mare to a slow walk as they crossed the wintry, hilly landscape.

Evergreen trees glittered with ice as did the trunks of the bare mimosa trees that lined the banks of Mimosa Creek. They rode across Diamond J land for a few minutes before seeing the barns then the house at the bottom of the rise. They passed a large corral full of horses before they reached the massive barn that stood closest to the sprawling ranch house.

Icicles dripped from the eaves and the sill of the big picture window at the front of the house. She and William dismounted at the barn and she followed the boy inside. Her eyes slowly adjusted to the dimmer light of the lanterns hanging on three walls.

Smith stood beside a black mare, bent over her left rear hoof with his back to the door.

Without looking up, he said, "William, we lost a cow. Her calf is in the last stall, feeding from a mama cow who recently lost her baby. Check on them and see how it's going."

Smith's typically smooth deep voice sounded rusty and hoarse. Caroline's gaze skimmed over his wide shoulders and the big hands cradling the horse's hoof. Hands she knew were gentle and soothing.

Stop. She gave herself a mental shake and started to announce herself. Before she could, William cleared his throat.

"Um, Mr. Jennings?"

Smith lowered the horse's leg and turned, the openness on his face disappearing when he saw Caroline. Surprise flashed across his handsome features before they hardened and his eyes went flat. Flinty. He seemed to stare right through her.

Involuntarily her gaze went to his mouth. All she could think about was him kissing her the other night. The hunger, the heat. The *need*.

Kissing was definitely not on his mind, she realized as his eyes narrowed.

"What do you want?" His voice was clipped.

William seemed surprised at the older man's brusque tone. Caroline wasn't. "I need to speak to you. Alone, please."

He hesitated, which irritated her. Finally he nodded.

She glanced at William then back at Smith. "Perhaps outside?"

Smith's gaze flickered to the boy who slowly started toward the back stalls.

Her student looked worried and she gave him a reassuring smile as Smith limped past her. She followed, noting that his dark shirt didn't seem as loose as it had before. It emphasized his broad shoulders and strong back. Unable to help herself, her gaze moved over his backside then his sleek powerful legs.

The sight of him filled up an emptiness inside her that she hadn't known she had. With a shock, she realized that she had missed him.

His limp might make him move slower, but that just gave her more time to study him. She wondered what his bad leg looked like. She wanted to see for herself. Was it scarred? Twisted? Her throat ached at the thought.

How many times had she prayed he would come back? Now he had.

Reaching the side of the barn, Smith turned, his dark eyes flat and remote. He looked like a stranger—hard, rough.

She should've been intimidated. Instead her blood hummed with excitement. And awareness. On the cold air, she caught a scent of clean male sweat and horseflesh.

It was a struggle to focus on the reason she'd come. She licked her lips, her stomach fluttering when his gaze lingered there.

"William told me he's been working for you after school," she said.

"He said he needed money."

"That's what he told me, too, but his schoolwork is suffering. He's falling asleep during class."

"You think that's my fault? I send him home every night before dark."

Caroline's gaze jerked to his. "Not after?"

He bristled. "I just told you—"

"I'm not doubting you."

He barked out a laugh.

"I didn't come here to attack you, Smith," she snapped.

He arched a brow, clearly not believing her. She tried to think past her irritation at that. Why had William lied to her?

"Caroline?" The word was pure impatience.

She moved closer and Smith backed up a step, as if trying

to escape her. His shoulders bumped the weathered wood of the barn.

Was this how things would be between them now? Sadness dragged at her. "Something is going on with him. Something bad."

She explained about his poor schoolwork and her conversation with him before trying to see Mrs. Dorsett. "He seemed desperate to keep me from speaking with her."

The tightness of Smith's burnished features slowly gave way to concern. "What do you think is wrong?"

"At first, I thought it was due to his working out here."

"Thanks," Smith bit out.

"Which is in addition to his job at Peterson's livery," she said evenly. "The problem seems to be at home, but I can't put my finger on it."

"You think there's something more than him being worried about his ma's illness?"

"I don't know." She paused. "He's still wearing last year's coat."

Smith looked baffled.

"Helen always makes sure he has a winter coat that fits and he's outgrown this one."

"Maybe she's been too busy to tend to sewing. She takes in laundry this time of year."

"Yes, maybe she's been too busy. Or maybe she's been sick for a while." Caroline tried to recall if she had noticed anything amiss before today.

Admittedly the man in front of her had ruled her thoughts since his return.

She sighed. "William won't tell me anything. I thought you might be able to talk to him."

Smith frowned.

"He looks up to you."

"If he won't tell you, he won't tell me."

"I think he might. Smith, there's no one else."

He didn't speak for a moment, just stared over her shoulder, his breath frosting the air.

Caroline realized she hadn't felt the cold until now. She knew it was because of the way Smith stirred her blood.

"All right," he said. "I'll see what I can find out."

"I appreciate it. And you'll get back to me?"

He leveled a look on her, a muscle ticking in his jaw. It was hardly fair of her to ask him, but she needed to know. Besides, Smith wanted to help William as much as she did.

"I'll let you know," he said grudgingly.

"Thank you." She expected the relief that went through her when he agreed, but not the anticipation. Pleasure at the opportunity to see him again. Pleasure?

That drew her up short. She shouldn't want to see him again, should only be glad he intended to help her find out about her student.

Right now, shamefully, she only seemed focused on the way he affected her. Despite the frigid air stinging like needles against her skin, there was a warmth unfurling in her belly. A heat that was due to Smith, plain and simple.

It was wrong that he still affected her that way. She was engaged! Guilt and alarm hit her at the same time.

He must have seen something in her face because his eyes narrowed and he limped around her.

Giving herself a mental shake, she followed. As the two of them reached the front of the barn, he said grudgingly, "Ivy's coming home. My ma's having a Christmas shindig."

"I'd guess the party is also to welcome you back."

"I reckon. The whole town's invited. It's on Saturday."

She would see him again in two days. Instead of dreading it, Caroline was impatient to see him again. That was wrong.

"I can't wait to see your sister. It's been too long. Since Tom's funeral." Caroline smiled. "I'll be here."

"Don't you mean you and Galloway will be here?" Smith asked in a low, tight voice.

Heat flushed her body. She'd forgotten about Ethan. "Of course. Both of us."

The fierce look on Smith's face cut her breath. Dragging his bad leg, he moved to her mare and cupped his hands to help her mount. The expression on his face said he was plainly ready to be rid of her.

Caroline paused in the doorway of the barn. She wanted to scold William, ask why he'd lied, but she would let Smith talk to him first.

She called a goodbye to the boy and went to her mount, putting one foot in Smith's large hands. He boosted her up and she seated herself, watching as he walked haltingly back into the barn.

He'd barely touched her, but her body vibrated with awareness. She had put her feelings aside and his, too, in order to talk to him about the boy.

She turned her horse and rode away, shaking so hard that her teeth chattered. Not from the cold, but from seeing Smith. And what she had just realized.

She had really believed she was ready to move on, leave the past behind, but she wasn't.

She still loved Smith Jennings and always would.

Chapter Four

Smith didn't go to Caroline's after getting William home that night. He just couldn't.

Seeing her so unexpectedly at the ranch had caught him completely off guard. And left him half-hard and aching. During their excruciating conversation, he had gone between wanting to kiss her and wanting to toss her off the property.

But the next evening, he forced himself to pay her a visit. He didn't want her throwing him off balance again. This way, he controlled the time and duration of the visit.

That seemed to be the extent of his control, though, because when she opened the door and he got a look at her, his whole body went tight.

The flash of heat, of welcome in her eyes, kept him rooted in place for a long moment. It wasn't until she said his name that he was able to move. He stepped inside and she closed the door.

Determined not to let her get to him, he took off his hat. A fire heated the small space, but Smith was plenty warm just from being close to Caroline.

She wore a cherry-red wool dress with a white collar and cuffs trimmed in red velvet. She looked pretty enough to eat and he wanted a taste.

The soft familiar whiff of vanilla made him want to put his mouth in the hollow of her throat where he knew the scent was strongest. He pushed the thought away. Just tell her about William and leave, he ordered himself.

She moved around him, toward the stove. "Would you like some coffee?"

"No, thanks."

"Are you sure? It's awfully cold. It would warm you up for the ride home."

He just wanted to get this over with. "No."

"All right," she said quietly. Seeming to finally get the message that he was here for only one reason, she clasped her hands together then unclasped them.

"Did you learn anything about William's situation?" she asked.

He shook his head. "When I rode home with him last night, he said his ma was asleep, that she was real sick. I offered to have Stephen check on her."

"But he declined."

Smith nodded.

"He did the same to me," she said.

Feeling penned in, too stirred up to stand still, he limped across the room. Trying to escape her gut-twisting fragrance, her warmth.

He passed the sofa where he'd laid her the other night, the chair positioned close to the stove, and stopped at the corner of the dining table.

Appearing anxious, her gaze darted to a spot behind him. He glanced over his shoulder, but saw nothing.

He shifted his attention back to her. "When I left William a few minutes ago, he said his ma was much better today and had been out."

Caroline frowned. "I haven't seen Helen Dorsett anywhere in town."

"I'll look around before I head home, try to find out if anyone has seen her."

"What if no one has?"

"Well, she has to be around here somewhere, doesn't she?"

"I guess so."

Smith drummed his fingers on the polished wood. With his other hand, he kept a tight grip on his hat.

Caroline threw him a nervous look.

He took in the rocking chair near the stove, the well-used coffeepot. A small shelf on the wall beside the fireplace held a porcelain redbird she'd inherited from her mother.

It was a moment before he realized there was no Christmas tree. She had always put it in the corner across from the small dining table that sat opposite the chair at the fireplace. There had been no tree in her classroom, either.

He glanced at her, still standing on the opposite side of the sofa. "You don't have a tree."

"No." The curt word didn't invite further questions, though he considered asking just because it was obvious she didn't want him to.

She used to love Christmas, especially decorating the tree, draping it with red ribbon and tiny angels made from starched white doilies.

Several handmade ornaments from her students always adorned the branches. A straw doll, a swan fashioned out of brown paper and colored with chalk, a cluster of jacks strung together to resemble a bell.

Smith didn't see any of that, didn't see anything that hinted at the holiday at all. He looked at the space over the door. Neither was there any sign of the one thing that had always hung there. Her gaze followed his and he knew by the sudden color in her cheeks that she realized he had noticed the empty space. No sense letting his mind go there. He was here about William, not the past he and Caroline shared.

He shifted his focus back to her. "How did the boy do in school today?"

"Better." She glanced behind him again.

Why did she keep looking back there? Was she on edge about him being here? Afraid he would see something?

"He stayed awake, though I could tell it was an effort. What could be going on with him, Smith?"

"I don't know, but we'll—I'll do my part to figure it out."

"Thank you."

The softness of her voice made him want to move closer to her. He wasn't going to. "I'd better go."

"I'll see you tomorrow at the party."

His mouth tightened. Why the hell did she have to remind him of that? "Sure."

He started to move and his bad leg cramped. A painful breath-stealing twist of muscle caused him to jerk and he gripped the edge of the table. He cursed as his hat fell to the floor.

"Smith?" She moved around the sofa and came toward him, concern darkening her green eyes.

"I'm okay. My bad leg knots up sometimes, especially in the winter."

"Is there anything I can do? Something I can get you?"

"Just need a minute." Gradually the agony shifted from a stabbing throb to a bone-deep ache. It still hurt like blue blazes, but at least he could walk.

"Maybe you should sit? Just for a moment?"

He shook his head. "That just makes it worse."

He rubbed it, digging deep into the muscle tissue with his knuckles, trying to work out the knot. Finally he straightened. "There. It's easing up."

She frowned. "Are you sure I can't do something?"

That sounded like flat-out trouble. "No, thanks."

He bent awkwardly to scoop up his hat. When he did, he bumped the chair behind him. Something thudded to the floor and he looked over his shoulder to see what it was. A faded round hatbox lay on its side, the lid slipping off.

Caroline made a strangled sound. Smith would've looked at her, but he couldn't move.

The contents of the box had spilled out. The engagement ring he'd given her spun to a stop next to the chair leg. The silver brush and mirror he'd chosen for her when she received her teacher's certification skittered under the table. Then there was the mistletoe.

Bunches and bunches of mistletoe sprigs tied with red ribbon that filled the deep container had scattered on the floor.

Something sharp shoved up under his ribs. Had she really saved them?

One look at her stricken, pale face told him she had. Her gaze lifted to his and the memory unfolded between them.

Two years ago before he'd left on that ill-fated cattle trip in early December, they had been in her doorway kissing under the mistletoe. Tradition held that a man removed one berry each time he kissed a woman beneath the greenery.

When the last berry was gone, Caroline teasingly insisted there could be no more kissing under that plant.

"I'll fix that," he'd said.

The next day, he had shown up with an armload of cut mistletoe, telling her that now he could kiss her forever because he didn't intend to run out of berries ever again.

She remembered. It was there in her eyes.

She had laughed and given him a big kiss. After cutting the greenery into separate bundles, she'd tied them with red ribbon, making sure each cluster had several berries.

From the quantity of now dried-out plants and shriveled white berries, it appeared she had kept every bit of that mistletoe.

The realization knocked the breath out of him and all he could do was stare.

He would never forget the way she had looked at him when he had walked through the door with greenery overflowing his arms. Like he could do things no other man could.

Heady, intoxicating stuff. How many times had he replayed that look while he was in prison? How many cold dark nights had that memory gotten him through?

The years fell away. Smith saw a softness in her green eyes, the same softness he used to see. Was it only nostalgia? It was more than that for him. It was love, stronger and hotter than he'd felt for her two years ago.

Before he knew it, she was in front of him. Reaching up to pull his head down to hers, plainly intending to kiss him.

He almost met her halfway, but something stopped him. Every muscle protesting, he shifted away. She didn't belong to him any longer. She didn't want him.

At his withdrawal, hurt chased across her features. Then in a split second, her face changed. Closed up. Reminding him that things were different now. He'd done the right thing even though it didn't feel right.

The moment broken, she rushed around him and knelt to gather the mistletoe and scoop it back into the box.

Smith stared down at her bowed head, the way the fire played against her silvery-gold hair, the elegant hands he would never feel on him again.

He didn't even offer to help. He couldn't. He just limped to the door and walked out.

On her porch, cold air searing his lungs, Smith leaned against a painted wood column. His legs wouldn't work. Nothing worked. Not him. Not her. It was a long while before he could pull in a full breath without pain carving through his chest.

Back then, she'd said she couldn't live without him. That had turned out to be a damn lie, hadn't it?

It didn't matter that she'd kept mementos of their time together. What mattered was that she had packed them away. The same way she had packed him away.

Smith's past with Caroline had tumbled right out in front of him last night and he wished he'd never seen it. He'd been riled up ever since.

He didn't want to see her, but thanks to this combination Christmas and "Welcome Home" party, she was right here in his huge front room.

She stood on the opposite side of the gleaming pine floor with Galloway as they spoke with Glen Peterson, who owned the livery as well as the restaurant in town.

Her fair hair was swept up on both sides and left to fall past her shoulders in a cascade of curls. The deep green velvet dress was one of her best, saved for special occasions. Against the rich color, her elegant neck and face were like polished ivory.

Smith's gaze traced down the row of buttons on her snug bodice and his grip tightened on the dainty cup his ma had given him earlier. Punch sloshed out, snapping his attention away from Caroline. He surreptitiously dried his wet wrist against the leg of his trousers.

All of the furniture, including that in the dining area, had been pushed to the side and the center cleared for mingling and the occasional dance.

A few people whirled around the small space to the lively strains of "Lorena" played by his pa on the fiddle.

It seemed as if the entire town of Mimosa Springs had come to welcome him home. He kept his distance from Caroline, but he couldn't stop watching her, which blistered him up good. Now, just as he had last night, he wanted to kiss her.

When Galloway slipped an arm around her waist, Smith's jaw clenched so hard he was surprised he didn't break a tooth.

He had danced once with his ma and once with his sister, if his hitching step could be called dancing. He had no intention of dancing or anything else with Caroline. There was only so much he could stand and holding her close, breathing in her subtle vanilla scent, was too much.

Besides, he hadn't forgotten what had happened between them at her house. Caroline would've kissed him last night if he'd let her. Smith had wavered between being glad she hadn't and cussing for the same reason.

As much as he enjoyed seeing his friends and his sister, he was ready for the party to be over.

A small hand slipped through his arm and he looked down to see his petite sister. Ivy's hair and eyes were the same black as Smith's, set off tonight against the pale pink of her silk gown.

He smiled. "You look pretty."

"So do you." She gave him an impish smile before gazing out at the crowd.

She was nowhere near his six-foot-plus height. She barely reached his shoulder.

She tugged him down, her voice loud enough for only him to hear over the music. "I finally had a chance to visit with Caroline. I can't believe she's engaged."

He grunted. "Well, she is."

"I guess there's no chance that the two of you—"

"She made her choice," he bit out.

Ivy squeezed his arm. "None of this would've happened if you hadn't been wrongly imprisoned and presumed dead."

"Maybe it would have. Maybe she wouldn't have remained true."

His sister searched his face. "You don't believe that."

He didn't want to, but everything he'd believed about Caroline had been shattered. "Didn't take her all that long to move on. Look at you. Tom's been gone for a year and a half, almost as long as I was, and you're not sweet on anybody. Are you?"

"No."

"I can't imagine the men who live near you keep their distance."

"There's at least one who doesn't and I have no idea who it is."

"Come again?" Smith raised a brow.

"Someone has been leaving anonymous gifts."

"Like what?"

"Drawings, poems."

Smith grinned. "So, somebody *is* sweet on you."

"I guess so." A shadow passed over her face.

Smith covered her hand with his. "What's wrong?"

She shook her head. "The gifts are lovely, but it makes me uncomfortable not knowing who's leaving them."

"How long has it been going on?"

"About three months."

"And you have no idea who it could be?"

"No."

"Did you tell Pa and Ma during their visit?"

"No. I'm sure it's harmless." She glanced up. "Mother said you discovered why you were listed as dead."

"Bart found out it was a clerical error made when I was transferred from Fort Smith to the prison in Kansas."

"Someone should have to answer for that!"

"I'm home now. That's what matters."

"I know," she grumbled. "But still."

"You want to dance with your crippled brother?"

"Maybe after another cup of punch." She released his arm. "Do you want more?"

"No, thanks." He needed something stronger.

Wondering why Ivy had changed the subject from her secret admirer to him, Smith watched as she made her way across the room to the table laden with cake and cookies at one end, punch at the other.

Smith felt someone's gaze on him and looked around to find

Caroline studying him. His skin grew tight. Every nerve in his body pulsed. Hell. He'd caught her watching him a few times this evening. The expression on her face wasn't longing, but he couldn't figure out what it was. He just wanted her to stop.

The crowd and the walls closed in on him. The air turned stifling, suffocating, just like prison. He had to get out, get away from her.

He ducked into the parlor that sat off the dining room and found a bottle of whiskey hidden in the back of a small cabinet that held Ma's good silver. Slipping the liquor under his suit coat, he crossed the dining area to the kitchen and stepped out the side door.

Headed for the massive bare oak several yards away, he hardly felt the cold as the whiskey burned a path down his throat to his gut. Bracing one shoulder against the sturdy trunk, he looked across the hills to the shadow of cattle dotting the landscape beyond.

The night was crisp and clear, stars glittering like frost against the inky sky. Out here, away from her, he could breathe.

He couldn't abide watching Caroline and Galloway any longer. Why had she even come? Last night, she had almost kissed him and tonight she was with another man.

He took another swallow of liquor. He heard the swish of skirts and glanced over to see her rushing toward him.

Why was she out here? To torture him? He already felt like a lit stick of dynamite.

He couldn't—wouldn't—put himself in the same position as he had last night. Close to her, alone with her and on the edge of control.

He scowled, resenting the whiff of her soft scent. "What do you want?"

The moonlight gilded her hair like silver, made her flawless skin appear translucent. She looked over her shoulder, as if she were worried about someone seeing them. Who? Galloway?

Something inside Smith snapped and he turned on her. "If you're going to be with Galloway, then be with him. Stay away from me."

"I came to tell you something!" Anger sparked in her eyes. "I looked out the kitchen window and saw Ivy in the barn doorway holding a man at gunpoint! I couldn't tell if he was armed, but he is *big*."

Smith cursed, striding past her and into the kitchen. Even though his sister was capable of taking care of herself, he grabbed the rifle from behind the door. "I'll check on her."

He rushed outside and around to the front of the house. In the spill of lantern light from inside the barn, he saw his sister in the open doorway, her petite frame rigid, her gun leveled steadily.

"Explain yourself," she snapped.

The man answered though Smith couldn't make out the words. The sound of a gun cocking had him picking up his pace.

"I told you not to move," Ivy ordered.

"Lady, if you'd just let me explain—"

Smith grinned, relaxing as he lowered his weapon. He knew that voice.

"Why were you skulking around in our barn?"

"Skulking? I was unsaddling my horse."

"Why? This isn't a boardinghouse or a livery."

"I know—"

"Where did you come from? Are you armed?"

"I'm more prone to answer questions when there isn't a pistol stuck in my face."

"Then you can just ride on."

"I'm trying to tell you I'm here for a job."

Smith stepped into the light beside his sister.

The man's gaze snapped to him and so did Ivy's. Smith laughed.

The big man, hands still in the air, glared. "Jennings, it ain't that funny on the business end of a barrel."

Ivy's eyes narrowed, but she didn't lower her weapon. "What's going on?"

Smith squeezed her shoulder as he moved past her, extending his hand to the man. "Gideon, how are you?"

His friend scowled at the woman in the doorway. "Be a sight better if she'd put that gun down."

Grinning, Smith turned, motioning to his sister. "C'mon, Ivy. Put your pistol away. I invited him."

Slowly she released the hammer on her revolver and lowered the weapon.

Gideon put his hands down, keeping a wary eye on her.

Smith stepped to the side and drew the big man forward. "Gideon Black, meet my sister, Ivy Powell."

She cocked her head. "I thought I knew all your friends."

"I met Gideon in prison."

"Oh!" she exclaimed, a flush cresting her cheeks. "You must be the one who saved his life. Thank you."

She held out her hand and Gideon hesitantly shook it.

With the lantern turned up as high as it would go, Smith knew she could see the cruel, jagged scar that bisected the man's neck. And the thin scar along his jaw. There were others where she couldn't see them.

Gideon had gotten all of them watching Smith's back. If it hadn't been for the enormous quiet man, a broken, twisted leg would've been the least of Smith's injuries.

The swish of skirts and the rush of footsteps had him tensing until he saw it was his ma and pa hurrying toward him. Caroline was close behind and Emmett had his revolver drawn.

Smith held up a hand. "It's okay, Pa. Gideon's a friend."

Even as the older man put his weapon away, he looked at Ivy. "You okay, honey?"

"I'm fine, Daddy. It was just a misunderstanding. I was startled."

Smith introduced his parents then Caroline. His friend's face didn't change, but he felt Gideon's reaction. The man had heard plenty about the woman Smith had planned to marry.

Gideon palmed off his hat, his dark hair ragged and past the collar of his coat. "Nice to meet you all."

Smith clapped him on the shoulder. "Let's get you something to eat."

"Yes, come in," Viola invited.

As they walked toward the house, Galloway came out with Caroline's cape. He slipped it around her shoulders, keeping an arm there. "Ready to go?"

"Yes." She glanced at Smith before turning to his sister. "I'll see you at church tomorrow?"

"Yes."

The women embraced then Galloway helped Caroline into their buggy before climbing in beside her. After the couple said their goodbyes, Ivy and Smith's parents started for the house.

Gideon stared after the departing buggy. "I don't recall you mentioning she had a brother."

"She doesn't," Smith said baldly. "He's her fiancé."

"Her *what?*" The other man's gaze sliced to him. "I thought *you* were going to marry her."

"She thought I was dead."

"Hell."

"Yeah. I'll explain after you've had some food."

Gideon nodded then shifted his attention to Ivy, keeping his voice low. "Just how good is your sister with that gun?"

"Pretty good."

The other man didn't respond, but Smith noticed his friend now studied Ivy warily.

Still able to hear the faint jingle of harness, Smith gave one last look back at the buggy carrying Caroline. Damn it, would he ever stop aching for her?

He wanted to move on just as she had. He wanted to forget her and everything they'd shared. The only way he knew to do that was to stay the hell away from her.

Chapter Five

If you're going to be with him, then be with him.

The next afternoon, Smith's words still rang in Caroline's ears. He was right. If she was going to honor her engagement to Ethan, she had to commit fully. She thought she had, but she'd been wrong. The realization had hit her like a blow when Smith had discovered she'd kept their mistletoe.

She shouldn't have been going through the reminders of their time together, but she had and now he knew it. Disbelief had flashed across his burnished features, then naked longing. The way he looked at her had put a quiver in her belly, just as he'd done last night at the party. Ethan had never made Caroline quiver. Anywhere.

She didn't want to think about Smith or what had happened after church today with Ethan.

She was determined to talk to William's mother and waited until late that afternoon before walking to the Dorsett's home. Tomorrow was Christmas Eve and Caroline wouldn't rest until she knew everything was all right with her student and his mother.

Nose buried in her wool cape for warmth, she approached their small frame house and knocked on the front door. When there was no answer, she knocked again. Still nothing.

She went around back. Their chicken coop, a sturdy shed

with a padlock on the door, was open and she heard movement inside.

Once in the doorway, she let her eyes adjust to the dimmer light. William stood a few feet away, bent over a long shelf that ran the length of the back wall.

"William?"

The sandy-haired boy jumped and spun to face her. Through the dusky light, she saw panic then fear flash across his thin features.

Why was he afraid? "I didn't mean to startle you. It's me, Miss Curtis."

"Yes, ma'am." He backed up against the shelf, the middle of three where the chickens typically nested and laid their eggs.

There were no hens. As Caroline looked around, she realized there were also no feathers, no feed and no ammonia smell. This was the cleanest chicken coop she'd ever seen.

"What are you doing in here?"

"I'm, um—"

Now she could make out a bulky shape lying on the long shelf behind him. She stepped closer, her breath a frosty puff in the air. Gray watery light slid through the clapboard walls enough for her to identify a blanket. "I came to speak to your mother, but there was no answer."

"No, ma'am." The boy's voice trembled.

Caroline moved closer and touched his shoulder. "William?"

"She's gone, Teacher!" He threw his arms around her and burrowed close.

Caroline started to ask where Helen had gone, but her brain finally worked out what the bulky shape was on the length of wood behind William. Her arms tightened around his slight frame and she fought to stay calm and steady for him. "What happened?"

"She died." He pulled away, wiping his wet eyes. "She was real sick, like I said. One night, I told her I was going for Dr.

Miller, but she got worse and I was afraid to leave her. Then she just stopped breathing."

"Oh, William." Caroline hugged him to her, stroking his hair. "How long has she been gone?"

"Almost two weeks."

The words jolted her. He had been alone for almost two weeks? Living with the fact that his mother had passed on? "And you didn't tell anyone?"

Blue eyes troubled, he shook his head. "I almost told young Mr. Jennings, but then I didn't."

Smith. He needed to know.

Her stomach dipped at the thought of seeing him. She wasn't ready. Still, this wasn't about either of them.

He had agreed to inform Caroline if he learned anything new and she'd done the same. She had to send for him whether she wanted to or not.

Almost an hour later, Caroline and Smith stood in Dr. Miller's office with William and his mother's body. She had finally convinced the boy to let her call for the doctor who also served as the undertaker. He had come at once with Glen Peterson and the two men had carefully transported Helen here, laying her on one of the exam tables.

Now Smith sat on a chair in the corner of the room and William stood in front of him, visibly fighting tears.

The big man laid one hand on the boy's shoulder as he gave details about what had happened to his mother.

He hadn't gone for the doctor after realizing she had passed on because he didn't have money to pay. She insisted they always pay for everything, especially the doctor.

So he had cleaned out the unused chicken house and wrapped her in several quilts, padlocking the door to make a safe place for her until he could get a casket. The reason he had asked for a job at the Diamond J was so he could buy the wood to build her a pine box.

Smith's gaze met Caroline's and she knew they were thinking the same thing. Either of them would have been happy to provide for the burial.

Her heart twisted. She had known something was wrong. Why hadn't she insisted on seeing William's mother before now?

Guilt bit deep as she moved toward him. "Why don't you come home with me for tonight?"

"Thank you, Teacher, but I want to be here," the lad said fiercely, his voice cracking.

She sent a pleading look to Smith.

He squeezed the boy's shoulder. "Just to rest. You can come back whenever you want."

Dr. Miller looked over at William. "You can leave your mother in my care, son."

"I want to stay with her."

Caroline trusted her friend, but she wanted William close. "I think it would be better if you stayed with me."

He shook his head.

Before she could react to his uncharacteristic defiance, Smith wrapped one big hand gently around her upper arm and pulled her aside.

A chill still clung to his deerhide coat though she could feel the warmth of his touch through her cape. Fighting the urge to lean into him, she met his dark gaze.

"Let the boy do this," he said. "He feels responsible for her."

The thought of it tightened her throat. "He's only ten."

"Caroline," Smith murmured. "It's always been only him and his ma. He needs to know he's the one who took care of everything."

Inhaling his familiar musky scent, she searched his face,

comforted by his nearness, his certainty. She didn't feel certain of anything except failing her student.

Stephen smiled at her. "Kate and I will look out for the lad."

She glanced at Smith, who nodded.

"All right." She turned back to William. "You stay here tonight. I'll see you tomorrow."

"Thank you, ma'am." His eyes were red from crying, but there were no tears right now. Just a soberness and a flash of gratitude.

Smith took her elbow and steered her outside. He could tell she didn't want to leave.

The uncertainty on her delicate features had him wanting to reassure her, which irritated the hell out of him. She had a fiancé for that.

Still, it didn't stop Smith from saying, "It's okay, Caroline. This is right. The boy needs to do this."

They stepped off the doctor's porch and started across the cold frozen grass toward her house.

"Are you okay?"

"I think so."

Smith noticed that her voice trembled, and against his better judgment, he eased closer. Her gray skirts brushed the tops of his boots.

He almost hadn't come. The messenger had said, "Miss Curtis needs you." At the time, Smith had bitterly wondered why she hadn't sent for her fiancé. Then he realized her summons probably had to do with William. Why else would she contact him?

So he'd gone. And it was a good thing he had.

She glanced over, regret on her face. "If I'd been paying attention the way I should have been, I would've known something was wrong."

"You did know," Smith said firmly. He didn't like her blaming herself. "You just didn't guess his mother had passed. No one could've guessed that."

They walked through the chilly night, the full moon barely peeking out from behind thick hazy clouds that signaled they might get more snow. The two of them passed the school then the church.

As they approached her house, she said thickly, "I should've tried harder to see Helen."

They stepped up on Caroline's porch and she reached for the door, her hand visibly shaking. So much so that she couldn't turn the knob.

Smith had planned to say goodbye here, but he couldn't. He opened the door and ushered her inside.

Quickly he lit the lantern hanging beside the door, filling the front room and kitchen area with light. He moved around the sofa to the wood stacked beside the fireplace and soon had a blaze going.

Skirting the dining table, he noticed the hatbox was gone, the mistletoe cleaned up. He wondered if she'd thrown it away. Forcing the thought out of his mind, he turned to find her still standing where he'd left her, door wide-open. She huddled into her wool cape.

"Caroline?"

She blinked, tears welling in her eyes. She appeared wobbly. And pale.

Smith limped over to shut the door and draw her farther inside.

"Smith, he's been on his own for almost two weeks! I know how alone he must feel."

So did Smith. His whole prison time had been like that. And a good part of his recent return, too. He was glad to be home, grateful for his parents and sister, but there was a part of him that was empty and always would be because he no longer had Caroline.

Her hair slid around her shoulders like gold silk. She looked lost and sad. And so beautiful he had to clench his fists to keep from touching her. He needed to see her settled then get out of here.

Moving behind her, he removed her cape. Her soft vanilla fragrance slid into his lungs, tightening all the muscles in his body. He hung the garment on the peg beside the door then steered her to the sofa. When she sat and peeled off her gloves, he started to leave.

She buried her face in her hands and a quiet sob escaped.

Oh, hell. Smith wanted to reach for her, pull her into him, but he wasn't strong enough to stop with that. Still, he couldn't go yet.

He looked around the small kitchen area, wondering if there was any of his whiskey left. Before he'd left two years ago, she had finally agreed to let him keep a bottle at her house. He made his way over to the cupboard on the other side of the sink and went through the cabinet until he found the liquor.

He grabbed a delicate teacup from the top shelf then splashed some of the amber liquid in a cup and passed it to her. "This will help steady you."

Her hands trembled as she took a tiny sip.

"Stop blaming yourself, Caroline."

"I should've known, should've tried harder."

"He hid it from me, too. The boy didn't want anyone to know. He kept it from everyone."

A tear slid down her cheek. "I just feel that I failed him."

Smith felt that way about her right now. Every protective instinct he'd ever had surged to life. He wanted to stroke her cheek or gather her against him. But he no longer had the right to comfort her, to try to stop her tears. And he just couldn't be this close to her without touching her.

Where was her damn fiancé?

She returned the empty cup to him.

"Better?" he asked tightly, trying to control the mix of resentment and the gut-deep need to make things better.

"Yes." She still looked sad, but not distraught. "What can we do for William? I recall Helen saying once that they have no other family."

"He can live at the Diamond J."

"Or he could live with me."

Smith wondered if her fiancé would be amenable to the idea. "That wouldn't cause problems?"

She gave him a funny look. "No."

Being near her, drawing in her feminine scent, chipped away at his resolve to keep a distance. He had to go. "We'll figure something out."

"I know. You always do." She smiled, sending a bolt of heat right through him.

He walked haltingly to the door.

She blinked, her gaze following him. "Are you going?"

"Yes. Are you all right?"

She nodded.

Even though he hated the idea of another man being here with her, she shouldn't be alone. Through clenched teeth, he asked, "Would you like me to send for your fiancé?"

"I don't have a fiancé," she said quietly, looking away.

He froze, making sure he understood her words. "What?"

"We ended things this morning after church."

His heartbeat roared in his ears as he studied her over his shoulder. She was no longer engaged. She no longer belonged to another man.

The words snapped through his brain then…

She was *his*. *His*.

Caroline hadn't asked him to stay, hadn't said he figured into her decision to call off her engagement. Smith didn't care.

Carefully he shut the door and made his way slowly back to

the sofa, tugging off his gloves. He tossed them on the couch with his hat then shrugged out of his coat.

She stood, a question in her green eyes. Stepping around the sofa, he eased to a stop in front of her, close enough that her breasts touched his chest.

He slid a knuckle under her chin and tilted her face to his. Her eyes darkened as she looked up at him. "Things are over with him? Really over?"

"Yes."

He started to ask why, but he didn't care. At least not right now. What he wanted to know was—

His mouth came down on hers. She made a sound of surprise then melted into him. Her kiss was welcoming, as hungry as his.

Oh, yeah, this was what he wanted to know.

He curled her tight into him, buried his other hand in her hair. It felt like hot thick silk. She tasted of his whiskey and a dark sweetness. Warmth spread through his chest. For the first time since returning, Smith felt whole. Steady.

Gripping the front of his shirt, Caroline moaned.

Slowly he lifted his head, his breathing rough as he drew in her subtle scent. She was flushed, her eyes soft with desire.

She blinked up at him. "What are you doing?"

"What I've wanted to do every time I've seen you."

He kissed her again, harder this time, demanding everything from her. Her arms curved around his nape then her fingers delved into his hair. He could feel every inch of her, from the press of her full breasts against him to the last button on her bodice that marked him right below the waist of his trousers.

Hard with need, he throbbed against her belly. The soft noise she made, the way she clutched him tighter, had his thoughts scattering.

With great effort, he drew back. Her pulse thrummed wildly

in the hollow of her throat. He glided a thumb over her cheek, flushed a becoming pink.

"Smith," she breathed, feeling outside herself.

His eyes glittered hotly. "I'm not leaving you again. Ever."

Her heart ached. Oh, how she wished that could be.

Sliding both arms around her waist, he pulled her into him, flat up against his arousal. "If you don't want me, tell me now."

Not want him? She would always want him, but she could never have him, not for forever anyway.

She opened her mouth to say so. She knew she should send him on his way, but any ability she'd had to maintain a distance between them had weakened when he kissed her.

"I love you, Caroline. And I know you still love me."

She did and she was so tired of pushing him away. She needed him. This man touched the heart of her like no other ever had or would.

He stroked a hand through her hair. "You belong to me and you know it. I should've made you mine before I left for that cattle sale two years ago."

Caroline had always believed Smith would be her first, her only.

The small bit of resistance she had crumbled. She could have him for tonight. One memory to last a lifetime.

Her arms tightened around his neck.

"Caroline?" His voice was husky with desire.

She knew what he was asking and there was only one answer.

"Yes." She cupped his cheek. "Yes, Smith."

The hue of arousal deepened the bronze of his features. He scooped her up in his arms.

"Oh! Your leg. Should you be carrying me?"

"I want to. Besides, it isn't far." He moved haltingly to the bedroom, heat from the fireplace wafting around them.

Her skirts frothed over his arm. The warmth of his hand

burned through her stockings where he held her, sparking a sudden impatience.

She wanted to feel his skin on hers *now*. He let her drift down his body, thumbing open the buttons on her bodice. She unlaced the leather strip that closed the placket of his black shirt, pushing the garment up and over his head.

Admiring the deep broad chest of burnished copper, she ran her hands over hard muscle and dark hair then down the well-hewn plane of his belly.

He backed her toward the bed as she unhooked her skirt. She slid the garment off with her petticoats then sat on the edge of the mattress. He palmed off her shoes and rolled down her stockings. After pulling the tapes on her drawers, she shimmied out of them. She shrugged out of her bodice, shivering when Smith scraped his teeth gently across the place where her shoulder met her neck and nipped her lightly.

She tugged at his waistband, watching as he toed off his boots and got rid of his socks. Her hand slid down his taut stomach and undid the top button of his pants, then the next.

He put a hand over hers. "Hold on."

His eyes were hot with raw need, the same need that burned in her. Before she knew what he was about, he untied her chemise and whisked it over her head.

He stripped off his trousers and laid her back. His callused hands were on her breasts, his thumbs circling the hard nubs of her nipples. "You are somethin'."

As his mouth closed over her taut flesh, she arched into the wet velvet heat, moving her hands to his hard shoulders.

She pushed at him until he rolled to his back.

He squeezed her waist. His muscles were coiled tight, his breathing labored. "What?"

"I want to see you."

This night was all she would ever have of him. Of *them*. She wanted to remember everything.

Muscles drawn tight, he lay still as her gaze moved over him. The light spilling from the front room slid over his broad shoulders, the flat ridged belly, his manhood. A thrill rippled through her.

Her attention caught on his left thigh—powerful and well formed. Shifting so that the light from the front room fell over him, she looked at his injured limb. Less muscular than the other, it was scarred and crooked from his groin to his ankle.

Smith caressed her naked hip. "It didn't heal right."

She stroked his leg down to the knee. "Does it hurt?"

"Not unless I've done a lot of standing or walking."

She knew he did plenty of that every day.

She bent to kiss his thigh, lightly smoothing her hand over the scarred flesh.

"Enough of that for now." He pulled her up his body and rolled her under him. "You had your turn. Now I want mine."

"You already had yours."

"Not hardly." He stared at her in arrested silence—every bit of her from her hair to her shoulders to the curve of her waist and the flare of her hips. "You are so beautiful."

He kissed her mouth then her neck, moved his lips to the valley between her breasts.

She shifted restlessly, her smooth legs brushing his hair-dusted ones. "Smith."

"Don't hurry me. I've waited a long time to look at you." He cupped her breasts then took her in his mouth. He lingered there until she squirmed, an unfamiliar tension coiling sharply inside her.

His lips glided over her ribs, causing her to wiggle. He nuzzled her belly then stopped altogether when he reached the scar. Several inches below her naval, the ugly furrowed mark stretched across the lower part of her stomach.

Feather-soft, his finger traced the puckered skin. "I'm sorry I wasn't here for your appendix surgery."

He brushed his lips across the spot. Once, twice.

Tears burned her eyes. She wanted to confess that the scar wasn't from appendix surgery. She wanted to tell him why she wasn't the same woman he had left behind, why she couldn't be with him after tonight.

Instead she reached for him, stroking the supple skin of his back. "Kiss me."

He did, sliding his work-roughened palm down her stomach then between her legs, easing a finger into her silky heat. He raised his head, watched her as he added another finger.

A sliver of moonlight flashed beneath the oilskin shade then disappeared. There was no mistaking the possessiveness in his face or the tenderness and desire.

"Smith," she panted.

"Right here." His thumb circled the sensitive knot of nerves at her center until her body went soft. She gave a small cry and her inner muscles tightened around him.

He levered himself between her legs, muscles tight as he eased his way slowly inside. The feel of his hot rigid flesh against her slick softness had her drawing in a deep breath. Moving her hands from the lean tautness of his hips and up his iron-hard arms, she kissed his chest, tasting his salty heat.

"Caroline?" he asked hoarsely.

"I'm fine." She tightened her legs around him. "Don't stop."

He pushed inside. She didn't care about the pain. In the amber lantern light, she could see his eyes blazing with such naked emotion that it brought tears to her eyes.

She tugged his head down for a kiss. He moved experimentally a couple of times and when she made a sound deep in her throat, his hips began to stroke hers. Steadily driving her up a dizzying peak, he laced their fingers together.

He slid deep, then rocked inside her in a slow, steady motion until she felt tiny urgent pulses inside her. When she let go, so did he.

She came back to herself to find him smiling down at her.

"Now you're really mine," he said softly. "Like you should've been all along."

He rolled over, taking her with him.

They lay there as their pulses slowed, their skin damp and warm. Caroline stroked a finger over a scar on his rib then one in the middle of his breastbone. "How badly were you hurt?"

"Would've been killed if not for Gideon."

"Your friend who arrived last night?"

"Yes."

"Were you in a fight?"

"Yes, but not of my doing. I was attacked because I was the newest arrival."

He really could've been dead, just as she had believed for almost two years. Caroline's throat closed up and she held him tight.

Her legs tangled with his as she relaxed against him. She drank in every detail—his dark tousled hair, the lean taper of his torso, the solid sun-bronzed arms that held her close. She savored the feel of his hard lines against her body, knowing she would remember this every night for the rest of her life.

He dropped a kiss on her head. "Why did you break things off with Galloway?"

She stiffened, but he only held her tighter. She knew she had to answer. "I don't love him the way I should."

"What do you mean? You don't love him at all?"

She inwardly winced at the hope in Smith's voice. "I don't love him as much as he loves me. He deserves someone who feels the same about him as he does about them."

She knew Smith expected her to say that she had ended things with the other man because she still loved Smith, but she couldn't say that.

Smith nuzzled her temple, stroking her bare shoulder as he said drowsily, "This is how things were meant to be."

Soon, the slow evenness of his breathing told her he was asleep. Caroline knew he believed they were together once again, but they weren't. They could never be.

And she was going to have to tell him.

A chill in the air woke Smith the next morning. Judging from the grayish-pink light peeking under the oilskin shade, it was barely dawn. Christmas Eve.

He had dreaded this Christmas Eve, just as much as he had the ones he'd spent in prison, because he believed he wouldn't be spending it with Caroline. Now things were different.

They'd be spending this Christmas Eve—and every Christmas Eve for the rest of their lives—together. Which meant he had better get more mistletoe.

Grinning, he slid out of bed and stoked the dying fire in the front room then added more wood before climbing back beneath the covers with Caroline.

He pulled her tight into him, sliding a hand to her breast and enjoying the feel of her bare silky flesh. Her hair fell in a golden tumble over her shoulders. Burying his face in her neck, he inhaled her sweet womanly scent. He could tell by her sudden stillness that she was awake.

"Merry Christmas Eve," he whispered.

"Merry Christmas Eve."

He brushed a kiss across her shoulder. When she pulled away slightly, Smith frowned. "What's wrong? Are you worried about William? He's probably still asleep."

"We should get up anyway."

He tickled her ear with his tongue. "I thought we could talk about getting married."

She gathered the top quilt around her and slid out of bed.

Smith levered up on his elbows, watching as she slipped on her pale blue flannel wrapper. "It would be great if we could get hitched while my sister's here. She could stand up with you."

"We can't."

"Why? Not enough time to plan what you want?" He swung his feet to the frigid floor and yanked on his pants then bent to pull on his socks.

Caroline had put on a pair of socks, too, probably her father's. Now she stood at the foot of the bed, looking as if she were bracing herself for something.

He went to her. "Caroline?"

She swallowed. "I haven't changed my mind about marrying you."

He barked out a laugh. "If that were true, you wouldn't have let me into your bed."

She turned away as if she couldn't bear to look at him. "That was goodbye."

"It damn sure wasn't!" He fought to stay calm, to figure out why she was saying these things. "Your chance to get rid of me was last night before we made love."

"I wanted you. I *needed* you, but...I can't marry you."

He snagged her wrist, his heart squeezing painfully when she pulled away. "If you say you don't love me, I'll know it's a lie."

"Last night is all we can have."

"Maybe not all." Smith shoved a hand through his hair, frustration clawing at him. "What if we made a baby?"

Pain flared in her eyes and he felt a sudden spike of dread. "Caroline?"

"We didn't make a baby."

"You don't know that."

"I do." She sounded as if she were having trouble breathing.

He slashed a hand through the air. "There was nothing to prevent it. You could be pregnant right now."

"I'm not."

He gripped her shoulders, wanting to shake her for being

so dang stubborn. "There's no way you can possibly be sure of that."

"There is." A tear rolled down her cheek and she looked straight at him, her eyes deep green and wet. "I can't have children. Ever."

Chapter Six

"What?" The words jarred him like a kick to the head. "What do you mean you can't have children ever? Why would you think that?"

"Because it's true!"

He could see she believed it with everything in her. He reached for her, but she moved away. "Caroline—"

"I need to tell you something."

"I wish you would." He tracked her as she paced back and forth in front of the bed. She was huddled into herself, looking small and helpless and sad.

She shivered. Because she was cold or because of nerves?

What did she need to say? Impatience sawed through him, but he reined it in. She was obviously distraught.

"Let's go into the front room where it's warmer," he suggested.

Her fine-boned features were pinched as she preceded him through the bedroom door and past the cookstove to the fireplace.

Concerned now, he touched her shoulder. "Don't you want to sit down?"

"No." Tension lashed her body as she blurted out, "The surgery I had wasn't to remove my appendix."

He frowned.

"About six months after you left, I began having some...female trouble. I went to see Stephen and he found a tumor in my stomach. Actually on my uterus. That's where a baby grows."

"I know what it is," he said hoarsely, apprehension snaking through him. "I have a sister."

She nodded, her cheeks flushed a deep rose. "Anyway, he had to remove my entire uterus as well as everything else so there's no way I can become pregnant."

"Ever?"

"Ever."

No children? Smith's chest hollowed out as he tried to take it in. It was a blow, to be sure. So many of their plans had included a big family. The possibility that they couldn't have one had never crossed his mind and yes, it changed things.

Regret and a sense of loss rolled through him. If he felt this way, she must've been devastated. The news would take some getting used to, but he was more worried about her.

He edged closer to her. "I'm sorry I wasn't here for you."

"You couldn't have done anything."

"We could've gotten through it together," he said softly.

She shook her head.

"Did you recover all right?"

"Yes. It took almost two months, but I did."

"That's when Della and William and Galloway helped you."

She nodded, but she wouldn't look at him. She was trembling, her arms wrapped tightly around her middle. Was she really okay?

Hit with a sudden alarming thought, Smith went still inside. "Last night? Did I hurt you? What did the doctor say about making love?"

"He said it was fine as long as I was fully recovered, which I am." She finally met his gaze. "You didn't hurt me. Not at all."

"Good." He exhaled heavily in relief. "I couldn't stand it if I caused you any pain. That's what I care about."

"Didn't you hear me say I couldn't have children?"

"Yes. Why didn't you tell me this that day at school when I asked about your surgery?" He recalled their conversation about the operation. When he had referred to her appendix, she had seemed confused and nervous. Because, he realized now, she hadn't wanted him to know the real reason for the procedure.

His chest tightened. "You lied to me. You've never done that before. Did you think I wouldn't want you?"

"No," she said flatly. "I knew you would say it didn't matter."

"Of course, it matters."

She flinched.

"Because it's upsetting to you."

"And you."

"And me," he admitted. "Still, it doesn't change the way I feel about you."

"I expected you'd say that, too."

"That's a good thing, Caroline," he said drily. "Being childless isn't what either of us prefer, but it doesn't mean we can't be together."

Tears filled her eyes and she turned away. There was something more going on here, Smith realized.

Moving to stand behind her, he gently laid his hands on her shoulders. "Are you having trouble coming to terms with it?"

"I've accepted that I'm not a whole woman."

"Of course you're a whole woman!" Smith turned her to face him. Was that what was bothering her?

He should've figured it out. She had always wanted to be a mother, expected to be one. It made sense that she would see herself differently now.

He stroked her cheek with the back of his finger. "Do you really believe that about yourself? Because I don't. If you'd let me, I'd prove again just how much of a woman you are."

His attempt to coax a smile from her didn't work. Nothing seemed to be working. Another thought hit him out of nowhere.

"What about Galloway? Is this why you ended things with him?"

"I told him about it, but no. I broke the engagement because he deserves to be happy, to spend his life with the right woman. I'm not that woman."

"That's because you're the right woman for me. Do you think all I care about is having kids? You think that's the only reason I want you?"

This was why she'd been pushing him away. Relieved to finally know the reason, Smith cautioned himself to remain patient. He just needed to reassure her.

"You want a big family. You should have one." Her words were clipped. "You can't have that with me."

"And we're dealing with it."

"You can't tell me you're willing to give up the future you wanted."

"The future *we* wanted." He searched her tortured green eyes. "It would've been nice to have children, but I can live without them. What I can't do, won't do, is live without you."

"You might feel that way now, but when our friends begin having children, you'll want them, too. And you should have them."

"As long as you and I are together, I'll be just fine."

She shook her head, looking defeated.

Smith's heart ached. "You've accepted that you can't bear children. Why do you think I can't accept it?"

"You shouldn't have to."

"Neither should you, but that's life." He dragged a hand down his face, unsure if he should reach for her or not. Every time he got close, she backed away. "I don't know how to reassure you."

She wiped at her wet eyes. "My mother died trying to give

my father one more child. Do you know how many times she miscarried? Do you remember the two babies who were still-born?"

"We aren't your parents, sweetheart."

"They were happy and in love when they married," she cried. "But with each failed pregnancy, my father's resent-ment grew. I couldn't bear for you to look at me like that, to blame me."

"Don't paint me with the same brush as your father. I know what's more important—our being together, staying together. You think my parents haven't had problems?"

"I'm sure they have."

"As a new bride, my ma didn't want to move here from Missouri, but she did. Now she loves it as much as my pa. It took years for that to happen, but she stuck by him. Just like I'll stick by you."

"I can't marry you."

He pinched the bridge of his nose, feeling as if he were drowning. "Not being able to have a family is hard, a loss for both of us, but it's not a reason to spend our lives apart."

"I'm trying to put your feelings first!" Her voice cracked. "The way you've always done for me."

"If that's true, then marry me."

"You've always wanted children and I can't—"

"I've always wanted *you*."

"When I fail to give you the family you want and deserve, you'll despise me just as my father did my mother."

"Gil Curtis was a fool," he snapped. "He treated you and Adelaide as if you were failures, didn't recognize what he had in your mother or you, either. I know exactly what I have in you, *with you*. Do I like the idea of having a child that's part of both of us? Yes, but I don't need it. Not like I need you."

How could he make her understand? Anger edging out the patience he'd managed until now, he struggled to keep his voice down. "When I was in prison, you know what I dreamed about? Just you. Not you and a house full of kids. I figured out real quick what was important and what wasn't. A life with you is what I want. Why can't you accept that?"

"I wish I hadn't told you."

Her words were so soft he almost missed them. His eyes narrowed. "If I hadn't pressed you on this, you wouldn't have told me that you can't have children?"

"Not if I could help it."

It was as if she'd just punched the breath out of him.

"I know your sense of duty. You're too good, too honorable to walk away from me because of this, but I know how it will be when you finally accept that our lives will be childless."

"Staying with you doesn't have one damn thing to do with duty or being honorable! You're the only woman for me, Caroline. You always will be." He snagged her hand. "I love you. That means through everything, not just for the times when I get what I want."

Pulling away, she went on as if he hadn't spoken. "My father said the same to my mother and in the end, it was the only thing that *did* matter. She died from childbed fever after delivering a stillborn son, her eleventh attempt to give him the family he wanted. I couldn't bear for you to look at me the hateful hideous way he looked at her."

"You know me better than that." His chest cracked open. Desperate to change her mind, he searched for a way to make her understand. "Don't you think there will be times in our marriage when you'll be disappointed in me? That I'll sometimes hurt you, deliberately or not?"

She blinked and he could tell she hadn't considered that, but before he could say more, she jumped in.

"It's not the same thing. Every couple has disagreements and fights, but you calm down, apologize and move on. This is more than a disagreement, Smith. This is something you want at your core, something we both thought we could have and we can't because of me."

He wanted to put his fist through the wall. "And I say I want you. Only you."

"You should have the kind of life you've always wanted."

"I can't have that without you, for better or for a hell of a lot worse. Do you think you're somehow protecting me? Is that what this is?"

"I only want you to have the family you planned."

"What about what I want?"

Every soft line of her body was rigid and tears spilled down her cheeks.

He cursed. Why couldn't he get through to her? "You thought I was dead and would never return. After all the time we've lost, you want to throw us away?"

"I'm giving you what you won't admit you want more than anything."

It was as though she'd grabbed hold of his heart and twisted. For a moment, he couldn't speak around what felt like shards of glass in his throat.

"No," he finally managed quietly, coldly. "You're deciding my life for me."

Black fury razored through him. Barely aware of moving, he limped to the bedroom for his boots and jerked them on.

Seething, he grabbed his coat, hat and gloves from the sofa and headed for the door. Once there, he turned, stabbing a finger toward her. "You don't get to decide what I want or what I should have."

But she already had and he wasn't sure he could forgive her for it.

Even worse, he didn't know if he should even try.

The look Smith fixed on her before he walked out was savage enough to weaken her knees. *Come back!* Caroline wanted to cry out, but she didn't. She couldn't.

The slam of the door reverberated in the early morning quiet, rattled through her small house. A chill lingered and behind her the fire crackled and hissed. Heat warmed her backside, but she was numb, eaten up with misery and resentment over what life had dealt her.

Smith loved her and she loved him. It just wasn't enough.

Legs wobbly, she curled one hand over the back of the sofa. As much as she hated what had just happened between them, it had been the right thing to do. If not, it wouldn't hurt so terribly, would it?

The look on his face—disbelief then raw naked pain then derision—was seared into her brain and a pulsing pain filled her.

All she wanted was for him to have everything that was within her power to give.

She wanted to crawl under the covers and cry until there were no tears left. If it hadn't been for William, she would have, but she didn't want the boy to be alone when he woke up. Didn't want him to be alone any more than he already had.

She made biscuits, put them in the cookstove to bake and went to dress. In no mood for cinching up today, she went without a corset. She donned her flannel chemise and petticoats then her thickest wool stockings. Leaving her hair loose, she pulled it back with a kerchief.

She stared at the bed, the rumpled sheets that reminded her of her night with Smith. His masculine outdoorsy scent lingered.

He would probably always think of last night with bitterness, but she wouldn't. Until she had ruined things earlier, it had been all she'd ever hoped and she was going to remember it that way.

Anxious to get to William, fighting thoughts of Smith, Caroline cooked a large helping of bacon, covered it and packed it with the biscuits. She was washing the skillet and baking pan when a knock sounded on her door.

Her pulse skipped at the thought that her visitor might be Smith, but that was foolish. The vicious hurt and anger in his eyes when he'd left had told her he wouldn't be coming back.

Untying her apron and wiping her hands on the garment, she made her way to the door and opened it. Her breath seeped out. It *was* Smith, tall and dark with a cold forbidding look in his eyes she had never seen.

Was he here to try to change her mind? If so, Caroline knew she wouldn't be able to resist.

No, she could tell by the way his face closed against her that he hadn't come for reconciliation.

There was no forgiveness in his midnight-black eyes. A muscle worked in his jaw and he turned his head away as though he couldn't bear to look at her.

A sob caught in her throat. Everything in her wanted to reach for him. Instead she clasped her suddenly clammy hands together and waited.

Snow fell in fat wet flakes behind him. Everything was covered in white. It must have snowed all night.

Her gaze moved down his full length and back up, searching for some clue as to what was wrong or if he was hurt. "Smith?"

His big frame rigid, face like stone, he thrust a piece of folded paper at her. She took it, recognizing the careful printing on the outside flap as William's.

To Teacher and Mr. S. Jennings

She fumbled the note open and quickly scanned the first few lines then scanned them again. Her breath backed up in her lungs.

Shocked, she looked at Smith, her voice cracking. "William's run away because he's afraid he'll be sent to an orphanage?"

She gripped the door frame to steady herself.

Smith's rugged features softened then hardened again so quickly she thought she imagined it. He stepped inside, nudging her back and closing the door.

Still struggling to understand, she read more of the letter. "His mother was put on an orphan train when she was a child. He's afraid he will be, too. Doesn't he know we would never let that happen?"

"Evidently not."

The resentment in Smith's voice registered as she pushed the letter back at him. "We have to find him."

She grabbed her cape from the peg beside the door as Smith walked over to bank the fire in the fireplace. The fire he'd started after they had woken up together. It felt like days had passed since then.

While he tamped out the flame in the cookstove, she rearranged her kerchief so that it covered her ears. She wrapped a shawl around her head, pulled on her gloves.

"I woke Stephen and Kate," Smith said stiffly. "They didn't know the boy was gone. Stephen is gathering the town together for a search."

"Okay." Her gaze went to the small basket she'd packed. "I made breakfast for him. Should I take it?"

"Good idea."

She picked up the woven container. "We should check his house first."

"Already did. He's not there, not at church or the school, either."

"Where could he be?"

"I've been to the livery." Smith's big hand covered the doorknob. "His mule's gone."

"He really doesn't mean to come back," she whispered. Something about Smith's arrival nagged at her, something other than William's disappearance. "Where did you find the letter?"

"Tacked to your door frame. On the outside edge."

Which explained why she hadn't seen it when Smith had left. "It's a good thing you noticed it."

He nodded sharply. "Ready?"

She skirted the sofa and met him at the door. "How long do you think he's been gone?"

"Hard to know."

"Long enough for you to check everywhere—" She broke off, suddenly hit with a realization. Her gaze sliced to him. "When did you find this?"

"When I left your house."

"And you're just now showing it to me?"

He scowled. "We need to get going. Bart and I figured out how to split everybody up. We need to get busy searching. It's snowing again."

"You weren't going to tell me!" Anger slid past the hurt and grew.

He opened the door, impatience stamped on his rugged features.

"Don't deny it."

"I'm not," he said flatly.

"I can't believe you were going to keep this from me."

"But I didn't." He leaned down until he was in her face, his gaze leveling into hers. "Because it would've been wrong."

"Why would you even think about not telling me?"

"I didn't want to upset you. And I don't want you out in this weather any more than I want William out in it."

"I am perfectly capable of deciding if I should go out in this weather."

"That's right. You're perfectly capable of making your own decisions so I thought you should."

He could easily have ridden off in search of William without telling her, left her to find out from the Millers or someone else. But he hadn't. He was giving her what she had denied him—the chance to make her own decision. It hit her like a smack upside the head.

Though Caroline understood the significance, there was no time for talking about it now. Nor did Smith appear interested.

Ushering her outside, he hurried her to the church where everyone was gathered. His Appaloosa was hitched to the post in front of Whitaker's. He must have saddled and fetched his mount when he'd checked the livery for William's mule.

Smith's parents as well as Ivy, and Smith's friend Gideon, arrived just as everyone was divided into teams of twos and threes. Smith and Sheriff Newberry made sure at least one person in each group had a mount or wagon.

"I saw tracks leading from the livery so I'm going west," Smith announced.

The residents quickly spread out so that a ring of people surrounded Mimosa Springs and began to move away from town.

Smith unlooped his horse's reins from the hitching post.

Caroline hurried over to him. "I'm going with you."

His mouth flattened. She could tell he wanted to protest, but he didn't.

"Fine," he said. "I'll meet you at the livery."

She rushed down the street and saddled her hardy bay mare. Moving to the mounting block, she stuck the basket under her arm and slid into the saddle.

Once she was outside, Smith glanced at the basket, then reached back to open one of his saddlebags. "Put the food in here."

She quickly did, tossing the small container inside the livery for later retrieval. They rode out, following the tracks Smith identified as belonging to William's mule.

A gust of wind swept across the hilly landscape. Caroline drew the shawl tighter around her head and huddled into her cape. She noticed that Smith had turned up the collar of his coat and pulled his hat down low. Thick white flakes soon coated the crown.

He half turned in the saddle. "I can still see a few of the mule's hoofprints, but the snow is covering them up quickly. Before long, the impressions will be gone."

"You're not stopping, are you?" she cried out.

He gave her a glacial look. "I'll be out here until I find him, but there's no way of knowing how long that will be."

"You think I should turn back, is that it?"

He didn't answer.

She shivered. "I'm not heading home until we have him."

"Didn't think you would," he muttered, kneeing his horse into motion.

Caroline followed, indignant that he would even think about sending her back. Then she reminded herself that he hadn't really tried. Though he plainly didn't like that she was going with him, he hadn't ordered her to return home, hadn't refused to let her join forces with him.

As she followed him through the blowing snow and needle-sharp cold, she realized with a sinking heart that was exactly what she had done to him.

Chapter Seven

Though Smith managed to stay focused on the search for William, it would've been a damn sight easier if Caroline weren't with him. The occasional blast of frigid wind cut like a razor. His hands and feet were frozen to the point of aching. Hers had to be, too.

More than anything, he wanted to send her back home, but she wanted to be here and he understood that. Why couldn't she understand what he wanted?

Their horses plodded through the snow. Because visibility was so limited, they moved much slower than Smith wanted. Still, he wouldn't risk missing any possible sign of William.

Time seemed just as frozen as everything else. He glanced back at Caroline. All he could see of her face was her eyes, and the worry there mirrored his own. The longer the boy spent in this harsh weather, the greater the chance they wouldn't find him alive.

Yard after yard, Smith tried to stay positive, relieved when the snow let up and almost stopped completely. The rolling landscape, blanketed in white, flattened out. They passed stands of green cedars and pines, bare-branched oaks.

They topped a rise. Caroline drew her mount to a stop beside his. The freezing temperature had his eyes watering and hers, too, he noticed.

Through the gray-white haze, he saw a pond at the bottom of the hill. A layer of thin ice covered the water and from a spot near the center, the surface was cracked all the way to the bank.

"There!" Caroline grabbed his arm, pointing to a dark motionless blur on the bank.

Smith leaped off his horse and half slipped, half ran down the snowy slope. As he neared, he was able to determine it was an animal. William's mule.

Then Smith saw the boy huddled up against the animal's belly. The mule had lain down, sharing its body heat.

His chest tightened.

"It's William," he yelled over his shoulder. "Bring my bed-roll!"

The animal was covered in snow, its body angled to block the worst of the wind. The mule raised his head as Smith knelt beside the pair.

William's legs were in the water. His ratty gloves were muddy and wet and dug into the bank like claws so he wouldn't slide back into the pond.

The animal's dark eyes followed Smith's movements. His throat closed up as he gathered the boy near.

Caroline stumbled to a stop beside them, sobbing. "Is he—"

"He's alive, but frozen clear through."

When Smith rose with William in his arms, the mule struggled to stand. Caroline leaned in and pressed a kiss to William's mud-caked forehead then rubbed the mule's muzzle.

"Teacher?" the boy mumbled.

"Yes, William. And Smith is here, too."

They reached their horses with the smaller animal plodding behind. Smith turned to her. "He's losing consciousness off and on. We need to him get him warmed up as soon as possible."

"I can carry him under my cape."

"If you hold him against you, his clothes will get you

soakin' wet. In this cold, that would undo any help you'd be giving him."

"What do we do?" Alarm creased her features.

Smith glanced at the bedroll she held. "Strip him and wrap him in that."

"Strip him?" She sounded horrified.

"Caroline, we don't know how long he's been out here. It's lucky his mule stayed close, but if William's clothes freeze, we could lose him. The best thing for him is to be as close to body heat as possible, without icy water-soaked clothes. We aren't that far from town. Now that I can see where we're going, it won't take us long to get back."

"All right."

With shaking frozen hands, they struggled to get William's clothes off. Smith had the thick blanket wrapped around the child as quickly as Caroline removed the garments.

He took the boy and held steady as she gripped his shoulder for support and climbed into her saddle. Once she and William were settled, she held him close and gathered her cape completely around him, sheltering him as best she could.

Smith knotted the mule's reins to the latigos that laced through the framework of Caroline's saddle. The leather strings typically used to tie ropes or a bedroll would hold just fine until they reached Mimosa Springs. Smith vaulted onto the back of his own mount then took Caroline's reins and set off in a quick trot. Her mount and William's kept pace.

The boy would be all right. He had to be. Smith glanced back, seeing only the top of Caroline's shawl-wrapped head as she hugged William close. He would do everything he could for the lad. His gaze moved to the woman who cradled the boy close.

Overwhelming emotion tugged hard at Smith's heart. Her attempt to push him out of her life might have come from a good place, but she had gone about it all wrong. She had hurt him. Infuriated him.

And yet despite the anger, he still wanted her.

His mind went back to those months in prison, remembered the desperation he'd felt to see her, hold her. He would've given anything to be with her. He still would.

After the way she had rejected his desires, dismissed him, he had thought he couldn't forgive her, but he could. He just wasn't sure he could convince her to change her mind.

Caroline and Smith took William straight back to town. On their way, Smith fired one gunshot then two in quick succession, the signal that the ten-year-old had been found.

Stephen saw their return and came running. He carefully took the boy from Caroline and laid him on her sofa as Smith fed more wood into the smoldering fire.

William shivered violently, his words slurring. "My mule?"

"He's fine," Smith soothed.

"Wh-where am I?"

"At Miss Curtis's house with me, Doc Miller," Stephen answered. "Miss Curtis is here, too."

Shrugging out of his coat, Smith stepped into the boy's line of sight.

"Is it Christmas?"

"Almost."

William gave a drowsy smile, his eyes fluttering shut.

Caroline draped her chilled damp cape, shawl and gloves over the back of a dining chair then went to warm herself by the fire. Smith stayed at the foot of the sofa, his broad shoulders rigid. Worry carved lines on his weather-reddened features.

Stephen handled the boy gently yet said nothing. He was focused, almost somber. Dread flared and Caroline moved to stand beside Smith.

She slipped her hand into his, barely aware of doing it until she felt him jolt. She looked up, murmuring, "I don't know what I'll do if he doesn't make it."

"He will," Smith said fiercely. "He will."

Her nerves were shredded. "Stephen? Tell us something."

"He has mild hypothermia." The doctor drew back to eye his patient. "The mule likely saved his life. If William had been out there alone, I wouldn't have much hope, but I believe he'll recover fully."

Her eyes burned as Stephen rewrapped the boy in Smith's bedroll.

Their friend glanced over his shoulder. "Bring as many blankets and quilts as you have. Bundle him up and lay him in front of the fire."

Caroline hurried to do as he'd said. When she returned, Smith helped her layer the coverings on William.

"Don't rub his hands or feet," Stephen warned. "It would be a dangerous shock to his system. When he's able to swallow, give him something warm. Broth or milk."

Smith carefully settled William in front of the fire. Caroline arranged the blankets so that his head was covered, too, leaving only his face exposed.

Seeing Smith kneel and place a hand on the youngster's head put a knot in Caroline's throat. Relief swirled inside her. Thank goodness they had found William in time. She couldn't bear the thought of losing the boy who had become more than a student to her.

She couldn't bear the thought of losing the man she loved, either, she admitted as Smith rose to speak in low tones with the doctor.

She lay down beside William, the blaze causing her to perspire, but she didn't care. The patient needed as much heat as he could get.

"Caroline?"

Smith's voice rumbled over her head and she looked up.

"Stephen's going to answer everyone's questions. I'm—"

"You're not leaving?" she asked in a half whisper.

"No."

"Good."

A strange look crossed his face. She watched him, growing drowsy. The next thing she knew she woke cuddled against his brawny chest, his strong arms around her. He limped toward the sofa.

Drawing in the scents of man and leather, she blinked up at him. "What are you doing?"

"You fell asleep," he said gruffly. "I'm putting you on the sofa. I'll sit with William for a while."

"All right." She searched his eyes for the hurt she'd put there earlier.

She didn't see it. She didn't see anything. His gaze was unreadable.

When he bent to lay her down, her arms tightened around his neck. Though the movement was automatic, it made her realize she didn't want to let him go.

He gently yet firmly unclasped her arms then lowered them to her sides.

He cocked his head. "Caroline, just because our future isn't the one we pictured—"

She waited. And waited.

Then he shook his head, stepping toward the dining table and the pitcher she'd filled with milk this morning.

"What were you going to say?"

"Never mind." He removed the piece of cheesecloth covering the earthen container and poured some of the liquid into a pan.

She stood. "Please tell me."

After a long moment, he gestured toward the boy. "Don't you see what we did here?"

She frowned. "We found William."

"We found him together. We're caring for him, together."

"Like a family," she said slowly, realization unfolding inside her. "*We* could be his family."

"We already are." Smith's gaze locked on her as if he were testing her reaction to that statement.

Legs shaking, she closed the distance between them. He stayed motionless, his expression apprehensive. Almost pained.

She laid a trembling hand on his chest. "We would be a family for William."

"With William," Smith corrected gruffly. He put his large hand over hers. "This will be good for everyone, Caroline. I know you're afraid things might turn out for us like they did for your folks, but we work, sweetheart."

She thought about all the ugly things her father had said and done to her mother. Smith's words came back to her. They were nothing like her parents. He, especially, was nothing like Gil Curtis.

Smith slid a knuckle beneath her chin and tipped her face to his. "I want you to change your mind about us being together. I want you to give us a chance. Just because our future won't be the one we pictured doesn't mean we can't have one."

Beneath her palm, she felt his heart thump hard. She inched closer, a different kind of warmth moving through her. "When I thought you might not have told me that William was missing, I was furious. I realized that must've been how you felt when I made a decision that should have been yours."

"Listen—"

"I love you, Smith." She hadn't let herself say it, not even last night when he was deep inside her. "Can you forgive me for deciding our lives without giving you a say? Without taking your wishes into consideration?"

"Depends."

Her heart sank. "On?"

"There are other kids like William who need families and a home. We could give them one."

She almost asked if he was certain, but as she stared into his eyes, she knew the answer.

It didn't matter that those children wouldn't come from her and Smith. William and others like him needed love and she had needed Smith to make her see it.

Her heart swelled. "Yes, I want to provide a home for William and children like him."

Smith's free hand slid to her nape, his fingers flexing in her hair. "There's one condition."

She held her breath.

"You marry me."

"Are you sure?"

He arched a brow. "I've always been sure."

He had. Sure and steady. Ready.

Her hands framed his face. His head lowered and his mouth covered hers. She held him tight, never letting go again.

After a moment, he drew back. "I thought this was going to be the worst Christmas of my life, worse than the two I spent in prison. Instead it's going to be the best one ever. Let's get married tomorrow."

"On Christmas Day?"

"Yes."

She glanced at the little boy stirring in front of the fire. "What about William?"

"He should be fine by then."

By this time tomorrow, she would be married to Smith and they would have a family, two things she'd thought forever lost to her.

She smiled. "I can't wait until we can tell William."

"I can't wait until we're hitched," Smith growled. He kissed her and kissed her and kissed her.

They were both breathless when he lifted his head. "You

should know I aim to have plenty of mistletoe on hand at our wedding."

Laughing, she tugged his head down to hers. "We don't need any."

* * * * *

REQUEST YOUR FREE BOOKS!

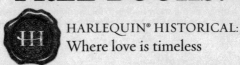

HARLEQUIN® HISTORICAL:
Where love is timeless

2 FREE NOVELS PLUS 2 **FREE GIFTS!**

YES! Please send me 2 FREE Harlequin® Historical novels and my 2 FREE gifts (gifts are worth about $10). After receiving them, if I don't wish to receive any more books, I can return the shipping statement marked "cancel." If I don't cancel, I will receive 6 brand-new novels every month and be billed just $5.19 per book in the U.S. or $5.74 per book in Canada. That's a savings of at least 17% off the cover price! It's quite a bargain! Shipping and handling is just 50¢ per book in the U.S. and 75¢ per book in Canada.* I understand that accepting the 2 free books and gifts places me under no obligation to buy anything. I can always return a shipment and cancel at any time. Even if I never buy another book, the two free books and gifts are mine to keep forever.

246/349 HDN FEQQ

Name _____ (PLEASE PRINT) _____

Address _____ Apt. # _____

City _____ State/Prov. _____ Zip/Postal Code _____

Signature (if under 18, a parent or guardian must sign) _____

Mail to the **Reader Service:**
IN U.S.A.: P.O. Box 1867, Buffalo, NY 14240-1867
IN CANADA: P.O. Box 609, Fort Erie, Ontario L2A 5X3

Not valid for current subscribers to Harlequin Historical books.

Want to try two free books from another line?
Call 1-800-873-8635 or visit www.ReaderService.com.

* Terms and prices subject to change without notice. Prices do not include applicable taxes. Sales tax applicable in N.Y. Canadian residents will be charged applicable taxes. Offer not valid in Quebec. This offer is limited to one order per household. All orders subject to credit approval. Credit or debit balances in a customer's account(s) may be offset by any other outstanding balance owed by or to the customer. Please allow 4 to 6 weeks for delivery. Offer available while quantities last.

Your Privacy—The Reader Service is committed to protecting your privacy. Our Privacy Policy is available online at www.ReaderService.com or upon request from the Reader Service.

We make a portion of our mailing list available to reputable third parties that offer products we believe may interest you. If you prefer that we not exchange your name with third parties, or if you wish to clarify or modify your communication preferences, please visit us at www.ReaderService.com/consumerchoice or write to us at Reader Service Preference Service, P.O. Box 9062, Buffalo, NY 14269. Include your complete name and address.

HHI1B

HARLEQUIN® HISTORICAL:
Where love is timeless

Explore a land as wild and beautiful as the men
who rule it with author

BLYTHE GIFFORD

**WORD IN THE ROYAL COURT HAS SPREAD
THAT THE WILD SCOTTISH BORDERS
ARE TOO UNRULY AND ONLY ONE MAN
CAN ENSURE PEACE....**

*Return of the
Border Warrior*

With failure *never* an option, John Brunson returns home
to persuade his family to honor the king's call for peace. But the
Brunson Clan will kneel to no one....

To succeed, John knows winning over Cate Gilnock, the daughter
of an allied family, is the key. But this intriguing beauty
is beyond the powers of flattery and seduction. Instead, the painful
vulnerability hidden behind her spirited eyes calls out to John
as he is drawn back into the warrior Brunson clan....

Available from Harlequin® Historical October 16.

RUNNING FROM THE PAST...
SHE BUMPS INTO HER FUTURE!

*Read on for a sneak peek of Lauri Robinson's fresh and
exciting debut novel from Harlequin® Historical.*

UNCLAIMED BRIDE

Not only was she out of her element, her wardrobe was
as out of place in Wyoming as the ocean would be. What
she wouldn't give for the red velvet cape lined with rabbit
fur she'd left England with. She'd sold it, along with a few
other of her more elegant pieces, hoping to find a way to
financially support herself. The amount she'd gained had
paid her room and board for the week, but hadn't been
enough to replace the overcoat, let alone anything else. That
had contributed to her ultimate decision—become a mail-
order bride.

The way Ellis Clayton glared down his nose at her made
Constance doubly wish she'd never seen Ashton's first
letter.

When his gaze met hers, he asked, "Are you interested in
coming home with Angel?"

Constance forced herself to breathe. The men across
the road still leered, but other than the wind, it was deathly
quiet. Besides herself, Angel was the only trace of a female
she'd seen.

Knowing the man waited for an answer, Constance
prayed the thickness in her throat would allow words to
come out. "Perhaps, I…" Her mind couldn't fathom a
single suggestion. Fighting to hold an iota of dignity, she
voiced her options, "I apologize, but at this moment, your
generosity appears to be my only hope."

The man's expression softened and the sight did

something to Constance's insides. She couldn't figure out exactly what, but then again she'd been greatly out of sorts since stepping off the stage.

His gaze went to his daughter, who smiled brightly. After shaking his head, he gestured to one of the men. "Put her stuff in my wagon, would you, Jeb?"

Angel grabbed Constance's hand, and tugged her in the man's wake. "He's not as grumpy as he makes out to be."

The girl's assurance didn't do much for the quaking in Constance's limbs, nor the churning in her stomach. She willed her feet not to stumble as she matched Angel's quick pace into the building. Nonetheless, Constance sighed at the relief of being out of the wind.

*Will mail-order bride Constance Jennings
be able to make a home and find love in
Cottonwood, Wyoming?*

Find out in
UNCLAIMED BRIDE
by Lauri Robinson
Available October 16 from Harlequin® Historical